Ragnvald Hrolf:

Book 6 in the Norman Ge

By

Griff Hosker

Contents

Ragnvald Hrolfsson

Published by Sword Books Ltd 2016

Copyright © Griff Hosker First Edition

Cover by Design for Writers
Thanks to Simon Walpole for the Artwork.

Ragnvald Hrolfsson

Hrolf

PART ONE

The Gift of the Gods

Prologue

The Haugr

I am Hrolf the Horseman. I came to the land of the Franks and carved out a land for myself and my family. When I came, we were the Raven Wing Clan. Now we are the Clan of the Horse, for many of my warriors ride to war. A dream and a visit to a witch made this so. I was told that my blood would rule not only the land of the Franks but the land of the Angles too. Now that I had seen more than thirty summers we had a toe hold on the land the Franks called the Cotentin. My warriors and I fought hard to keep a part of the land of the Franks for us. It is called the land of the Northmen. The land we hold is not a large land. You can ride across it in half a day and the length of it in one. But it is a rich land. The grass is green and lush. The trees are laden with fruit and the wheat we grow is much sought after. The seas team with fish and we can hunt in the many woods and forests. It is a good life. After the last battle, the Franks gave up trying to retake their land. They built walls to protect their towns as the Saxons had and we raided much as we had before. I am not a fool and I do not believe that we are done with the Franks. We have been lucky that their king and his sons have been fighting each other for Charlemagne's old empire.

We had drawn to us others who wished to live in the land and to use it to raid. Jarls brought their drekar and followed my banner. They raided with me and some stayed for they liked the land and they liked the way I ruled. I was no king. I was not even a count. I did not order warriors to do my bidding but every warrior who came to my land swore to obey our laws and to defend it against all who try to wrest it from us. We built walls around our homes. The walls were made of stone and wood. They had small towers and I had men riding the borders to watch for enemies. We were well protected. The men who rode my borders

1

had been Franks. Alain of Auxerre was the captain of the men we had rescued from south of the Liger. They did not farm or hold land as my Norse warriors did. They went around each of my towns and made sure that we had early warning of any danger. They wore dark blue cloaks with a white sword upon it. They all carried the same shields and they had the helmet with the nasal. They were oathsworn but they were not oar brothers. When we raided they watched the road from Rurik One Ear's home in the south to Flambard the Fisherman's home in the west. Then they rode to Bertrand of Ċiriċeburh in the north, east to Bárekr's Haven and finally to the Haugr. In two days, they could ride around my land. It allowed us to raid.

Jarl Thorbolt Sweynson and Jarl Sigtrygg the Left-Handed were two jarls who had brought their warbands to join me. They had both chosen to live in my land and we had given their men farms. It was with these warriors that we raided. They had helped me to defeat Henry of Carentan and Jean of Caen. As the Franks built defences and gathered men to stop us raiding we looked to the north and the land of the Saxons. Jarl Thorbolt hated the Saxons more than any man I had ever known. They had almost taken him and his ship. Had we not arrived then he would have been in Valhalla already. Since King Egbert had defeated the Viking fleet led by Klakke Blue Cheek and the men of Om Walum led by King Mordaf ap Hopkin, the King of Wessex had tightened his grip on his land. That did not deter us. We would raid them again. I had another reason to. I had been close to death after the last battle. A Saxon had almost ended my life. I think that I had visited the Otherworld but my son, Ragnvald Hrolfsson, had kept faith with me and that had brought me back from the brink of death. He was to be married to the daughter of Flambard. He wanted his own hall and he wanted it with the coin he collected himself. We would raid the land of the Saxons again and I would exorcise the ghost of the Saxon who had almost taken my life.

Chapter 1

Our knarr traded with Dorestad and it was from the men there that we learned our news. It had once been part of the Empire but Louis the Pious had lost his grip on it and now it was a free port. Ships could raid and then trade safely there. The port was inland on a mighty river. The land around it was swampy and some said that one day it would become landlocked. That was the future. The gods would decide that. For the present, it served our purpose to use it and its markets. There was an unwritten rule that there would be no fighting within its walls. All obeyed the rule for it would have been foolish to do otherwise. The men of Dorestad prospered. It was said they had begun to expand their land beyond the Walls of Dorestad. It did not concern us. We sent our knarr to sell our surplus and to buy that which we did not produce.

Siggi Far-Sighted returned from one such voyage. It was not a long one. A drekar could easily do it in a day and a night but a knarr, such as *'Kara'* could sometimes take two or three days if the winds were not right. While his men unloaded his ship, he hurried to my hall. We had been warned of the arrival for the anchorage was not an easy one even for a skilled seaman such as Siggi. We did not mind it for it gave us protection from the sea. My son and I were at the gate waiting to speak with him. His gait showed that he was keen to deliver news.

He nodded as he reached us, "Jarl Hrolf, I have news."

My son was growing into a man quickly but he was still impatient. "We can see that from the haste with which you joined us. Tell us your news."

Siggi gave me a sideways look. He had known Ragnvald since he had been a boy and he knew he was my heir but, like me, some of my son's ways irritated him.

"Of course. King Egbert and his son Æthelwulf made a journey to Cantewareburh. There they visited Ceolnoth. He is the holy man the Saxons call Archbishop."

Ragnvald looked disappointed, "And how does that profit us?"

This time I shook my head, "I know, my son, that soon you are to be married. Mathilde will lie beneath you and sigh over every word you utter but learn to speak less and listen more. You should show respect to Siggi and allow him to speak."

He looked chastened, "I am sorry, Jarl."

We had raided the land of Cent before now. It lay to the south of Lundewic. That was a huge trading port. "It has a rich church there, is it not?"

"It is Jarl and it is now richer. The king and his son have made a large donation to the church so that when King Egbert dies Archbishop Ceolnoth will ensure that Æthelwulf becomes king."

"And how did the men of Dorestad learn this?"

"The holy men came to trade and to spend some of their new-found wealth. They like the pots made and traded by Dorestad. They also bought much of the linen and lace which they make in the lands of Frisia."

I saw realisation dawn on Ragnvald's face. He had learned his lesson. He would listen more. "The burgh is a strong one, is it not?"

"Aye, jarl. They have appointed a thegn, Ethelbert, and he has a warband there. He has fifty men. The church pays them to protect their church and the relics there." Siggi knew that I would wish to raid and he was giving me as much intelligence as he had been able to gather. The priests would not have come alone. They would have had guards and servants. They would have talked over ale. Dorestad was a hive of gossip. Siggi was like Sven the Helmsman. He was a captain who knew how to listen and how to sift out the truth from the lies.

Ragnvald said, "We should raid them."

I shook my head, "Ragnvald, it is not all about treasure and gold. Did you not hear Siggi's words? That is but one part of the story. Kings play the game of thrones. King Egbert is preparing the way for his son to become king. That tells us that the king fears he has not long left."

"I do not understand."

"And that is because you have much to learn. Listen!" He nodded. "When a king dies, especially a strong king like Egbert, then there are always those close to the throne who will try to take advantage. There will be discord in the land. I did not say that we will not raid Cantewareburh, we will. The gods have given us this morsel and we will not waste it. However, when King Egbert dies that will be our opportunity to takes slaves and treasure."

"But the Franks!"

"King Louis and King Egbert are allies. When King Egbert dies then King Louis will also be weakened. He will lose an ally. King Louis has problems with his sons. The gods are sending us sheep to be fleeced. Do not waste the gift of the gods."

"I understand. But are you well enough to raid? You were near to death."

"I am recovered. The wounds have healed. A raid will tell me how well." I smiled, "Unlike you, my son, I do not have to row! I shall enjoy a pleasant sea voyage north. Now, send riders to Jarl Thorbolt and Jarl Sigtrygg to ask them to visit with me."

He was keen for something to do. I turned to Siggi. "We had good trades?"

"We did. The Holy Books we sold are much in demand. I was able to get the pots the women crave. Of course, Jarl Hrolf, it might be easier to simply raid inland where they make them. It would be cheaper than trading for them."

"One day, Siggi, when my men are all competent riders, then we will do so. Gilles and Bertrand, along with Alain of Auxerre are the only leaders whom I would trust to lead men into battle on the back of a horse and if we raided further inland then we would need to be mounted. I think the seas and the rivers will be our roads for the foreseeable future."

He nodded, "That suits us. I prefer a wooden hull beneath my feet. I will go and ensure that the pots are unloaded properly. We cannot afford to have damage." He smiled, "Your wife has a sharp tongue, jarl!" My wife had been the daughter of a Frankish noble. She liked well-made objects and it was she who had ordered Siggi to trade for the pots.

After he had gone I headed back into my hall. I had been less than truthful with my son. I had recovered but I would not trust myself to battle yet. A raid against a church was something which I could manage but a raid or a battle might expose my weaknesses. I had had dizzy spells. I had felt a pain in my head, especially late at night. I had ridden Allfather's Gift and Dream Strider but I had been too worried about falling off to enjoy the ride. I really needed to speak to a healer. I would have asked Father Michael but he was my wife's priest. Perhaps he might tell her. I did not want her worrying. Perhaps I rode with my death in my own head. I knew not. What I needed was to speak with Aiden, Jarl Dragonheart's healer. He was a wizard and he was gifted. He had removed part of Haaken One Eye's skull and put in a metal plate. Perhaps that was what I needed. However, I had a clan to watch and my personal problems were secondary. If I died then Ragnvald would lead the clan. My jarls and others such as Alain of Auxerre, Gilles and Rurik could guide him. He was rough clay and he still had a journey to take but I was pleased with the way my son was growing.

Mary was busy teaching our daughters how to read and sew. She was doing this by having them sew verses of scripture onto cloth. They would be displayed around my hall. I know that Mary thought that one day I would suddenly see the light and become a Christian. That would not happen. I followed the old ways and the old gods. They had given us much already and I could not see what this White Christ did for the Franks. If he was any kind of god he would not have allowed us to take their land so easily. She looked up when I entered. My daughters did too. "I did not tell you to stop just because your father entered. If you are going to be ladies then you must learn to read and to sew!"

I smiled. She was a hard taskmaster. "Siggi Far-Sighted has returned. He has pots."

That brought a smile to her face as I knew it would. It also meant that she would curtail the sewing and the reading lesson. My daughters would be able to go outside and play with the other girls! I went to my mail. I had not worn it since they had taken it from my body, thinking I was dead or dying. I had used sand and water to clean it. I had left it hanging from one of the rafters in my hall. Mary did not like it and the girls were frightened of it for they said it looked like a hanged man. It had not helped that Ragnvald had used a piece of rope to make it move one night as they were heading for bed. I needed it there so that I could see if the rust worm was eating into it. A weak suit of mail could spell the end of a warrior.

I took my mail down and, after putting on my padded byrnie, donned it. It felt heavy but, then again, it had been some time since I had worn it. Self-consciously my hand went to my head. The wound had bled but Father Michael had had to cut away my hair. It was growing again and made my scalp itchy. He had cleaned the wound with vinegar and it had scabbed over. The scab was now gone but I could feel the scar. I wondered what was going on inside my head. My smith, Bagsecg Bagsecgson, had not repaired my helmet. He had told me that there would always be a weakness. Instead, he was making me a new one. I walked over to his forge. If I was going to raid then I needed a helmet.

He was beating out some iron. From its length, I guessed it was for a sword. He was sweating and he was red but he had that look of joy upon his face which accompanied the making of swords. He and his father made the finest of swords and they were highly prized. He looked up when he saw me approach. He frowned upon seeing that I wore mail.

"Are you well enough for war, Jarl?"

"I am, Bagsecg, and I am here to ask if my helmet is ready."

He nodded. "It has been ready for some time." I frowned and he said, "If I am to be truthful with you, Jarl. I did not wish to tell you. I feared you might go to war. We almost lost you in the last battle. The clan cannot survive without the jarl."

"Your helmet saved me. Where is my new one?"

He picked up the bucket of water which was next to his forge and poured it over his head. "Ah, that is better. Firstly, I have changed it a little." He went to a chest and took something out. "Put this on first." He gave me a leather helmet. It was lined with sheepskin. I pulled it on. It was a tight fit. It rubbed a little against the scar. There was no pain but I was aware of it. My smith nodded as though satisfied. He adjusted it slightly. He made it square. He took a hessian sack from the chest and took out some mail. He handed it to me. "Put this on your head."

I saw that it was like a hood. I slid it over the leather helmet. It was a tight fit. The bottom half of the opening covered my chin and bottom lip. The top of the opening covered my eyebrows. Once again, he adjusted it. "I used Erik Long Hair to test the size. You and he have the same size heads."

6

He then took out the helmet. It was round but the top was more conical than my old one had been. I saw that he had made it cover my ears. There was a band of metal that went from my nose to the back of the helmet and a second one that went the other way. Finally, there was a third band that bound them and ran around the rim. He had used a different metal to the other two bands so that it stood out. The lighter coloured band ran around my eyebrow line.

"Try it jarl and I can adjust it while you are here."

I put it on. It was a tight fit and I felt an ache in my wound. I was a warrior and I gritted my teeth and bore it. Once it was on It felt good. Bagsecg seemed satisfied. "There are three layers of protection now and yet you have good vision. I have made it more conical so that the blow of an axe will be more likely to be deflected down. The top is protected by those two bands of metal. You cannot have a plume as I know the Franks favour. This is a helmet to protect you and not make you look pretty. The hood and the leather cap will absorb blows and the mail hood will prevent a blow to the throat."

I did not say that I could not hear as well as I would have liked. I was trading my hearing for the triple protection I would now enjoy. I took the helmet off and then the mail hood and the cap. I put the cap and the hood in the helmet. I reached into my purse. Bagsecg shook his head, "No, jarl. This is my gift to you." He smiled. "Besides the young warriors, like your son, will see it and they will pay whatever I wish to be dressed as Hrolf the Horseman. You wearing it will make me a rich man." He waved to his sons. "Already I have my boys making these hoods." I saw that his sons were toiling to turn out mail hoods.

He would accept no payment and I returned to my hall. I took off my mail. My wife said not a word. She and the three girls were examining the pots Siggi had brought to make sure that they were all perfect. She would say something when we were alone. That was her way. She did not like the way of the warrior. Her father had enjoyed the life of a noble. He had hunted. He had played politics and he had only gone to war when his king demanded it. I did not demand that my men raid. I offered them the opportunity. I poured myself a horn of ale and sat in my chair. I did my thinking there.

Although we had lost men in the war we had young men who were now old enough to take an oar. Warriors still came to join us. Some had come after Klakke Blue Cheek had been defeated. I had heard that some had joined Jarl Dragonheart and we had taken a few of the warriors we felt would be of our mind. We rejected more than we accepted. We did not do it with any malice but we were firm. Most of those we rejected headed north to Frisia or the land of the East Angles where Danes were growing in numbers. Our clan grew. Warriors like Erik Long Hair and Beorn Fast Feet had sons of their own and one day they would become warriors.

I worked out that we could set sail with almost a hundred spears. If that was not enough to take what the priests of Cantewareburh had robbed the king of then we should all become farmers. The raid was of practical value too. Ragnvald needed coin for his bride. He intended, for he had already spoken to me, to build a hall in the south close to Valognes. He did not want to be too close to either us or his wife's father. He had a hall close by the coast at Flambard's Stad. If he built one further south then we would no longer need one there. I think that my son relished the thought of raiding over the border into the land of the Franks and stealing more of their land. Mathilde was young but so was Ragnvald. When I had moved into the hall on Raven Wing Island with Mary then I had been young too. My son had begun to gather about him the young warriors who would take over from those such as Rurik One Ear, Erik Long Hair and Beorn Fast Feet. None of us were old warriors but Vikings did not live long lives. They lived eventful lives. The problem would be Mary. She would not approve of such a raid. It was not only my wound, it was the fact that we were raiding a church.

I looked up as she came in. "What is up then, husband? What do you plan that you hide from me?"

I knew that I would have to tell her. It was easier to get it out and then live with the silence and the looks. They would both pass!

"They have a great deal of treasure in Cantewareburh. We will raid there. Ragnvald needs coin for warriors and his hall."

"You would rob the church?"

Arguing with my wife was like walking through a boggy field. You considered where you placed each foot with great care. "We raid the Saxons. Do not forget, my love, that it was a Saxon who almost ended my life."

"And you would go along with the warriors?"

"I am jarl."

She looked to the heavens and clutched her cross. "Sometimes, Hrolf, I do not know you. Let others raid."

"Our son?"

She hesitated and then nodded, "I know that he must prove himself a man. It is in his blood. You, my headstrong husband, do not. You have proved more than enough that you are a brave man."

"I promise that I will not lead the attack and besides these are the priests of the White Christ. What can they do?"

It was the wrong argument to use and I knew it. However, she had a cunning look on her face as she said, "Of course our son will have to be married in our Church by Father Michael for Mathilde is Christian. Will our son be prepared for that?"

She was a clever woman and she had set me a puzzle. She was right. Flambard's daughter would wish a Christian marriage and our church was now the only one in my land. I compromised. I would speak with Ragnvald and let him make that decision. I smiled, "Of course, my dear."

I would be able to raid but it might cost me my son being married in a Christian church. That was a bridge we would cross but not until we had raided the Canti! I went out to seek Asa. She had been a slave who had been taken from Cent. Now freed, she had married one of my men and was one of our clan. I needed her knowledge. She told me all I needed to know about the land to the north of the church.

It was late when Ragnvald returned. "The jarls will be here on the morrow. They are keen to blood their young men." He looked at me. "Will I lead?"

"You will lead those men who have chosen to follow you."

"And the profits?"

I smiled, "You and your men will be given the share which is owed to *'Dragon's Breath'* once the jarl has taken his share."

"Which will not be as much as the jarl."

"When you are jarl you will have the profits and the responsibility. You will have to use your own coin to make the town safe and keep the people fed." I shrugged, "You can marry and spend your coin on your hall and your wife or you can spend it on a drekar. With your own drekar then you could raid where you wished. Then all the profit would be yours."

He laughed, "And this is how you make me a man! I will get my hall first. I am a patient man, father. I will have my own drekar and then the Franks should watch out." He was growing. A Viking grew up quickly. He had been fighting alongside me since he had been ten summers old but that did not give a warrior wisdom. The fact that I nearly died had helped. He had realised the responsibility which might be his. When he had decided to marry that completed the process of making the boy, the man.

Jarl Thorbolt and Jarl Sigtrygg the Left-Handed were very different warriors. They led their men in different ways but the one thing they had in common was that they were both more than happy to fight under my command. Both had had far more success since they heeded my advice and, when necessary, orders. As I had been not been raiding for some time due to my wound, they had both raided independently. Neither had brought back as much treasure nor as many men as when I led them. That was partly the fact that the more ships and spears you took the more likelihood there was of success but, in the main, it was because of their tactics and techniques.

It had been the scout, Ulf Big Nose, who had taught me how to scout and I used those skills before we raided. It meant we had fewer surprises. When I had followed the Wolf Banner of Jarl Dragonheart I had seen how the use of stealth could bring rewards. However, it had been Ulf who had taught me those skills.

My two jarls were happy that I was well enough to raid. I did not think their concern for my health was motivated by anything other than profit. They could smell the riches we would accrue. "It is good to see you recovered Jarl Hrolf. My men were keen to see your banner leading us to victory again."

9

"Thank you Thorbolt. It was a good fight and the Franks will think twice before attacking us again."

"Perhaps we could raid them again, they lost many good men. We did not."

I shook my head, "No Sigtrygg. The ones close by us were weakened but there would be little glory and no treasure there. The richer Franks live closer to the Issicauna. Paris is the place to raid but three drekars will not be enough."

"It is a stronghold?"

"They have an island and they have walls around the island. The king lives there and he is well protected. We would need as many ships as Klakke Blue Cheek took to Carhampton."

"That was over three hundred!"

"We have some way to go to match that."

The door of my hall opened and Ragnvald entered. I had sent him to Harold Fast Sailing and Sven the Helmsman to ask them to prepare my drekar for sea. I nodded and gestured for him to sit next to me. My eyes commanded silence. I saw him nod.

"We raid Cantwareburh. King Egbert has paid a great deal of treasure to the church to ensure that they support his son's claim to the throne."

"His son Æthelwulf who is King of Cent?"

"That is he. I know not exactly what the treasure is but King Egbert is rich. It will be worth the raid. The problem we will face is the men who guard the church. Thegn Ethelbert is a lord who serves the King of Cent. Our brethren's raids have taught them the wisdom of guarding their holy places. He has a hundred men."

Thorbolt nodded. "And there will be the fyrd. As soon as our drekar are seen then they will be summoned. Even the ordinary Saxons will die to protect their holy places."

"And that is why we will not land close by in our drekar."

They both leaned forward as I took out the calfskin upon which were marks I had made. It was a map. I had learned how to use them when serving jarl Dragonheart and his wizard Aiden. Mine was crude and could not compare with theirs but it served me well. My jarls thought it wizardry that the marks on the skin could be translated into victory and treasure.

"Remember when we raided the Isle of the Sheep?"

"Aye, we took many slaves."

"It is here just ten miles from Cantwareburh." I pointed to the coast to the west of Cantwareburh. "Here they have ports and burghs. There is a ring of them: Hrofecester, Sondwic, Doverre, Eopwinesfleot. The Isle of Thanet also protects the north and east. We have raided the Isle of the Sheep and we know the waters. There are channels that head south and east. From what Asa, a slave we took from Cent, told me there are few homes there. The ground is full of marshes.

There are families who live there but they are solitary creatures who trap eels and wildfowl. We could make our way through them."

"But you do not know the waters?"

"No Sigtrygg. My plan is to sail up them in the dark. We will first sail to the island of Walcheren. There are Vikings there. We will not land, we will just lie up during the day. If we leave in the middle of the afternoon then it will be dark when we approach Thanet. By the time we are at the channel, it will be dark."

"You would risk an unknown channel in the middle of the night?"

I shook my head and saw Ragnvald smile, "Sigtrygg, it is not the unknown. We are not sailing off the edge of the world. I spied the channel when we raided the Isle of the Sheep. At its mouth, all three drekar could sail side by side. I have no doubt that it will narrow. When it does then we stop. The closer we are to Cantwareburh the better. We leave men to watch the ships and to turn them around and we march however many miles it is to the church."

Thorbolt nodded, "It is a good plan for the priests of the White Christ rise early to pray. We will hear their singing and it will guide us."

Sigtrygg nodded, "Then I am happy too. What is your plan for this Ethelbert?"

I shrugged, "That depends where we find the hall of these warriors. They are there to protect the church. I am guessing that they will have their hall to the east of the church for our brethren normally raid from that direction. We will be approaching from the west. I intend to use my son and the younger, untried warriors to capture the church and the treasure. The more experienced warriors will form a shield wall and prevent the thegn from interfering."

Sigtrygg looked at my son, "He is young." He was not afraid of upsetting Ragnvald.

"He is but one day he will lead the clan. If you still follow my banner then you will serve him. Do you not want to follow a leader who has experience? This way my young warriors become blooded and we use our best warriors to defeat the Saxons. I hope that by the time dawn breaks we are heading back to our drekar, and as the fyrd is roused we are sailing home."

I could see that Sigtrygg had his doubts but they both nodded.

"We leave the day after tomorrow at dawn. My drekar is ready now and I will summon my crew this afternoon."

When they had gone Ragnvald asked, "Am I ready for this, father? Do you trust me to do as you say?"

"Are you ready? You can answer that for you can look into your heart and seek the truth. If you think not then tell me. I will not be upset. As for trusting you; I would not have suggested you had I not the utmost trust in your skills. This will be your chance to lead a large number of men. It is not easy. You will make mistakes but these are priests you fight. A mistake may not be as bad as if you faced a housecarl! You have those who follow you. They can have oars on

11

my drekar. I remember that there was a time when you said you would rather be on the back of a horse than taking an oar. Do you feel the same way still?"

He gave me an honest smile, "Of course I would rather be on a horse, father. There you are in control. On a drekar, you are subject to wind and tides. But I know that I must raid or I will not have enough coin for my hall. I cannot marry until I have my own hall and my own hearth weru. I will row and I will find those who will become, one day, my oathsworn hearth weru. However, I will only choose those who are good riders. My men will be the best of the best."

He left and I was satisfied. Had he lied to me then I would have been worried. Gilles and Bertrand would not be raiding, they were both horsemen but Folki Kikisson and his men would. They had sworn to follow me. The remnants of a large band who had tried to carve out a piece of Frankia for themselves, they hated Franks more than any other of my men. Before I rode to speak with Gilles, Rurik and Bertrand, I would speak with Folki. He would help me choose the men who would row my drekar.

He was happy to be going to war. Folki was a warrior. "There will be much treasure, Jarl?" A leader needed treasure to keep his men happy.

"There must be for he buys the support of the church. King Egbert is rich but what are coin and gold when you are dead? It is worth paying to ensure that his blood continues to rule his land."

"Then I will choose men wisely. There are some who only wish to raid when it is a worthy adversary and there is honour to be had. The priests of the White Christ and the men who guard them are not the Franks who wear mail and ride horses."

"Good. I leave that to you. I will return tomorrow after I have spoken with my three lords."

I rode alone and I rode my old horse, Dream Strider. His days were drawing to a close. He was old and I would not ride him to war. I had taken a Frankish warhorse in the last battle and he would carry me in mail. However, I enjoyed riding Dream Strider. We were comfortable with one another. We had been riding since Raven Wing Island. He was my first horse and he would always be my favourite. I knew that if I dropped my hands he would still obey every movement of my knees and my voice. All that was missing, to take me back to my youth, was Nipper my dog. The three of us had been inseparable. When Dream Strider went to the Otherworld then that part of my life would be over. I found that sad.

I rode first to Gilles. He had been my first warrior and he had looked after my horses on Raven Wing Island. He was the closest of my lords. He had a horse farm and a wall to protect his people. Like me, he was Norse and, like me, he loved horses. It was he who bred horses for war and it was he who trained young Vikings who wished to become horsemen.

His boys were now grown. They knew how to fight from the back of a horse and they wore mail. They would never row a drekar. That was what made my clan unique. We had horse warriors and those who fought in the shield wall. He was, like all of my men, concerned about my health, "You gave us all a scare, jarl."

"I know not why. Any of us can die. None of us is immortal."

"We all hope that you will be. You are the heart of the clan. It is good that you do not war with the Franks yet. Although we defeated them we lost riders and they take time to train. It is good that your son has a good eye for warriors who can fight on a horse. They are like him and like my sons, they are young. They will be the ones who conquer the rest of the Cotentin for the clan."

"Do not worry. We will not war with the Franks this year." After I left him I headed to Valognes. It was the first town we had captured from the Franks.

Rurik One Ear was, probably, my oldest friend. The others: Siggi White Hair and Ulf Big Nose were both dead but Rurik was a survivor. He had started a family late in life and now had eight children. His wife, Agnathia, seemed to be perpetually with child. I teased Rurik, now calling him Rurik Five Bellies for he was fat and would not fight outside the walls of his town, Valognes. He was still a doughty fighter but he would not stand in the shield wall.

I saw the twinkle in his eye when I told him of the treasure. "That will be a mighty treasure, Hrolf. I am tempted to join you on the drekar."

"I fear, old friend, that with your size we would be somewhat unbalanced."

He nodded and patted his belly which resembled that of his pregnant wife, "Aye you are right. I will have to make do with the tales you tell when you return." He became serious and put his hand on my arm, "You will return, Hrolf the Horseman, for life would be dull without you."

"Of course."

I stayed the night with him and left as dawn broke to ride to Bertrand in Ciriceburh. Bertrand was a Frank and a true horseman. When we had taken Ciriceburh from our enemies he had been the obvious choice as lord. He had made it even stronger and it was now our major port. It had a good harbour. Ships could land and unload at the dock which lay outside the walls. Bertrand and his men were not seamen but they were warriors and my northern port was the most secure place in my whole land. After I had spoken with him I rode back to my home with the eight men who wished to go raiding. They were the warriors who had no mail and wished to buy some. Mail was expensive and the best way to afford it was to raid with Jarl Hrolf.

We would be away for up to five days. I hauled up my chest and began to sort it out. I had two pairs of sealskin boots. I packed my older pair. I had a wolf skin. I was not Ulfheonar but I had hunted and slain a wolf. Along with my sealskin cape, the cloak was a necessary piece of clothing when at sea. I took my Saami bow and spare strings as well as arrows. In all likelihood, I would not need my bow but if I did not have it then I would need it. I did not take my spear but I had my seax and my sword. Heart of Ice had been made by Bagsecg's father. It was my oldest possession and, with a spell from Kara the volva upon it, had never let me down.

It set me to thinking about Ragnvald and his need for a sword. He had one. Bagsecg had made it for him but it was five years old and he was now bigger and stronger. When we returned from Cantwareburh we would have him one made. A warrior needed a good sword. A spear was used to get you warmed up when in battle. It cleared the chaff from the field but a sword enabled you to get close enough to see the fear in your foe's face. A spear was a clumsy weapon but even an incompetent warrior could kill with one. A sword, on the other hand, was an extension of a warrior. When I fought with Heart of Ice I did not have to think. The sword was of me. I knew that Jarl Dragonheart was now an old man and yet he was feared because of his sword, Ragnar's Spirit. It had been touched by the gods. If my sword was good then his was great. I would like a sword like that for Ragnvald.

The evening before we sailed, I visited with Sven the Helmsman and Harold Fast Sailing. They had been almost old men when we had sailed from Raven Wing Island. They were now shipbuilders. The skeleton of a drekar lay on the slips. We had no need of a drekar yet but one day we would and they were working on our new vessel. It was a labour of love. They had built '**Dragon's Breath'**. I thought her perfect but they knew ships and had identified weaknesses. There would be none in the new drekar.

"Jarl."

"How is '**Breath**'? Ready for sea?"

"Aye, jarl. She has no weed and we checked her keel for worm. She will fly."

Sven added, "And Siggi is ready. We have gone over the charts and the coast. He is nervous but that is understandable. He carries the heart of the clan with him."

I nodded, "He will do well. I leave enough men to guard the Haugr but I will need the eyes of you and your men to spy out danger too. I have spoken with Alain of Auxerre. The land is his domain but you watch for the wolves of the sea."

"Danes."

I nodded, "The Dragonheart was attacked by Danes and they are growing in both numbers and confidence. The land of the East Angles is almost theirs and I have heard that Eoforwic is known as a Danish city now. They call it Jorvik."

Harold smiled, "When we came here the gods guided the steering board. The sea, the island, the rocks and the tides protect us here but we will watch."

Chapter 2

We headed north and hugged the coast. The winds were warm and from the southwest. We did not have to row. Our three drekar were making good time. We had left at dawn and used the winds sent by the gods to speed us on our way. We feared no one. The Franks were notoriously bad sailors and their boats little better than tubs with a sail. The Saxons, on the other hand, were learning and now built better ships. I knew that one day they would build ships that were almost the equal to ours. Of course, their warriors could never match us on land or sea but they were a numerous people. They were like fleas on a dog and they multiplied as fast. We pulled in at the mouth of the Scheldt. It was as wide as a sea. Further upstream lay Dorestad but we would not venture there on this part of our voyage.

With a sea anchor thrown out and our sail lowered we ate. The swampy, insect ridden island did not invite a landing. Since my wound, I had not had as much of an appetite as before and I ate sparingly. I prepared my war face. The Ulfheonar had taught me how to do so. It began with the donning of padded byrnie, mail and sealskin boots. My seax and sword came next. I always used a whetstone before a raid to ensure that they were both as sharp as they could be. I saw my son giving me a curious look as I donned the leather cap. When I took out the mail hood I had the attention of all my warriors. Erik Long Hair knew of it but not the others. Folki watched, seemingly mesmerised as I slipped it over my leather cap and then held the helmet.

"I have never seen the like, jarl."

"Bagsecg was concerned that another Saxon might take it into his head to swing an axe at my helmet. Our smith thinks this will add protection. We shall see." I smiled as I saw them talking amongst themselves. Bagsecg was right. They would seek to own the same hood and helm.

I had the most interesting crew. Aboard we had the most experienced warriors. There were warriors from the Raven Wing Clan, Folki's band and there were the young untried warriors whom Ragnvald had brought and Bertrand had sent. Many would not return. The less experience you had the more likely you were to die. I was not underestimating the men of Ethelbert the Thegn. They would have mail and they would have battle honours. I could do no more. This was now in the hands of the gods or, even worse, in the hands of the Norns. Hitherto they had been kind to me but I knew just how precocious they could be. I stood and looked east. The Empire of Charlemagne was crumbling. Louis the Pious, his son, was clinging on to Frankia by his fingertips. I was raiding in the west but would my future be in the east?

We left in the middle of the afternoon. We had been fed. We had drunk our beer and we had put on our war faces. We headed west and we rowed.

It was Erik Long Hair who began the chant. It was my song. Many of those who had first sung it were now dead. This was a paean in their honour.

The horseman came through darkest night
He rode towards the dawning light
With fiery steed and thrusting spear
Hrolf the Horseman brought great fear

Slaughtering all he breached their line
Of warriors slain there were nine
Hrolf the Horseman with gleaming blade
Hrolf the Horseman all enemies slayed

With mighty axe Black Teeth stood
Angry and filled with hot blood
Hrolf the Horseman with gleaming blade
Hrolf the Horseman all enemies slayed
Ice cold Hrolf with Heart of Ice
Swung his arm and made it slice
Hrolf the Horseman with gleaming blade
Hrolf the Horseman all enemies slayed

In two strokes the Jarl was felled
Hrolf's sword nobly held
Hrolf the Horseman with gleaming blade
Hrolf the Horseman all enemies slayed

I saw my son at the bow oar grinning and singing along lustily. One day he would have his own chant. Men would honour his deeds. It was *wyrd*!

The coast had been a smudge on the horizon when we saw the sun slowly start to set. We would be in the dark and with an adverse wind we did not have our sails up. We would be hidden from view. We had stopped our singing now. Sound could carry and the songs had worked. The crew were in rhythm.

Siggi Far-Sighted had sailed here before but never as a captain. I knew that he was nervous. The last time we had sailed to the Isle of the Sheep he had been at the bow looking out for danger. His ship's boys did that now. I went to stand with him and I said quietly, "You are a good captain and you will find the channel. Sven and Harold trained you well. I spoke with them before we left and they had no doubts about your skill."

"But if I make a mistake, jarl? There are two other drekar behind us."

"And do they not have captains holding a steering board too? This is your responsibility, Siggi, not the two who follow us."

When the sun set and darkness fell we were reliant on the sharp-eyed ship's boys who stared into the blackness. The mouth of the Temese was wide but we sought the smaller channel around the Isle of the Sheep. I wandered to the bow and stood with my hand on the prow. The dragon's head had been cunningly carved so that it had a mane yet it still looked like a dragon. Those who carved such prows had skill. It is said that they used their own blood when carving to make the dragon's head come to life. Some, like my wife and the Franks, said that showed they were careless. I knew that was not true and my drekar breathed and lived. She was as much a part of the clan as any warrior.

Finni Audunsson was precariously poised on the sheerstrake holding the stay. He glanced down at me. "Watch for the land Finni! Forget that I am here too."

"Yes, Jarl Hrolf."

Ulf Big Nose had taught me to use all of my senses. I could smell the land. This part of Cent was swampy. I could smell the bogs. They lay on both sides of the drekar. That was good for it meant we were approaching the channel. The sound of the oars slicing through the water was the most dominant sound but, far off, I could hear waves as they broke on the shore. My eyes stared into the dark to seek the tell-tale lightness that would be the waves breaking on the shore.

Finni suddenly pointed to steerboard, "There jarl! I see land."

I looked to where he pointed. I could not see it but I trusted his judgement. "Well done. I will go and tell Siggi."

My men knew as I walked down the drekar, that we were close. Siggi would soon slow them down. I pointed, "There Siggi, to steerboard, is land."

"Then that will be the Isle of the Sheep." He turned to Lars, the ship's boy who held the light in the pot. "Signal '*Cold Drake*' three times."

Lars used the cloak to flash three times, warning Sigtrygg that we were about to slow.

"Half speed."

The men at the oars slowed down as we headed towards the invisible shore. We had a mile at most to travel before we would be close to the small river which would take us closer to our target. I went to the larboard side to try to spot

17

the river. It was its motion which told both Siggi and me where it was. The current fought the steering board. I saw the gap between the white of the waves and I pointed. Siggi nodded and pushed the steering board over. As we fought the current my men strained once more. Once we were in the river then our motion became easier. I glanced astern and saw the dark shapes of our other two drekar.

The breeze was from the southwest and it brought the smell of Saxons. It was the smell of wood smoke; the sheep dung mixed with the smell of pigs and cattle. We were passing through farmland. The swampy land close by the river was shunned by the Saxons. The islands of higher ground were their preferred homes. We would be hidden. I went back to the bow. We would have to find somewhere we could turn around. When the river became too narrow then we would stop.

As I passed Ragnvald he asked, "Are we close?"

"We are."

I reached Finni and he said, "The river is wide enough for three drekar Jarl."

I stared to the larboard side and saw what looked like open water. It was an illusion. The land was prone to flooding. If we crossed to the seeming pools we would ground. We had to keep to the centre of the channel. We had rowed a mile when Finni said, "Jarl, the river narrows."

I saw that he was right. There were trees that clearly showed where the land began. We could still turn around but any further and we would not be able to. I turned and, as I walked back said, "Stop rowing!" By the time I had reached Siggi, I said, "In oars."

Siggi said, "Lars, the signal. We are here."

I picked up my helmet and went to take my shield from the side of the ship. I hung it over my back. I wanted my hands free. I picked up my bow and arrows. I handed them to Ragnvald. He nodded. He knew what he would have to do. I would leave Siggi and the men assigned to guard and turn the drekar to their task. The warriors who were going ashore were busy preparing to land. Finni had jumped into the water and, after swimming to the bank was pulling the rope around the tree to draw the drekar closer to shore. I was ready and I walked to the prow and jumped in. The water came to my waist. I nodded to Finni as I passed him. When we were all ashore Siggi would use his crew to turn the drekar. Finni would secure it to the shore. There would be eight men to guard each ship. Armed with bows they would be more than a match for any Saxons who chanced upon them.

I clambered up the bank and then knelt to examine it. There was a path. We would be heading south and east. Until we came closer to houses we would stick to the river path. We would smell the church. The priests of the White Christ used candles and something Father Michael had told me they called incense. It would draw us as a bee is drawn by nectar.

Despite the fact that I was jarl, I led as scout. I had been the clan's scout. There were others who were good but I had been taught by the best. There would come a time when I would hand over the duties to another but this night I wanted to be at the point of our arrow as we carved our way through the undergrowth by the river. I saw that the river widened again. We could have come another five hundred paces further upstream. I stored that knowledge for the future. It would be marked on my charts and I would remember.

Sound carries at night and I heard a bell tolling. It would summon the priests to prayers. It acted as a beacon. I wondered if the Saxons who were the priests' protectors would be there at night too. If they had the sense then they would. Vikings liked to attack at dawn. When the river turned south we left the path and made our way through the swampy, boggy ground to the trees I saw two hundred paces away. It was a hard two hundred paces but we were rewarded by a greenway when we reached the trees. It was a wide and well-worn green road. A long way in the distance, for the greenway, was straight, I saw a dim glow. That would be a church. They had wind holes in the church to allow air in and they showed the glow of their candles. On a dark night, a tiny light was clearly visible.

We ran. It was not a breath sucking heart-pounding run it was a loping run. It was a rhythmic run. If we were not trying to stay hidden we would sing and keep up a pace as we did when we rowed. I knew that my men were doing as I was, they were chanting in their heads, and that kept the pace for us. The hard and compacted sod was better for running than stones. I could see a long way ahead and the trees were thin and well back from the sides. There would be no ambush. I sniffed the air and the sweet smell of incense swept towards me on the breeze. We had covered a couple of Roman miles when I realised that I had not had a pain in my head since we had landed. What did that mean? I remembered when Haaken One Eye had had his head opened. The warriors who witnessed it spoke of a black blob of blood which Aiden had removed. Was there one of those in my head just waiting to kill me? I would have preferred a wound I could see. I forced myself to chant again in my head and rid myself of these unwelcome thoughts.

I stopped and held up my hand when we were less than a mile from the walls. There had been Romans here and they had constructed a wall. The Saxons had reused part of the wall. I could see the familiar gatehouse. They had added a wooden palisade around it. The church was stone and surprisingly big. It was bigger than the one I had seen at Wintan-Ceastre. It had been built on a raised piece of earth. We would have to drop into a shallow valley and climb up. There was a Roman Road. It led directly to the walls. As I recalled it was called Watling Street and went from the coast at Dover all the way to Caestir in the far west. The Romans were mighty builders.

The wall prevented me from seeing the other buildings inside. I guessed that the Saxon hall would be close by. I waved Sigtrygg, Thorbolt and Folki to my side. The singing and chanting from the church, less than a mile away, would drown out my whispered words. "There will be another gate on the far side. The road to the coast passes through it. Folki and Sigtrygg take your men and attack the eastern gate when you get there. I will attack this one with Einar Bear Killer and Thorbolt.

They nodded and loped off. Thorbolt asked, "What if we attack before they are in position?"

"Then they will have an easier task for the Saxons will open the gates to send a messenger for help."

There were forty men behind me as we ran down the greenway. I saw that it merged with the Roman road. I suspected it carried on further south. There was little cover close to the walls. The darkness would hide us until we were a hundred or so paces from the walls. I wore a wolf cloak over my mail. Others had dark cloaks or seal skin capes too. Most of us would discard them before we fought. A Viking likes his arms free to swing. For big men, we could move remarkably quietly. As we headed up to the gates there was no jingling of mail nor thud of feet. Greased mail does not jingle and sealskin boots are silent. I stopped two hundred paces from the gates. I could see two sentries above the gates. They were the watch. They would open the gates at dawn. Until then they were barred to keep the burghers safe.

I waved forward Ragnvald and his six archers. My son was a fine archer. With my Saami bow, he was the best that we had. The six with him were equally good. I pointed to the sentries. The seven of them scurried across the open ground. I saw one of the sentries turn. Ragnvald was ready and his arrow struck the man in the chest. Two arrows from his companions hit the other. Their falling bodies would be seen by someone. Ragnvald waved half of his men to the wooden tower to the west and he led the others to the tower to the east. They would deal with any other sentries. We ran to the gate. There was a ditch but there was also a bridge to the gate. It was not a bridge that could be raised. It merely channelled all traffic through the gates.

Erik Green Eye and Gunnar Stone Face stood with their backs to the wall and a shield held between them. Two of Jarl Thorbolt's men did the same. I ran at the shield and, as I stepped on it, they boosted me up the wall. It was made of stone. The Romans were good masons. However, the Saxons had not bothered to keep it in a good state of repair. The mortar had fallen out in places. I grabbed hold of one of the stones and pulled as my foot found a ledge. I reached up and found another stone and pulled. My left foot found another crack. When I put my right hand up I found I had reached the top of the wall. I pulled myself up and tumbled over the wall to the fighting platform. I drew my sword and saw Thorbolt's hand coming over. I went to him and held my left arm to help him over. He nodded his thanks.

Swinging my shield around to the front I ran to the steps. It was then that we were discovered. A light shone from the guard hut and a Saxon stepped out. He saw the body of the sentry with the arrow in his chest.

"Alarm! Vikings!"

I jumped from the fighting platform. The man looked up as my sealskin boots descended. He broke my fall. There was a sickening crack as his back was broken by my fall. I did not keep my feet but I managed to roll and rise as the second Saxon emerged from the guard hut. I slashed instinctively and my sword tore across his chest and his middle. I quickly stepped into the guard hut. I needed the gate opening but the sentries had to be eliminated. There were two more inside. Neither had shields. I rushed at them. I hit one with my shield as I rammed my sword through the other Saxon's attempted parry and into his middle. As the last Saxon rose I stabbed him in the neck.

By the time I got outside Erik Long Hair and Jarl Thorbolt were there.

"Thorbolt! Open the gate. Erik and I will hold them off." Saxons were running from a hall which was forty paces from us. They were Ethelbert's men. "Erik, lock shields!"

With our left legs forward we braced our arms against our shields and held our swords above the rim. We had to buy time for our men to get through the gates. There were twelve Saxons racing at us but I was confident that we would resist their first assault. They should have formed a line and attacked us but they just hurled themselves at our shields and weapons. Perhaps they thought that their White Christ would, somehow, protect them. The swords of the first three struck our shields. Locked together they were like a solid wall. I stabbed over the top and my sword struck one Saxon in the throat. I tore it out sideways. Blood spurted as he tried to scream. A spear was rammed at my head from behind. This would be a test of my helmet. It glanced off the side and I did not even feel it. I swung my sword sideways in a long sweep. I caught one warrior on the side of the head and he tumbled into the next one. Erik had slain two warriors when I heard a roar from behind as the gates swung open and our warriors, led by Einar Bear Killer, rushed to the aid of their jarl. They threw themselves at the Saxons. They had been no match for two of us and the thirty who poured through the gates ended their defence rapidly.

I pointed to the warrior hall. "There is our target."

Ragnvald and his young warriors would secure the church and its treasure. We would eliminate the threat of the thegn and his men. The ones who had raced to fight us had been the watch. The Saxons who were supposed to defend the church now emerged from the hall.

"Wedge!"

While they tumbled out to fight us I formed us into the quickest formation we could; the wedge. I stepped forward and Einar Bear Killer and Thorbolt stepped behind me. Even as I was advancing towards the Saxons my men were filling in the rest of the wedge. Erik Green Eye, Beorn Fast Feet and Rolf Arneson stepped in to make the third line and we were just thirty paces from the Saxons who were still trying to organise a single line.

Behind me, I heard the chant begin as warriors banged their shield. It enabled me to move faster, in time to the beat.

Clan of the Horseman
Warriors strong
Clan of the Horseman
Our reach is long
Clan of the Horseman
Fight as one
Clan of the Horseman
Death will come
Clan of the Horseman
Death will come

In the time it took for the rest of the wedge to lock in as one I raised my sword and we struck the enemy line. It was not the thegn who was the target of my attack. He was still shoving men into a makeshift second line. The weight of forty mailed warriors takes some stopping. I did not even have to move my sword. I rested it on my shield and the weight of warriors forced the blade into the warrior's chest. He screamed as he fell and my foot almost slipped on his bloody chest. Their line was breached. I lunged at the only warrior before me. I made my sword swing sideways and into the neck of the young Saxon. He stood his ground and he died.

The Saxons were split and they were disordered and disorganized. We were a solid wall of metal, wood and steel. I turned to face the thegn. He had a full mail byrnie and a good sword. He swung it at my head. My shield came up. My arm shivered but the shield held. I had learned that striking a metal-rimmed shield or a shield boss was the best way to blunt a sword. I swung my sword high and tried to deliver a backhand swing at his neck. His shield could not block the blow and he had to bring up his own sword. Having just struck at my shield he was slow and he barely blocked the blow. I punched with the boss of my shield and it rapped into the knuckles of his right hand. I leaned into the blow and he had to take a step backwards. Unless you practise every day, such actions are not natural and he failed to swing his sword at me. It allowed me to sweep below his shield and his byrnie. It was a glancing blow but my sword tore through the ties on his leggings and into his leg. Bright blood stained my sword.

He had an open face helmet and I saw the fear on his face. It was compounded by the fact that, around him, his men were dying. They were being butchered my masters of the sword. A frightened man is defeated before he raises his sword. There is no belief behind the blows and he expects every strike by his opponent to succeed. He swung at my head again. I flicked up my shield and brought my sword from a high angle to sweep towards his neck. I think he had

22

been expecting another blow to his leg and his shield was held lower. It did not rise in time and my sword bit into his mail coif. My sword was sharp and well made. It ripped through the mail and into his neck. When the blood spurted in an arc I knew he was dead.

I looked to my left and right. The Saxons were dead. "Rolf, take three men and search the warrior hall. Beorn, go with Erik Green Eye. Find a cart or horses to take the mail and weapons back. The Saxons might be poor swordsmen but they make fine weapons."

I saw that two of Jarl Thorbolt's men were either dead or had suffered bad wounds. We would take them home with us. We did not leave our dead to be despoiled by Saxons. Cantwareburh was largely a place where they worshipped the White Christ but there were people there. They were the ones who served the priests. The men were being slain and, when it was all over, the women and children who might be of use to us would be enslaved. I turned and shouted to Erik Long Hair, "Come, let us see how my son fares."

We ran through the Saxon dead and dying. I saw the church door open and two Saxon warriors lay dead in the door. Inside I saw that eight priests were cowering before my son's men but my son faced a young priest who held a sword. Ragnvald had laid down his shield. The priest knew one end of a sword from the other and he swung a quick blow at Ragnvald's legs. My son had quick feet and he danced out of the way. He pirouetted and brought the flat of his sword across the back of the head of the priest. He tumbled unconscious to the ground.

I shook my head, "That was risky. Why did you not just kill him?"

He shrugged, "He was the first priest to fight back. I was intrigued. I will take him back with us and ask him why."

It was a reasonable answer. I looked around and saw the oldest priest who wore better robes than the others. He was a leader. I spoke in Saxon. It was not perfect but he would understand my words, "You! What is your name?" He did not answer immediately and so I punched my shield boss into the face of the young priest next to him. He fell with his nose a bloody mess. "Priest answer me or more blood will flow!"

"I am Archbishop Ceolnoth, barbarian. Do your worst. A place awaits me in heaven!"

I laughed. "Priest, all we want is the treasure Egbert gave you to buy the throne for his son." His eyes flickered to the altar. He stood obstinately silent. "Erik, Ragnvald, move the altar. There will be a door beneath it and a crypt. We will find what we need there."

"Aye, jarl Hrolf!"

"And bind these priests They annoy me!"

Leaving my men to do my bidding I went over to the altar. Einar Longlegs who was one of Ragnvald's men was already using the altar cloth to gather the candlesticks and dishes the priests used for their rituals. My men were strong but the altar was big and heavy. When they pushed it away, there was a wooden door. Jarl Thorbolt asked, "How did you know? Is this wizardry?"

I shook my head, "They often use such places." I took one of the candles that had been lit and held it close to the door as it was opened. The air which rushed out made the candle flicker. "Ragnvald, go down with three of your men. Bring everything you find there no matter how strange they seem. If they hide it then it is valuable to them. We can always sell it back to them!"

He grinned. It was almost a game to him. "Aye, jarl."

"I leave you, Jarl Thorbolt, to see to the treasure. Begin heading back to the drekar with it. Choose women and children who will not slow us down."

"Aye, jarl."

I left my men and headed to the eastern gate. I had not seen Sigtrygg and Folki. Had they encountered trouble? I soon found them. They were carrying bales of wool and sacks. Folki asked, "We have the church?"

"We do and we have killed the guards." I looked to the east. The sun was beginning to rise. "Did you have trouble?"

"Not really, jarl. When you attacked they did as you expected and opened the gates. We rushed them. They had twelve warriors guarding the gate but they were little trouble. We found a hall and it was filled with these bales of cloth and there were sacks of iron and copper. I know not where they were bound but they are a true treasure."

"Good. Jarl Sigtrygg have your men prepare fires. We will delay pursuit by firing the town."

"Will that not draw Saxons here?"

"It will. We know there are none to the west of us, where our drekar lie. This way we draw those from the east. That way they cannot pursue us in their ships."

He smiled, "Each time I think I am becoming a better leader you show me that I know nothing! I will make it so."

By the time we reached their church the crypt had been emptied. My son pointed west, "I have sent it to the ships. There were many things I did not understand. I found gold and jewels and crowns but I also found clothes and boxes of bones."

"They are relics of saints. To us they are worthless but to these priests, they are worth a fortune." Gudrun Witch Killer had the priests kneeling and his sword was ready to execute them. "Gudrun take the priests to the ships. Leave the old one here."

He looked disappointed, "Aye, jarl."

I took my sword and cut the Archbishop's bonds. Ragnvald was prodding the priest who had fought him. He pushed him, with the point of his sword, from the church. There was just the Archbishop and me left. "This is what you will do, priest. If you wish your priests returned and the relics which you value, then you will send a ship to my home in Frankia. It is called the Haugr and is south of Ćiriċeburh. The price for the relics and the priests is a thousand pieces of gold."

"And our treasure?"

"Is now my treasure. You can buy back that which we do not want."

"How do I know that I can trust you?"

I pointed my sword at his stomach. "You do not. You have two moons and then I will sell the priests and the bones. There are lords in Frankia who pay well for such things."

"God will have his vengeance upon you."

I shrugged, "As I have been doing this for years it seems he is a very forgiving god. Perhaps he hopes that I will have a change of heart. I will not." I turned to go and then said, "Oh and your town will soon burn. This building is made of stone. It should survive."

"Why, barbarian?"

"King Egbert is the enemy of the Jarl Dragonheart. If I can hurt Egbert then I serve Jarl Dragonheart still."

I could see that he did not understand. I did not care. Folki, Erik Long Hair, Einar Bear Killer and the rest of my men awaited me at the gate. I was the last one to leave the town. Already the flames were licking the east wall. Jarl Sigtrygg had set the fire there to allow the wind to bring it through the town.

"We go!"

With the sun rising behind us the trail was much easier to follow. We did not run. If enemies pursued us then we would turn and we would fight. The twenty men with me were the best that I had. Besides, it would take time to load everything on our three drekar. Folki asked, "Will the priest pay?"

"He will pay. I am guessing that he will go to Egbert. He will complain that he was left unprotected. The Archbishop is a clever man. He will argue that without his priests he cannot support the King's claim. Egbert will find the money. He may even send men to try to take the relics and the priests without paying."

"He is old."

"You are right. Perhaps his son will come."

"You have thought of all this, already?"

"It is what I would do. If someone took that which I valued then I would try to take it back by force. We will be ready."

I thought I was so clever. I felt that I had outwitted Egbert and the Archbishop. Of course, the Norns had outwitted me. When we reached the river, I saw that the three drekar had been loaded but all of them were stuck in the mud. The tide had gone out.

Poor Siggi looked distraught. "I am sorry jarl. I should have realised that when we loaded the ships, as the tide had turned out we would be grounded."

I smiled, "It cannot be helped. I thought the raid had gone too well." I cupped my hands and shouted, "Leave four men on each ship to watch the prisoners. Take off your mail and helmets. The Norns want to know if we can pull our boats to the sea. What say you?"

I heard a roared, "Aye, jarl!"

I joined my men and held the rope with them. We were waist-deep in the water. We would have to pull until it was up to our chests. Then the rising tide would float them and take us to the sea.

I began a chant. I chose one which my oathsworn would know. It was the song of Siggi White Hair. We owed all to Siggi. He had guided the clan to our new home and he had been as a father to me. We chanted and our hearts swelled with pride as we did so.

Siggi was the son of a warrior brave
Mothered by a Hibernian slave
In the Northern sun where life is short
His back was strong and his arm was taut
Siggi White Hair warrior true
Siggi White Hair warrior true
When the Danes they came to take his home
He bit the shield and spat white foam
With berserk fury he killed them dead
When their captain fell the others fled
Siggi White Hair warrior true
Siggi White Hair warrior true
After they had gone and he stood alone
He was a rock, a mighty stone
Alone and bloodied after the fight
His hair had changed from black to white
His name was made and his courage sung
Hair of white and a body young
Siggi White Hair warrior true
Siggi White Hair warrior true
With dying breath he saved the clan
He died as he lived like a man
And now reborn to the clan's hersir
Ragnvald Hrolfsson the clan does cheer
Ragnvald Hrolfsson warrior true
Ragnvald Hrolfsson warrior true

The song made us move together. At first, the drekar refused to budge. Lesser men might have given up but the three crews pulled together. When I felt a slight movement, it gave me heart. Suddenly the drekar slid off the mud, making a sucking sound, and the bow was in the water. The next pull took us further from the mud. Beneath our feet, the slimy, muddy bottom did not help us but we persevered and eventually, the drekar floated. The sweat was pouring from me but we continued our chant and continued to walk downstream. It took until the sun had risen higher in the sky before I felt the water lapping around my chest. "Warriors of the Clan of the Horse, you have shown the gods that you are worthy! Back to your ships and we will let the wind carry us home!"

They cheered. We had lost but a few men and we had gained great riches. We had been set a challenge and we had overcome it. We washed the worst of the mud from us before we clambered back aboard our drekar. We drank our beer and ate the salted fish we had brought. The work had made us hungry. We had time before we sailed home.

With our cargo, it might take two days to reach the Haugr. Our men would be able to row but not for a little while. My shoulder muscles still burned from the effort. The three captains of the drekar had to use all their skills to shift us along the river until we saw the estuary and the sea. As we edged into the water of the Temese the wind caught our sails and they billowed. It was a good sign.

My men were all barefoot. Our boots needed to dry out. Our cloaks, too, were laid out to dry. When we reached our home, our mail would need work. Luckily the grease we had applied would prevent too much damage to water. As the wind took us east I used my whetstone to put an edge back onto my sword. The more experienced warriors did the same. I smiled as I saw Ragnvald and his young warriors talking about the raid and their part in it. I saw that the priest who Ragnvald had laid out now had a bandaged head and was tied to the mast fish. My son meant what he had said. He wished to learn what made this priest different from the others.

Erik Long Hair and Folki joined me. They too sharpened their weapons. "Your son did well, jarl, but why did he let the priest live?"

"There would have been little honour in killing him."

"But he raised a sword to him."

"My son is like his mother. He is a thinker."

Folki smiled, "As are you, jarl. I confess that, like your son, I am intrigued by this priest who did not turn the other cheek but tried to kill your son. Perhaps he was touched by Loki."

"The Christians do not have a Loki. They have someone they call the Devil or the Unnamed One. He seems to fight their White Christ. My wife tried to explain it to me. I had thought it a good tale at first but it did not seem to have an ending. It could be he was touched by this devil. My son will discover the reason."

Erik Long Hair said, wistfully, "You are lucky to have such a good son. Not all warriors have the comfort of an heir who can carry on the work they have begun."

Folki nodded, "It is time I took a wife. I look at Thorbolt and Sigtrygg and see them settled on farms and siring children and I envy them. Now Ragnvald will soon be siring sons. I owe it to Fótr."

I nodded. Fótr had been a young warrior whom I had admired. He was a good leader but he had an untimely death. He would have sired warriors. I hoped that Folki would do the same. I wondered at Erik's words. Did he have problems with his son? I had no time to reflect on that and the thoughts disappeared for the Norns had been spinning again.

With the wind from the south and west, our men would not need to row again until the wind changed. Many now lay asleep as the sun reached its height. It was as we turned south and east that the ship's boy shouted, "Saxon ships! Six of them!"

We looked to where he pointed. From the land came the sails of six of the new Saxon ships. The Norns had grounded us for a reason. It allowed the Saxons to get to their ships and to prepare to retake their treasure.

I shouted, "Arm yourselves! We fight again this day!"

Chapter 3

"Break out the bows." My men hurried to their chests to take out their bows. It was our best offensive weapon until we could close with them. If they expected us to run then they had misjudged the matter. I turned to Siggi, "I want you to steer directly for them." I saw the question in his eyes. Had this been Sven or Harold they would have known the reason. I would have to explain. "The wind does not favour them. They have oars and they will have to row. We had the wind and our men can be ready to fight if we need to. You sweep towards them and, while we use our bows to slay those who steer them, you use *'Dragon's Breath'* to shatter their oars. After we have hit them then turn south and east. The wind will take us towards our home and they will lose time turning. If our ships cannot outrun them then there is something wrong."

He grinned, "Aye, jarl. I should have known myself."

I took the Saami bow. Ragnvald had only used six arrows. I had plenty left. After I had chosen the best one I glanced astern and saw that my drekar were following me in line astern. The Saxons were trying to make a barrier of their boats. They were rowing to meet us. I think they intended to use the weight of numbers to defeat us. The men who did not have bows would use either slings or the throwing spears. Using a sling they could hurl the javelins a long way. The gods were with us and we seemed to fly across the white-capped waves.

"Captain, I see two more Saxons further south. They are sailing east."

Siggi looked at me as he heard Lars' words. "The Saxons are learning. The other two ships will have the wind. They will try to stop us should we break this line. They must want this treasure badly."

One ship seemed to be leading the other five and I pointed to that one. Siggi nodded and adjusted his course. We were approaching rapidly and I pulled back my bow and released an arrow high into the sky. It was to gauge the range. The wind was helping. The arrow plunged down towards the steering board. They had not seen it and I saw a warrior fall. The arrow stuck out of his thigh. Shields were raised around the warrior on the steering board. Unlike us, the Saxons did not like to fight in mail. My men began to release their arrows. More than half fell into the well of the ship. There they had rowers. A man cannot use his shield and row. Their oars were disordered as rowers fell and their oars collided with others. The nearest Saxon began to turn towards us. It was a gift from the gods.

"Now Siggi!"

He put the steering board over. We were less than thirty paces from the Saxon. Arrows, stones and spears were hurled into the Saxon. Our keel struck the oars on their steerboard side. The drekar's hull splintered and shattered them. Inside the Saxon ship, it would be carnage as broken splinters of wood became deadly weapons. They would tear into flesh and be as dangerous as an axe wielded by a berserker.

The other ship was now within range and I shouted, "Larboard side!"

We switched to the other side and released our arrows, stones and spears. This time we were unable to shatter their oars for they turned away. Their captain had seen the effect of our hull. He moved further from us but we made the ship a charnel house. Just then one of the priests who had been a hostage broke free and, running to the side hurled himself into the waters. I do not know if he thought to save himself by walking, as his White Christ did, on the water. His head came up once and then sank beneath the waves. I looked astern and saw that the Saxons were in disarray. My other two drekar were adding their arrow storm to ours as the four Saxons who were yet untouched, tried to turn and use the wind.

I now saw the two Saxon ships which had left the shore to cut us off. I turned to see the Saxons behind us. It would take them some time to turn. "Siggi, make for the second Saxon. I want us to lay alongside his stern."

There was no question this time, "Aye, jarl."

"Folki, Erik, I want ten men to board the Saxon. We will cut their steering board and fire the ship. Have a fire in a pot. Ragnvald, have the men ready on the oars. When we are boarded again we will row until we are free of this Saxon trap."

"Aye, jarl."

I went to the chest with the deck weapons and took a hand axe. It had been sharpened before we left and would be the perfect weapon for what I intended. Our change of course had taken Jarl Thorbolt by surprise and his drekar was now parallel to us. I went to the stern and pointed to the leading Saxon. I saw him raise his sword in acknowledgement.

I saw that our change of course had confused the Saxons. Were we trying to sail to the landward side of them? They did not want to lose the wind and so they both turned slightly further south by east so that they could turn and cut us off. It made what we were doing easier. The new Saxon ships were not as tubby as the older ones but they were not the lean dragons we sailed. We closed rapidly with them. Siggi had learned well and the art of a good captain was knowing how to use the sails effectively. Siggi did. He gave orders and the sail was furled as we closed with the Saxon. I was at the prow with my axe in hand and I clung on to the stay. Saxons do not use bows or, if they have them, they do not use them well. Had they had a good archer then they would have been able to slay me.

As our dragon reared over the steering board I jumped down to land on the deck. I swung my axe and it hacked into the chest of the warrior guarding the helmsman. Folki, Erik and my men followed me. They raced to clear the stern and to form a protective wall. I turned and found the steerboard withy. I began to hack through the ropes which bound it. As soon as the ropes were cut I gave a mighty swing and sheared the steering board. It fell, with a splash, into the sea.

"Folki! Fire!"

"Jarl!"

He picked up the pot he had brought and he threw it on the deck. The dry timbers flared and flamed.

"Back!"

The Saxon warriors were advancing towards us. The fire was now a barrier. On my drekar, Ragnvald had taken it upon himself to organize the archers and they began to rain arrows on them. The ship's boys threw ropes and we swung back to '*Dragon's Breath'* I walked up the bows to clamber back. The wind had taken the Saxon sails and began to push the ship away from us. Without a steering board, they would have to run out oars and use them to steer. Their captain and sailors were dead. As the sail billowed above us and Ragnvald and his men began to row, we started to put clear water between us and the Saxons. The ship we had fired was now ablaze. I did not think they would save her. Her consorts would have to come to her rescue and that alone would stop their pursuit. I glanced to the larboard side and saw that Thorbolt and Sigtrygg has used arrows to clear the stern of the other Saxon. It was edging towards the stricken Saxon. We were clear. When they saw our oars they, too, began to row. With the wind and my men aiding us, our three drekar were soon far enough away from pursuit for me to order the men to stop rowing. The smoke on the horizon marked the Saxon ships.

Our raid had been successful and yet not without incident. My men began banging the decks and chanting, "Hrolf the Horseman! Hrolf the Horseman! Hrolf the Horseman!" I saw Ragnvald joining in. I nodded my thanks.

Siggi said, "With this wind behind us we should be back at the Haugr by dawn."

"Good. I like not travelling with so many captives for long periods." I took off my mail hood and my cap. "Ragnvald, come and help me take off my mail."

He helped me to pull it over my head, "I can see, father, that you have skills I do not possess. I know how to position horses for the best effect but not a drekar."

"You need to use your mind more to make a ship do as you wish. You use the wind. In some ways, it is easier. A ship has to obey wind and tide. A horse does not. You have chosen your path, son, and I am happy. You have chosen the way

31

of the horse. I can go from horse to ship. That is my path. I looked down at the bandaged priest. His face was full of fury still. "My men think you should have killed him. From his face, they may be right."

"I might throw him to the fishes but first I will question him. He had skill with the sword. It was not enough to defeat me but he fought like a warrior yet he wore the habit of a priest. I am curious. Come and listen while I question him. You have an ear for such things. You seem to know men's thoughts from the words they do not say."

I nodded, "I watched Jarl Dragonheart and Aiden the galdramenn. They taught me the skill. I will watch him for you."

Ragnvald showed how much he had grown by cutting the priest's bonds. I saw the surprise on his face. Ragnvald offered him the water skin. The priest looked dubious. I took the skin and drank from it before giving it back to him. He nodded and drank.

"What is your name?"

The priest hesitated. I almost smiled as I saw him trying to work out if giving his name was a sign of weakness. Ragnvald was patient. He took a piece of dried cod and began to chew it. His eyes never left the face of the priest.

"I am Æðelwald of Remisgat."

"Ah, the port from whence the Saxons sailed." I was impressed. My son was guessing but he did it well. The priest nodded. "Tell me, priest, why does a man who follows the White Christ carry a sword and how does he know to use it like a warrior?"

I saw the same debate. This was an angry young man. As he wrestled with his decision I examined him. He looked to be of an age with my son. He had the hair and build of a Saxon. Ragnvald had taken his sword and brought it on board. I picked it up. Æðelwald of Remisgat stared at me. There was a fierce anger that I held his sword. I could understand that. The blade was shorter than mine but it was well made. There were words etched into the blade. The pommel and hilt were plain but this was a true warrior's sword. I spun it in my hand. It was well balanced. I tried to bend it and I could not. My actions seemed to make up the mind of Æðelwald of Remisgat.

"My father and my brother were warriors. They fell at the battle of Carhampton and I was left with my mother. King Egbert took our land and gave it to another. My mother's heart broke and she died. It was either the church for me or starve. I chose the church."

Ragnvald nodded, "And you hate Danes."

"They killed my father."

"If you fight us then you will be beaten." He shrugged. "So, you learned the sword and chose the cross."

"I would that I could fight the Danes but I will not fight for King Egbert or his sons."

I liked the youth. He was honest and not afraid of speaking his mind.

He saw me looking at him, "Do I die now or when I get to your home?"

"That is not my decision. You are my son's prisoner. He will decide your fate."

He looked at Ragnvald who shrugged, "I have yet to decide."

That seemed to satisfy the young man but I saw him looking at the sword in my hand. He would use it if he were given the opportunity. I would have two of my men guard him.

I walked back to the stern. I was keen to examine the treasure but it was all stored below our decks. When we reached the Haugr it would be divided up between the jarls. I knew that they would defer to me. I was known as a fair and generous jarl. It was another reason why men followed me. Leaders who were mean with their booty soon lost support.

The wind continued to favour us but as we crossed the open sea between the land of Wessex and Frankia the drekar tossed in the powerful waves. Some of the priests began to wail and pray as though their god would save them. It was interesting that Æðelwald of Remisgat did not. He sat with his back to the mast fish and his eyes closed. Was he planning an escape or contemplating his fate?

I had Gunnar Stone Face and Erik Green Eye watch our prisoner. It would take a brave man to try to escape Gunnar. I slept but awoke before dawn. After I had made water I walked the length of the boat. The other priests were asleep. Some slept in pools of vomit. Siggi would make them clear it up before they left the drekar. Æðelwald of Remisgat was also asleep but, as I approached, his eyes flickered open. They briefly rested on me and then closed as he returned to his dreams.

I went to the prow and stared at the darker shadow that was the coast. I was pleased with the raid but I knew that I was putting off the inevitable. One day I would have to carve out a larger land for the warriors who followed me. The best land had already gone. South of Valognes there was rich farmland. It belonged to the Franks. We would have to take it from them. I knew that more men would come to us following our raid. Warriors would wish to follow the jarl who bloodied Egbert's nose. I was still standing by the prow when the sun rose in the east. The land of Frankia was favoured by the gods. That morning as the sun's golden rays lit it up I was happy that I had followed my dream and listened to the witch in her cave.

It took time to tack around to the anchorage. It was almost noon by the time we were at the wooden jetty where we landed our prisoners and our treasure. I had my men escort the priests to the church. Ragnvald had his own personal prisoner taken to my hall. The slaves were landed next and Sigtrygg and his men escorted them to the slave pens. Finally, after the handful of animals, we had taken had been landed we took up the decks of the three drekar and carried the treasures to my hall.

Father Michael walked over to us after the hostages had been taken to his church. "Is this wise, Jarl? King Louis is an ally of King Egbert. This might rouse the sleeping dog. Would you have war again with the Franks?"

"I know why you try to chide me, it is because they are priests, Father Michael. Do me the honour of speaking the truth. I do not use deception when I speak with you. We will have war with King Louis again. That is as sure as the sun rises. One day some relative of Henry of Carentan will complain to the king that Vikings hold the land which belongs to him. Or someone else will ask for land and he will give them that which we hold. I am not naïve. We have a truce and nothing more. Besides the Archbishop Ceolnoth can have the hostages and his Holy Books unharmed when he pays me a ransom. I have not hurt any. I even left the Archbishop in his church." I smiled, "Perhaps I am softening in my old age."

"Your wife will not be happy."

"My wife is never happy. To please her I would have to give up my sword and put up my feet. I may do that. Ragnvald is becoming a good leader. He could raid for me. However, she also wishes me to become Christian and that will never happen!" I saw the frown on the priest's face. He wished us to change completely. That we would never do. There would always be a Viking deep inside us. "I hope that you can watch over the priests for me? I will provide food and guards for them. Warn them that if they flee I will hunt them down and kill them. You know I would do it."

"I will do so. I would not have their blood on my hands." As I turned to go Father Michael said, "Lady Mary visited with me yesterday. She asked about Ragnvald and Mathilde's wedding."

I could hear the nervousness in his voice. My wife had visited while I was away for she, too, feared that I might react angrily. I smiled, "It is my son's wedding. If he wishes to please his bride he might well marry in your church. His father has paid enough coin to make it the beautiful place it is. However, do not expect him to become a Christian. He is a warrior and would lead a warband. I will tell him about his mother's plans. He is a man now and he can make his own decisions."

We laid the treasures out so that all the warriors who had fought could see them. As leader of the clan, I would have the first choice. I would decide which of the treasure was for the other jarls and which for my men. The only time there had been trouble was when the new men on Raven Wing Island objected to Siggi's division. We had not had that problem yet. The treasures were laid out logically. The Holy Books and the relics were together. The crowns, jewels and coins were in a second pile. The iron, metals, foods, cloths, candlesticks, candles and other items were also together. Finally, there was the largest pile: the weapons, helmets and the mail.

I made it simple. I first divided the gold and crowns into four equal piles. I saw the surprise on Jarl Sigtrygg's face. He would learn that was the way we worked in my clan. I waved over Bagsecg and pointed to the metal. "That is your share."

He picked up a piece of metal and spat on it. He rubbed it with his finger. His face beamed, "This is ore of the highest quality. This is the iron with which they make the best swords. He pointed to the crowns. This is the equal, in value of any of those."

"Good."

The domestic items I split into four. One quarter was for the people of the Haugr. Finally, I divided the weapons and mail into six. One share would go to Bertrand and one to Alain of Auxerre.

When the division had been made I said, "Is the clan happy?"

The warriors banged their shields and yelled, "Aye."

I saw that Æðelwald of Remisgat was talking with my son. The anger had gone from his face. It often happened thus. He was a clever youth and knew that his fate was tied to ours and he accepted it, for the present. I waved them both over. "Æðelwald, tell me what these relics are. I can see the books and know their value but there are five chests here." He hesitated. "I have said that the priests and the Holy Books will be returned to the Archbishop when the ransom is paid."

He nodded. He opened the first box, "These are the bones of St. Tatwine." There was a skull and what looked like the hands of the saint. I opened a second. "This is the cross of St. Bregwin." To me, it looked like a dozen other such crosses I had seen in churches I had raided. The third was the largest of the chests, "This is the vestment and ring of St. Theodore of Tarsus."

"Vestment?"

"The clothes he would have worn." Now that he was instructing me the young priest's tone had changed. He opened the fourth one. It was a long narrow box, "This is the crosier which is the archbishop's symbol of office. He is the shepherd."

The young man appeared reluctant to speak of the fifth box. I went to open it. He said, "That is not of the church. King Egbert placed it there. It was one of his gifts to the archbishop. It is not Christian, it is pagan!"

I saw now why the youth was reluctant to open it. What could King Egbert wish to keep in the church that was pagan? I opened it and saw that it was the hilt, pommel and sword guard of a Saxon sword. There was a blue stone in the pommel. The blade had almost rusted away. It was in pieces.

"A sword?" He nodded. "Tell me more." He seemed reluctant. "If it is pagan then the archbishop will not wish it back, will he?"

"He might."

"Why? Come, you have us intrigued. It is a sword and we are warriors. You were a warrior."

He sighed, "It is the sword of Hengist the first king of Cent. He was a Saxon. It was passed to his brother Horsa and then his son Octha. It was said he died in battle and one of his oathsworn took the broken sword back to his family. It has been passed down through all the kings of Cent. Once King Egbert's son, Æthelwulf, became King of Cent, it passed to him and King Egbert wished it to be safe."

I looked at Ragnvald and spoke to him in our language. "I see now, my son, the hand of the Weird Sisters. You were meant to spare this youth for we would have given back this box with the other relics."

"And we do not?"

"It is not a relic of the church. You were meant to have this. I was going to have Bagsecg make you a new sword. He has Saxon sword iron and we have parts of an ancient sword. This hilt, pommel and stone will be part of your new sword. It is *wyrd*."

I saw his eyes light up. "Aye, father, you are right. And with my share of the treasure and the weapons, we can build my hall. I can begin to become a leader."

I looked at Æðelwald of Remisgat, "And the priest? Does he live or die?"

"Our threads are entwined. If I cut his thread then I end my own."

"Then think carefully how you will use him." I pointed to the church. "You will need to speak with Father Michael for your mother is making plans for your wedding. Ask him about Æðelwald of Remisgat. Take him with you when you speak with the priest. I think it will help."

"You are wise, father, and you see beneath the surface of men's minds and words. We are lucky that you lead us."

"Remember son, that one day, and that day will be soon, you will be the leader. Prepare yourself."

I closed the chest and picked it up. Æðelwald looked at me as though he was going to object. I walked away, leaving him to my son. Bagsecg and his sons had just collected the metal and were sorting it. "Bagsecg, a word." He came over to me and I opened the chest. "I would like a sword for my son. I wish some of the iron I gave you, the stone, pommel and hilt from this blade. It belonged to the first King of Cent."

His eyes lit up, "That would be a mighty sword."

"I would have the best sword that you have ever made. It might not be touched by the gods but with the magic which is in the iron, this box and your hands it would be a blade which even the Dragonheart might envy."

"I will make the blank and then contemplate the design. This will not be a quick job, jarl."

"I know. You have other metals that you can use to decorate it. Do not stint. I will pay you well."

"You have paid me already by commissioning the sword. My father is known all over the world of the Viking. When I make this my name shall live forever too. It is *wyrd*."

My wife was in a difficult position. She had gone behind my back to the priest to arrange the marriage. She did not know, for certain, that I would be reasonable about it. On the other hand, she was unhappy with the relics and the hostages. It was like a battle with an unknown enemy. I would have to judge my words carefully and time them well.

My daughters were waiting for me when I entered. "What have you for us father?"

It had only been the men who had watched the division of the spoils. They had seen my slaves bringing in the pots, goblets and vessels which would please my wife. They smiled at me as though that would bring them greater rewards. I had three necklaces I had taken from some of the richer slaves. One was of jet and the other two, amber. I gave the jet to my eldest, Mary. She had seen ten summers. In three or four years, she would be married. The other two I gave to Anna and Clothilde. They were all happy and sported them before their mother.

My wife was less happy for each of my daughters had been baptised and Bagsecg had made them silver crosses. The crosses were now hidden by the jet and amber. They were the stones of the pagans. "Were the pots and goblets satisfactory?"

"You could have bought them! You have gold aplenty."

"We will sail to Miklagård and spend the money there. I am certain that you will find finer vessels."

She was mollified. She knew that the Byzantine Empire had the finest markets and the most exotic of goods. She smiled. "Where is Ragnvald?"

It was my turn to smile, "He is speaking with Father Michael. It is what you wished, is it not?"

She coloured, "Come girls, the food is being spoiled. Ragnvald will have to have cold fare!"

It was an excuse to leave and compose herself.

I went to change into a clean kyrtle. I would have enjoyed a bath but I was hungry and it would take time to heat the water. I would have one later. I shouted for ale and a servant brought a bowl of freshly brewed beer. Brigid was the finest of alewives and her husband, Erik One Arm, was another of my oldest friends. Drinking Brigid's beer was somehow comforting. It represented a world that did not change. When I drank her dark beer, I remembered the fallen. I thought of those who were now in the Otherworld and it gave me comfort.

The servants began to bring in the food and lay it on the table. I saw that there was a game stew with rabbit, hare and game birds. There was baked bread which was still warm from the oven. Freshly caught fish made up the first part of the feast and then they brought in the cheeses, apples and plums. I chuckled to myself. She must have been worried about my reaction to the wedding plans.

When Ragnvald returned, he was not alone. He had with him Æðelwald of Remisgat. The young priest had been washed for he had had much blood on him. His bandage was gone as Father Michael had tended to his wound. He looked almost shy as my wife and daughters stared at him. I gave a sideways glance to Ragnvald. He shrugged and announced, "The hostages did not wish Æðelwald of Remisgat to stay with them. They disapproved of his use of a sword. Father Michael thought it best for him to stay with us. He has sworn on his cross that he will neither escape nor do us harm."

I opened my mouth to say something and Ragnvald gave the slightest shakes of his head and said, "This is *wyrd*, father. Trust me."

I nodded, "I do, Ragnvald Hrolfsson."

Chapter 4

Riders from Bárekr's Haven brought us news of the Saxon fleet which approached the coast. The rider, Finni Larsson, told us that there were eight ships. It seemed to me that they were coming for war. Eight ships were too many for the ransom alone. I had my sentry sound the cow's horn which summoned all warriors within hearing.

Ragnvald was with me when the news came in. "I will fetch our horses." He was a horseman first and last. He might dress and fight like a Viking but, in his heart, he was happiest on the back of a horse.

I was donning my mail when my wife appeared. "Is there trouble?"

"There could be. King Egbert has come for his priests but he has come with more ships than he needs. You have naught to fear."

She smiled, "When you are threatened, lord, then I do not fear. You have a mind which is as sharp as any. It is when you fight that I hold my breath."

I put on my cap and hood but carried my helmet. Once outside and when I saw that my men were gathered, I mounted Allfather's Gift. I hung my helmet from my saddle. Alain of Auxerre and his men were there along with Ragnvald and his horsemen. The walls were manned by the warbands of Einar Bear Killer. I led my men through the gates of the Haugr. There were thirty of us on horses and another forty on foot. The boys who worked on the ships and fought with us tagged along too with their slings and bows. There were thirty of them. It was not an army, it was a healthy welcoming party.

I turned and shouted, "Close and bar the gates!"

As we neared the shore I said, "Folki, send six of your men to the church. Have the hostages taken back to the Haugr. If there is treachery then they will be the first to die."

"Aye, jarl."

I saw the masts and sails of the ships beyond the church. Perhaps they thought to sneak upon us. The position of the spit of land upon which the church sat and our anchorage meant that any ship which approached had to turn back upon itself. Unless you had rowers, it could not be approached rapidly. A sneak attack was impossible. I had plenty of time to array my men in a three-deep line.

Ragnvald looked behind me and said, "Folki's men have the hostages. They are marching to the gates."

I saw the royal standard fluttering from the mast of the third ship in line. The king had come. I knew that the Saxons could carry up to thirty men in each of their ships. I counted six ships. That meant they might have a hundred and eighty men. If Egbert thought that he could take my home with such a small number of men then he was a fool.

I saw that they were not coming in to the shore in line astern. Two of them were abreast of the king. It seemed to me that they were trying to protect the royal vessel. They had miscalculated and made a mistake as the tide was low and the channel clearly marked. Folki had an eye for such things. "Jarl, the far Saxon is perilously close to the rocks."

"I know. He must have a poor watch on board."

As the ship with the pennant began its last turn to reach the jetty I saw the mast of the far Saxon judder and then tip. He had struck the rocks. The ship behind made a sudden turn away from the danger and it became fouled in the shrouds of the ship behind the king's ship. It was becoming a disaster. I saw Father Michael and his servants run from the church to pluck Saxons from the water. The leading ship tied up but, because of the accident, none of the other ships could join him until their rigging was cleared.

"Folki, hold the men here. Ragnvald, Alain, let us go and greet our visitor."

"Just the three of you, jarl?"

I laughed, "Folki are you worried about Saxons who cannot even sail a ship into a harbour? We are mounted. I am sure that we can extricate ourselves if we need to."

As we rode along the stones of the jetty we had built Alain said, "I have never met this King Egbert, lord. What is he like?"

"I have never met him either. He must be old. From what the Dragonheart told me of him he has seen more than sixty summers but he has ruled Wessex for over thirty-five years. It shows that he is a survivor. I am just surprised at this. He has a cunning mind. Although defeated by the Dragonheart and Klakke Blue Cheek at Carhampton he managed to escape and then defeat both Klakke and the King of Om Walum. Why does he come here? Is this an attack or something else?" I knew that Saxons and Franks liked to play games that involved alliances and threats. Perhaps this was a game. Sadly, for Egbert, Vikings do not like such games.

We reached the ship which had tied up and we stopped. I saw warriors on board and they were donning mail as we reached them. I saw a discussion taking place. I recognised the archbishop amongst those in the heated debate but there were no old warriors. What did the pennant mean? I glanced to the wreck and saw that Father Michael had rescued the survivors and the other four Saxon ships were now edging nervously towards the jetty. Whoever this was, their arrival was not the magnificent gesture it had been intended.

A gangplank was lowered and four mailed warriors stepped off and approached us. They carried swords but the leader also held an axe. He looked to be of an age with me. He had been one of those involved in the argument aboard the Saxon. "I am Thegn Wihtred of Haestingaceaster. I command the king's warriors."

I nodded. He had spoken to me in Saxon. I answered him in the same. "And do you come for war Thegn Wihtred of Haestingaceaster or to deliver the ransom?"

He glared at me. I had not dismounted and he was forced to look up at me for Allfather's Gift was a tall horse. "If it was up to me, Viking, then my axe would have already made you kneel at my feet."

I laughed. Alain had not understood his words but Ragnvald had. Ragnvald said, "Let me kill him, father!"

I shook my head and said to the thegn, in Saxon, "My son here would have me slay you for your words but I can see that you are a warrior. Put aside your empty threats for we both know that if you raised your weapon then my men would be here in an instant and all of you, including the archbishop, would die. Tell me your message for I grow impatient."

"King Æthelwulf wishes to speak with you before he decides if we are to punish you for your raids."

"King Egbert is dead?"

The thegn nodded, "He died a month since."

Now it made sense to me. "Then tell your king he may land but," I swept my hand at the other four ships now tying up, "the rest stay aboard their ships. They do not land."

"You would command a king?"

"In this land, Saxon, there are no kings. This is the Land of the Horseman, the Land of the Northman and I command here. All men who land here obey me. Remember that and you might just keep your head upon your shoulders." He turned and, leaving his men to stop us boarding, went back aboard his ship. "That is interesting. What will this young king be like?"

Alain pointed to the man speaking to the thegn, "That must be the king. I think he is here to show you that he is not afraid of you." He laughed, "Had he and his men not made a mess of their entrance it might have worked. As it is his men will just be feeling foolish."

This time ten of his bodyguards stepped across to the jetty. The archbishop was with the new king. King Æthelwulf was younger than I was. I deliberately stayed upon my horse. It would annoy the king. He stood before me and glowered up at me.

"I understand that you speak our language, barbarian, and so I will speak directly to you. I would have my treasure and my priests returned to me."

I nodded, "Then fetch the ransom and they shall be yours."

"I am King Æthelwulf and I do not bargain with pirates and pagans!"

"Then you have wasted your time and lost a ship." I pulled my horse's head around, "Farewell! Your priests will be sold along with the bones of St. Tatwine, the cross of St. Bregwin, and the vestment and ring of St. Theodore of Tarsus."

Archbishop Ceolnoth said, "Wait, jarl, do not be hasty." I turned my horse's head around. The archbishop spoke quietly to the king but I still heard his words. "Your majesty the church supported your claim to the throne but these relics are irreplaceable."

The king looked from his thegn to the archbishop and then back to me. He was debating how to leave with some face.

I smiled and spread my hand. "Come King Æthelwulf this is not hard, either you pay the ransom or you do not. There is no negotiation. There is no middle way. I am a warrior who does not lie. I have told you my terms. You either accept them or reject them. Either way, I will profit." His hand went to his sword. My face hardened and my words threatened. "And if you choose to fight then we will also profit for when we have slaughtered you we will have your mail, your jewels and your ships. This is not Wessex. This is my land and here I make the rules."

I knew that he regretted coming but now that he had come, the only thing left was either to fight or to pay.

"Fetch the relics and the hostages and then we shall show you the gold."

"I will see the gold now!" I pointed to his feet. "There."

He tried to outstare me but it did not work. The glare from the sun behind me made him lower his glance. "Do it!"

Two of his men hurried back aboard his ship and brought out a chest. The Archbishop opened it and I saw the coins. I turned and waved to Folki's men. "Ragnvald go and bring the relics and the Holy Books."

Grinning my son said, "Aye."

I turned and saw Father Michael and his men bringing the survivors from the wreck. The ship itself lay at an untidy angle. When the Saxons had gone Sven and Harold would strip all of value from her. There would be a sail, ropes, masts and timbers which could be salvaged. It was an unexpected bonus.

The king seemed to see the church for the first time. "You have a church here and a priest?"

"We do. There are Christians who live amongst us."

The archbishop asked, "How can they countenance living with the likes of you?"

I was not insulted, "You will have to ask them but I will tell you this, priest, that the slaves we took from you are happier to be here than in either Cent or

Wessex. When they are freed, they do not attempt to cross the sea for a Christian land. They stay here with my clan. Think about that, priest."

Father Michael arrived. He did not speak Saxon and so he spoke to me, "We saved those we could. There are eight souls who drowned. When we have recovered their bodies, we will bury them."

I nodded and told the king and the archbishop what he had said.

The king shook his head, "I will not have my men buried in this pagan stronghold."

"As you wish but you will have to wait for the tide to turn and your men will have to be fishers of bodies."

The hostages arrived first and they dropped to their knees before the archbishop. "Have you been mistreated by these barbarians?"

I wondered if they would lie but they did not. The eldest of them said, "No, lord, we were treated well and stayed in the church. They fed us and ensured that we were safe."

The archbishop said, "For that, I thank you, Viking."

Ragnvald brought the books and the relics. They were handed over. Each one was checked to ensure that they were in good condition. Then the king frowned, "There is another chest missing."

I smiled. I had known this was coming, "You asked for the holy relics. I listed them. The last box contained a pagan relic. The archbishop did not say he wanted pagan relics."

"That is because it is mine! It is a link to the first king of Cent."

"I know, Hengist the Saxon and he was not Christian. You shall not have it. I have taken a fancy to it." My hand was resting on my sword. I had seen, while the books were being examined, that the king was speaking to Thegn Wihtred of Haestingaceaster. Now Wihtred pulled out his sword and shouted, "Have them!"

It was a mistake. Folki had ten warriors with him but there were three of us on horses and with swords. I whipped out Heart of Ice and brought it down across the shoulder of the warrior who thrust his sword at me. Blood spattered the archbishop as I tore into his throat. I pulled back on the reins of Allfather's Gift and he reared. His hoof clattered across the head of the thegn who collapsed. Ragnvald and Alain slew two more of the bodyguards and as Folki and his men levelled their weapons I yelled, "Hold!" My men stopped. The bodyguards who remained had gathered about their king while the priests and the archbishop had fled back aboard the ship. "If you wish to die, Saxon, then I will oblige. If not have your men throw down their weapons and then get back aboard your ships and leave. You have no honour!"

He had no alternative, "Do as he says!" The swords and spears were dropped. The king pointed a finger at me. "King Louis is an ally, Viking! I will have vengeance for this insult." He stepped back aboard the ship.

I pointed to the thegn. He lived still. "Your thegn lives. Take him with you."
They picked him up and began to carry him to the ship. One reached for the
thegn's sword. "I said you could have him. His weapon stays here with the
others."

We did not bother to pick up the chest until the Saxons had sailed from our
bay. I saw that the two ships which had been fouled were sailing sluggishly. The
collision had damaged them. If the king had thought to enhance his reputation by
cowing me it had gone horribly wrong. They had had to leave the bodies of their
dead and sail away seeing the skeleton of their ship and their dead on the jetty. It
was humiliating.

We took the gold and the weapons back to the Haugr. Ragnvald said, "Are
you worried about King Louis?"

"If he decides to come for vengeance then so be it. It is inevitable. But I do
not think he will. Not yet. Rurik One Ear has spies and riders who cross into the
land of the Frank. They have yet to finish their defences. They know we use
horses as well as ships. Alain here and his men had slain all of their scouts. They
are blind and know not what we do. Their fingers have been burned twice before
now. They will make it harder for us next time."

I examined the sword the thegn had left. It was a good sword. I kept it to give
as a reward for one of my warriors. I divided up the gold into three piles. My two
jarls would be happy with the coin. The weapons and the mail we had taken we
would keep for us.

I saw Æðelwald. He was looking at the weapons. "What do we do with him?"

Father Michael was behind us, "He is a priest lord. I have spoken to him
when I tended to his wounds."

I nodded, "He used a sword and tried to kill my son. He is my son's
prisoner."

Ragnvald looked thoughtful. "I do not know, father. I took him for I wanted
to discover if a Christian could be a warrior. Now I know the reason I have no
reason to keep him."

"But he is your responsibility, Ragnvald. You could keep him as a slave or
servant."

"I would not like that, lord. The man did serve God."

"And now Father Michael, he serves my son. You know our ways."

He held up a placatory hand, "I have a solution, lord, which might serve us
both. I have need of a priest to aid me. He could serve me and yet remain the
property of your son."

"He is yours, Ragnvald. What do you say?"

"If he is happy with that then I am content. Perhaps he will relinquish the
church and become a warrior. Then he could serve me. He had potential with a
sword. I will fetch him."

I saw Ragnvald speaking with the priest. When they joined me, he looked into my eyes and I saw that he had lost his belligerence. "Is it true, jarl, that King Egbert is dead?"

"He is."

"Then my prayers have been answered."

Father Michael looked confused and when I translated he shook his head, "That is not a Christian attitude."

I smiled, "Father you will have your work cut out. He only speaks Saxon. Ragnvald, explain to Æðelwald what Father Michael is offering. I must ride to Rurik. I fear that the Saxon king will sail to his ally. Rurik must be warned."

"Aye father."

Alain and his men were at the stables. "Come we must ride south." We took out spare horses. I rode Dream Strider.

As we rode I explained to my captain of horse what I intended. He nodded, "It might be easier, lord, if we rode into the land of the Franks to see for ourselves how the land lies. I do not doubt that Rurik is vigilant but we know horsemen and we know the Franks. We can discover more."

He had a point. "And I shall come with you. If we are to make our land greater then I need to see the size of our enemy."

When we reached Rurik's, it was getting towards evening and, as the gates slammed behind us, we accepted Rurik's offer of beds. As we ate he gave us the latest intelligence he had of the French king. "I doubt that he will do anything even if this new king asks it of him. The king is ill. His son, Lothair, is regent and rules for him. Although Charles the Bald, the king's favourite, disputes the matter. Until he has the throne he will look within his borders rather than without."

I laughed, "When did you become so wise? I can remember when all you were concerned about was where your next ale was."

"You are right and fine ale is still a priority but that was when I was single. I have a wife and children. Thanks to you I have a title and hundreds of people who rely upon my decisions. I have changed as have you, Hrolf. Those days on Raven Wing Island now seem to be another life." He frowned, "However, I do worry about you riding through the land of the Franks. They too have men who keep watch. My own riders have had encounters with them."

"The day that I fear to ride abroad is the day I hand over to Ragnvald."

"And that might not be such a bad thing, eh Captain?"

"I am happy when my lord rides with us. He is a fearless leader and has a mind as sharp as any."

"You see Rurik, I am not yet ready to become a fat old man!"

He laughed, "And I most certainly am. I have my sons and as they grow they can take over more of my duties. You see, Hrolf, how I became so clever when I married Agnathia!"

We left the next morning. Rurik sent a rider to tell my wife that I was staying with Rurik for a few days. Since our war, there was little south of Valognes that belonged to the Franks. Most had fled and the ones who had remained had chosen to obey and serve Rurik and therefore me. Alain's men's cloaks and shields were recognised as we moved along the narrow lanes. The farmers and their families waved. The nearest fortified town was Carentan. It was now a bastion against any further incursions south. I did not intend to ride close to it. I knew the land to the east of it. We could see it from the sea for Carentan lay just a mile or two from the coast and I needed to see what lay to the west. Now that we had the coin my son intended to build a hall south of Valognes. It would be on the west coast. I had to spy out the dangers which lay there.

Once we had passed the last farm, Alain sent out two outriders to give us a warning of danger. I had twelve men protecting me. We were all mailed, well mounted and well-armed. It would take a formidable foe to challenge us. We passed abandoned halls. The Franks who had lived there had fled. There were still a few farmers who eked out a living close to them but the lords had gone. We had slain many in the battle. King Louis had other things to worry about for his father's empire had crumbled. Frankia was the strongest and richest part of the Empire and the Emperor was now elected by the counts and princes who lived in Charlemagne's former Empire. I intended to ride to the coast and then head back through the centre of the peninsula.

We climbed a narrow track to a ridge and then dropped down into a valley. I could see the sea to the west. Fishing boats were there. Some might even belong to Flambard and his family. Others would be from the island of Angia. Alain pointed. "I have not been in this valley before, lord. Look there is a wall with towers. The Franks defend this place."

"Then let us approach cautiously. I would like a prisoner to question. I wish to know who rules here." I saw that they had built stone-based walls topped by a wooden palisade on a piece of high ground. The walls followed the natural contours. They had just one gate in and out. The river was a natural defence and it curved around the man-made defences. The houses were inside the walls. I saw that they had a hall such as I had within my own walls. The gate had two towers and there were two higher towers towards the northern side of the walls. If they had keen-eyed sentries then we would have been seen. It did not bother me but I was ready to draw my sword if we were threatened. We descended through the trees and lost sight of the towers. The track was slightly overgrown. Perhaps, when Henry of Carentan had ruled, there had been more trade to the north. I stopped and said, "Halt!"

I dismounted. There was horse dung on the greenway and it was not fresh. I saw hoof prints. There had been riders along this track in the last month. I mounted.

"Be alert, captain. I can smell danger."

Caution paid. The two riders who were scouting suddenly rode back. "Lord, there are horsemen coming."

"Into the trees and wait for my command."

I heard the hooves as the horses pounded up the track towards us. The Franks had not used scouts. They had ridden with their heads down, watching the track. They were about to pay for their mistake. There were eight riders who galloped up the track. None wore mail. All of them had a helmet and their shields hung from their cantles. They did not carry spears. I kicked my horse in the flanks as the first Franks closed with me.

I held my spear before me. The rider's horse baulked as I suddenly appeared. It reared and the rider had to fight to keep his saddle. Before the others could react my twelve men had them surrounded with spears held close to their chests. The leader, the man whom I had stopped, was younger than I expected.

"I am Hrolf the Horseman. You have heard of me?" He nodded but said nothing. "Who is your lord and what is the name of his stronghold?"

"I serve a Leudes. Lord Guillaume of Rauville is my master and his lady sent us to find out what raiders were doing in his valley."

"We are not raiders, my friend, if we were then you would be dead. We are taking the air and enjoying a pleasant ride around your land. I rammed my spear into the ground and held out my hand, "Your sword." He looked as though he might object. "If I wanted your sword to keep then you would be dead. My men have spears that could end all your lives with one thrust. Your sword."

He handed it to me. I held it and flexed it. It bent more than it should. This was not a well-made sword. I handed it back to him.

"Now you may return to your mistress and tell her that you have met the barbarian from the north and you lived."

"We can go?"

"Of course. We came not for war."

My men raised their spears. The Franks turned their horses and headed back down the slope.

After they had gone Alain asked, "What did you learn, lord?"

"That they have poor weapons, no armour and very little experience. Come, there is a track that heads west along the valley. We will ride to the coast and then head north."

We passed a couple of farms but they were in the valley bottoms. I saw that they had terraced some of the slopes. It was good farmland. When we saw the sea again, as we emerged from a thickly wooded part, I spied wood smoke and houses. We followed the track down along the stream. There were just four houses there and they were next to a strange bay. It looked big enough for a drekar. I saw that the channel was a deep one and yet the stream down which we had ridden was not particularly big. The huts were some way from the water. I saw why. There were thirty paces of stone between them and the water. I reined

47

in to allow my horse to drink from the stream and to let those in the huts see us. We came in peace. I had learned from Flambard that these fisher folks did not want to bother with other people. They were insular and lived alone. They were quite happy with their isolation. I took off my helmet and allowed my hood to slip down my back. I kicked my horse in the flanks and headed towards the huts. They had crude doors. There were no hinges, they just leaned against their opening. As we approached I saw one replaced.

I stopped outside it, "You inside, come. I mean you no harm and wish to speak with you."

The door opened and a woman, she looked to be just a little older than Ragnvald stood there. She had a knife in her hand. It was a gutting knife. Two small children clung to her legs. "What do you want? We are simple fishermen."

I nodded, "I know. Whom do you serve? Is there a lord who takes taxes from you?"

She allowed a smile to flicker across her face. "There was but he died in the war last year. Since then we have been blessed. No lord has bled us dry." She suddenly took in our mail and our weapons. "You are not a new lord, are you?"

I smiled, "I am not a Frank. I am a Norseman, what you call a Viking!"

She crossed herself and pushed the children behind her. She seemed to realise that she had a knife in her hand and she dropped it. "I meant no harm, lord, Spare us!"

I held my hands up with the palms showing. "I told you that I meant you no harm. "Tell your men that my men hold the town of Valognes. If you wish to trade fish there then you will be welcome. They have a market." I took out a couple of copper coins and threw them to her. "Here, for your trouble!"

We headed through the small hamlet and headed north along the coast. It reminded me of the Haugr. It was a natural harbour and there was a raised piece of ground where a castle could be built. I stored the information. I had learned much.

As we rode north Alain asked, "What is in your mind lord?"

"That it would make a good place to build a stronghold. We are about twenty Roman miles from Flambard's home and the same from Rurik at Valognes. This is a better harbour than that used by Flambard. It might suit my son."

We saw no more strongholds on the twenty-mile ride back to Rurik. We reached there just after the gates were closed. They opened them for us. When I mentioned the fishing port to Rurik he knew of it. "We named it Kartreidh."

I smiled, "The stony harbour. That makes sense. Do you know the men who live there?"

"When we have visited they hide from us."

"Flambard was the same. I think, if we build near there we will build further inland. I will speak to Ragnvald. It will be a challenge but it might be the answer to his problem."

Rurik leaned forward, "I have spoken with the Franks who live within my walls and trade with their brethren beyond. They say that King Louis has not long in this world and Charles, his son, is busy eliminating enemies and seeking allies. I do not think the Franks will bother us. At least not until they have spilt some family blood and decided who is to rule. Wessex is too far away to be able to come to his aid and from what you have told me the young king will do well to hold on to his crown."

I felt that we could go ahead with our plans to expand slightly further south. Louis' sons would not be able to do anything about us; not for a while. While he was preoccupied then we would strike. By the time I reached my home, I had come up with a plan.

Ragnvald was waiting for me. He sought me out even as I stabled Allfather's Gift. "I have spoken with Father Michael. I have agreed that I will be married in the church." He looked at me defiantly, "It does not mean I have given up the old ways. I will not become a Christian. Mother seems to think I will but she is wrong. Now I just need somewhere to build a hall." He looked at me hesitantly. "If I am some way from Mathilde's family then I should be away from here as well."

I think he was expecting an argument from me. I nodded, "That seems sensible. Of course, you are of the clan and you cannot simply hide in some backwater. My men would think I was protecting you."

He smiled, "Nor would I wish that. I am a horseman and my men and I will protect our borders."

"Then you need somewhere that is to the south of us."

He laughed, "You have found somewhere! That is what this is about! I begin to read your face now, father. Where is it?"

"It is twenty miles from Valognes and twenty miles from Flambard's home. It is a fishing village called Kartreidh."

"Stony harbour?"

"Aye. There are a few people there but I spied a hill which could be fortified. It is by a river."

"It sounds perfect."

"It would be were it not for the stronghold of the Franks at the head of the valley. A place called Rauville. It is less than ten miles from where you would build your hall."

"They have a garrison there?"

"They have horsemen but they do not wear mail."

"It matters not. I will accept it. Tomorrow I tell the priest that we are to be married as soon as possible. Then you can show me my new home."

Chapter 5

My wife thought that everything was arranged too quickly. She had wanted Siggi Far-Sighted to sail to Dorestad and fetch fine linen and better-quality pots. Ragnvald showed his character by insisting upon speed. His bride to be was just as pleased about the rapid arrangements. We told Flambard that he could have Ragnvald's old hall and that his daughter and Ragnvald would have a new one further south. With his new-found wealth, Ragnvald was able to buy more horses and arms for those who would follow him. However, the speedy wedding meant he did not have my wedding present for him, his new sword. That would have to wait.

Ragnvald used the last of his money to pay for stone. We had last bought some from the Franks. That was the closest quarry but I did not wish to risk losing my knarr. Siggi sailed to On Walum to trade for some. King Æthelwulf was still securing his northern borders with Mercia and the land of the East Angles. Siggi was able to sail in and trade without any trouble. When he had traded for stone he would sail directly to Kartreidh. The voyage would take him some time and so I joined my son and his men along with Alain and Folki. Building a hall took men. Building one under the noses of Franks who might interfere took warriors. With Alain and Folki we had the best of both.

Folki was in an ebullient mood for he had taken one of the Saxon slaves as his wife. Nanna was a comely young Saxon who seemed to like Folki. Perhaps she saw it as a quick way out of slavery. Whatever the reason, they were married and she moved into the hall which Folki's men and their families shared.

I had sent word to Rurik to let him know our plans. He promised to have his men south of Valognes as a deterrent to the Franks. Einar Bear Killer and his band came to aid us as did Folki. Thorbolt and Sigtrygg both chose to raid. In a way, I was disappointed. I had hoped that they might offer to help. Instead, they sailed to Dyflin where Thorghest the Lucky and Magnus Axe Hand were raising men to war with the Hibernians. Bertrand sent horsemen to help. They would not build but they were skilled and would give us warning of danger.

When Ragnvald saw the site I had chosen, he was pleased. The hamlet was just a Roman mile away but he could see it from the hill I had chosen. We paced out his walls and laid a line of white stones there. Then we did the same for the hall. They would be built first and then the other buildings would be added later. Mathilde and her women were with us and my men began to construct a hut for them. The men would sleep in the open until we had built the hall.

While my men toiled, I pointed to the hamlet. "If I was going to be the jarl of this land I would make friends with my people."

Mathilde nodded, "Your father is right. They are quiet and shy people. We need to let them know that we mean them no harm."

Ragnvald said, "I suppose you are right." He put his hand on the saddle.

His wife said, "No, husband, we will walk. It is less frightening for them and besides, it will be pleasant."

My son had chosen a wise woman. She would guide him. Agnathia had done the same for Rurik. While they were gone I helped my men finish the hut. It was a simple affair. My men had chopped down eight trees. By digging four holes they had the corners of the building up very quickly. Then, while half of the men cut turf for the wall, the other half hammered huge nails to tie in the four crosspieces. It would not be a light and airy building but it would keep them dry. The smaller branches from the trees were cut and laid across as the first layer of the roof and then more turf was added. By the time Ragnvald and his wife returned it was erected. All it required was a door. It was coming on to dark and so we lit a fire and began to cook the food we had brought.

Mathilde provided fish, "Once I explained why we were here they were more than happy to help us."

Ragnvald shook his head, "My wife promised them that we would not tax them."

"Quite right too!"

"But father, how will I have an income if I do not tax? I do not raid in a ship."

Mathilde shook her head, "They have no coins. They are poor. They catch fish and trade it. If you tax them then they will starve."

"You are a Viking, my son. You tax your enemies. We will make this a stronghold like the Haugr. When that is completed then you can extend your influence." Even as I said it I was imagining a drekar in this natural harbour. The Liger and the rich lands to the south were within easy reach of a drekar. A good leader never stopped thinking about how to make his clan stronger. The proof of my success would be in what I left behind.

One of Ragnvald's men was called Benni. There are some men who shine with a sword or riding a horse. Some can use a spear in a way you never imagined. And then there was Benni. He was a good horse rider and he could use a sword but he had an eye for building. He had often watched Father Michael as he had supervised the building of my towers. He had been a young boy then. Now he was one of my son's oathsworn. The first sign of his skill was when he questioned Folki's placing of the stones to mark out the wall. After we had finished the hut for the women we had eaten and then slept. When we rose to begin building Folki frowned as he saw that Benni was moving them.

"What are you doing?"

Benni smiled, "Making the walls stronger." He pointed. "If we build here then we can use the natural rock which lies there to give the walls extra support. And it gives an extra pace of space within."

Ragnvald tried to see what Benni meant. I saw it immediately. "You are right Benni. What else would you change?"

"The hall is too close to the wall. If we moved it north five paces then it would be higher and there would be less digging to make it flat. That way we could put more men here and they could use bows to release over the walls. It would double the defence."

I turned to Folki, "He is right. Benni, move the marker stones. Make the town the way you see it. We will go and hew trees. Come Folki." Leaving Ragnvald with Benni, we walked to the nearby trees. I picked up one of the axes we had brought and walked with Folki. "There was little wrong with your design but Benni's is better."

"But he has barely begun to shave!"

"We both know that means nothing. Besides it is he and my son who will have to live here. If they are happy with the way the walls are built then it is good. This does not make Benni a better warrior, Folki."

"I know but it does not feel right."

"You will soon be a father and have sons. One day they will do things differently to you. That is change and that is good. Regard this as practice for those days when your son shows you he is better than you."

"Has that happened to you, Jarl Hrolf?"

"Of course. My son is a much better rider than I am. Only Gilles is his equal. I would follow my son's banner into battle if we rode on horses."

With that thought to occupy him, Folki and the others threw themselves into the hewing of trees. We had many to cut. It served two purposes. It gave us the materials for the hall and it also cleared a killing ground around the hall. As the trees were cleared so we were able to see further. If we built a stone tower it would be seen from all around. That was important. It was like a stag marking its territory, it told others to keep off. As I took a break and looked around I saw that it would also give warning of any who might attempt to sail into the anchorage. The gods had given us the best of sites.

Once the smaller branches had been trimmed then the crucial task of splitting the logs began. Again, there were men who were better at this than others. We deferred to them. A badly split log could ruin the work of a morning. The planks were piled as the trees were split and I returned to see Benni's progress. He had finished. Ragnvald and Benni looked happy.

"Benni says that we could use some of the stone from Kartreidh. We might be able to build a tower such as we have at the Haugr. It would not be as high."

Benni said, quickly, "That would mean we do not have to build a crane. We could build it quicker. It would strengthen one end of the hall."

I looked at him in surprise. "It would be attached to the hall?"

"Aye, jarl. It would be bigger than the one at the Haugr but not as high. If the hall fell it could still be defended."

"It is a hard task you have set yourself."

"I would have my jarl's family safe." He smiled, "One day I will have a wife too and I would be happier knowing she had a refuge."

He and Ragnvald explained how it would work. I smiled as they did so. The hall would be stronger as the beams for the roof would have support from the stone of the tower. The entrance to the tower would be from within the hall making the tower more secure. It was a clever design. As the foundations were dug and the bones of buildings appeared I saw that it would be different from the Haugr. It would be better. There were others who would see it and make the next halls even better than this one. It was *wyrd*. My hall and stronghold looked different from those in the land of the wolf. We might have the same blood but we sailed a different course.

Mathilde was delighted with Benni's ideas. She hugged him as she saw his ideas come to life, "We shall call this Benni's Ville. My people use that word for towns. I would like to name it thus."

Ragnvald showed his maturity. He nodded, "That is good." He had learned that he could give into Mathilde on the things which were unimportant to him. The name sounded right and Benni looked as proud as a new father. The name was *wyrd*.

Siggi arrived with the stones. Hauling them up to the site proved harder than we had thought. We had strong ponies to pull them but we did not have the stone walkway we had had at Raven Wing Island. Ragnvald had more work ahead of him.

Once the trees had been hewn and split and the stones hauled we needed less labour and, eight days after we had arrived, I led Alain and his men to ride to Valognes. We rode along the valley but kept to the north of Rauville. I was not afraid of a confrontation but I did not want to initiate one yet. Winter would be upon us soon and my son and his men would need to have the hall finished by then. We did not need the distraction of war.

Rurik had been as good as his word. He had kept his men patrolling the far reaches of his lands. "The king is dead. Lothair has claimed the throne. However, his two brothers, Louis and Charles have allied to fight against him."

I smiled, "The gods smile on us. If there is civil war then they cannot try to punish us for our attack on Wessex."

"I thought you would be happy."

53

"More importantly, Rurik One Ear, it means that when the new grass is upon us then we can begin to raid with our drekar. The eyes of the Franks will be drawn within and we can take advantage."

"And we could advance further south. My people would like that. Perhaps Carentan might be a prize we could take?"

"Perhaps although I fear they have made it stronger. We do not have enough men to try to siege a large town. You should ride with us to see my son's new hall. Between the two of you, the west of this land should be secure."

My son was delighted by the news I brought back. He pointed up the valley, "Perhaps we could take Rauville."

"You have yet to see the hall and your own defences completed. Finish one job first and then scout. The time of the new grass will be time enough for you to think about war."

"Will you help me to take Rauville?"

I put my arm around my son's shoulders and led him away from the others. "I am jarl of the clan. My responsibility is no longer just to watch over you. My men will become restless if we do not raid. When the new grass comes I will take my ships and we will raid the Franks. Rurik will expand south. I can let you have Alain and Bertrand's men. Perhaps Gilles and his horsemen might be persuaded to accompany you. You would have to manage with those alone."

I wondered if he would argue with me but he showed that marriage had added years to him. "You are right. If I am a leader of men then I should lead them. This is good advice you give to me. I should spy out my enemy's defences. This way means that my home will be safe and we can use this as a base."

The weight I had placed on his shoulders seemed to make him redouble his efforts and he threw himself into his work. The building took shape. As the leaves fell and the days grew both colder and shorter so the stronghold we called Benni's Ville, took shape. The ditch followed the natural contour of the hill so that the bridge over it was at the highest point. It meant that carts and wagons struggled the last thirty paces to the bridge but that was a price worth paying for it meant that a ram would also struggle. The walls had a stone base and a wooden palisade with a wide fighting platform. Ragnvald had decided on just one gate and the gatehouse had two wooden towers.

It was the hall, however, which marked Benni's Ville as something new. The long wooden hall such as Ragnvald had had further north was now attached to a square tower that had a stone base. The stone base was not complete but the tower would be as high as the hall and then have a wooden palisade around the top. Even Folki was impressed, "Jarl, I was wrong about Benni. I would never have thought of this. We could build all of our new halls like this."

"You would need a hill. Ragnvald was lucky to have one already."

"Then we could make a hill. The spoil from the ditch would make a natural hill."

"Perhaps." It would take a great deal of work. At the moment, it was unnecessary but who knew what the future held.

I left when the first frost made the ground hard. The roof was in place and the palisade ran around the walls. Benni and Ragnvald would continue to build their tower. It would rise above the roof of the hall. The hardest part, placing the stones and mortaring them at the base, had been done. I led Folki and Alain's men back towards Valognes. This time, however, we did not take the twisting road through the uplands, we took the main road which went along the valley. Eventually, it forked for Carentan and Valognes but we would pass by the town of Rauville. I wanted the lord there to see my banner.

We were mailed and we were helmed. Our banners flew. There were forty of us and I feared no man. As we neared the walls of the town I saw that they had a tower but there was no banner flying from it. As we neared the gates were closed and the walls manned. There were more townspeople on the walls than warriors. I saw but two men with helmets.

I took off my helmet and turned Dream Strider to ride towards the gate. I held my hands open. Behind me, my men were ready in case of treachery. The two men with the helmets were above the gate on the fighting platform. Both were greybeards. This was the town watch.

They did not speak nor did their hands go to their weapons. When you are faced by a wolf you do not prod him. "I am Jarl Hrolf of the Haugr. I come to speak with your master Guillaume of Rauville."

"He is not here. He fights alongside Charles the Bald and Louis."

That explained why no one had come near to us or questioned our presence. "Then tell him that I now have men at the end of this valley. It is now our land. Kartreidh belongs to the Northman now."

They looked at each other but did not argue. One said, "We will tell our lord but he will not be happy."

"Then he knows where to find me. The Haugr is my home. If he wishes to serve me then he can visit with me there."

I had stunned them, "Serve a Viking? Why?"

"The wind is changing my friend. Charlemagne is just a memory. Soon the land he ruled will have other men fighting over it. Tell him to think about that."

After we had left Alain said, "It is still a mighty Empire, lord. I fought from one end to the other. It is not as big as the Roman one but it is large enough."

"If three brothers are fighting over the carcass already how many others will seek the opportunity to carve out their own kingdom? We are the future Alain. Their ships cannot match ours and our horsemen are becoming the equal of theirs. With stout warriors like Folki, we can take this land. It may not be in my lifetime but my son and his sons will inherit that which we have begun."

Mary was happy with my news. She was a wise woman and she understood the politics of the land of the Franks. "Our son will be safe until this war is resolved. Is our son's home well made?"

"It is but neither he nor his wife would be happy if you visited it yet. They will want to make it a home. At the moment, it is a refuge and it is the equal of the Haugr. They will be safe."

I visited Father Michael to pass on the news of the war. I saw that Æðelwald of Remisgat now wore the same habit as Father Michael. He nodded when he saw me. He spoke to me in our language, "Welcome Jarl Hrolf."

"You are learning our language?"

He answered in Saxon. "Father Michael is teaching me and I have but few words. But I am learning quickly and, in a few months, I will not need my Saxon tongue."

"Do you not wish to return to your home in Wessex?"

I looked into his eyes as he answered. I was looking for the lie. He shook his head, "I can see now that God chose me for this purpose. I am here to convert all of you to follow Jesus."

I laughed, "Then you enjoy a challenge."

"It is a challenge and it will be hard. I will make it my purpose in life. I will fight you and your people but it will be a fight of the mind so that I can save your souls."

He left us and I looked at Father Michael. He shrugged, "He is zealous and he truly believes he can succeed. I am a realist. I work with those who already believe. He may achieve his aim. I hope so."

"I admire him for trying but he should be careful. Some of my men may take offence and they tend to be violent men."

"And that is why he might succeed. He is a warrior. He can use his fists too. He will not turn the other cheek. It is not a trait I admire in him but I can see how he might need it. He wishes to build a church at your son's new hall." I gave him a sideways glance. "There is no church for your people on that coast, Jarl Hrolf. The nearest is at Ċiriċeburh."

"I will think about that. It might please my son's wife. She is a Christian."

"It was she who suggested it. After she was married she sought us both out and asked if we might consider building her a church."

"That would cost my son coin. He might not be willing."

"It could be made of timber. There is timber in abundance."

I left him with more thoughts racing around my head than I could handle. As Yule and the Christian Christmas were looming up I had to think of other things. Samhain and the animal slaughter and harvest were busy times. We had built more barns in which to store our produce. We had an excess that could be traded. When those in the land of the wolf of Hibernia had a bad harvest then they would buy from us. Their knarr came from Whale Island and Dyflin to trade with us.

They were our main source of seal oil and news. My wife sent Siggi in the knarr to Dorestad so often that he said the harbour master thought he must have a woman there that he was seeing. She was buying as many things as she could for Ragnvald's hall. My son put her off visiting by telling her the hall was too rough for her. Mary was a clever woman. She planned on surprising him at Gói. She had ordered carts to be built to enable us to carry everything to the new hall.

It was the end of Mörsugur when a knarr came from Dyflin. They had had rain at harvest time and storms. The crops had failed. Thorghest the Lucky sent gold to buy more from us. His captain, Leif Larsson, brought me a message from Thorghest. "The Jarl says that as he is an ally of the Clan of the Wolf he would have an alliance with the Clan of the Horse. He sends you this as a token of his good intentions."

He handed me a dagger. It was well made and I recognised the handiwork of Bagsecg's father the master smith. It was a smaller version of my sword with the same runes on the blade. The difference was that the handle was bone and in the shape of a horse's head.

I took it. "This is a fine blade. Tell him he had no need to buy my friendship. He married the Dragonheart's daughter and I am still oathsworn to the Dragonheart. Perhaps I can send him something back which might be of use. Tell your master that the Franks are fighting amongst themselves. At Harpa, I intend to gather a fleet to raid their river. If any of his captains wish to join us then they are welcome."

"I will tell him."

Sometimes it takes a small stone to roll down a gentle slope to begin an avalanche. That dagger was such a stone.

PART TWO

The Viking Fleet

Chapter 6

Jarl Thorbolt told me, when he came to visit, that they had had a successful raid in Hibernia but it had not been profitable enough. The weapons they had captured had been poor and the slaves had not fetched a good price. There had been so many slaves that it was hard to sell them. It had been their words which had instigated Thorghest the Lucky's invitation to ally with us. They had told the other jarls of our success and the riches. Neither Thorbolt nor Sigtrygg had profited as much on their own.

"I do not think that Jarl Thorghest will come. He has become like a king now. The Dragonheart has more grandsons and Thorghest appears contented. Dyflin is a fine slave market and the life there is not hard but the rewards are not as great as here or when raiding the Saxons."

"We know that."

"Will your son be raiding with us?"

I shook my head, "Now that he is married and has a hall he will make his position stronger first. The weakness of the Franks can be exploited on land and sea. Bertrand and Alain can join him. Along with Gilles and his warriors they can muster more than ninety mounted warriors. I am not sure that the Franks, so long as they continue to fight each other, can match those numbers."

"Sigtrygg will be here at Harpa." He pointed to the shipyard. "Sven and Harold are almost finished with the drekar. She is not large but she looks lithe."

"Aye, she is a threttanessa. She will be anchored at Kartreidh. If my son does not raid with her then there are others who would choose to do so. She will be my ship."

"Have you a name for her?"

"Not yet. I would see the figurehead and speak with my shipbuilders first. Their blood has seeped into her keel. They will know her name better than I."

Ragnvald Hrolfsson

At the start of Þorri, we launched her. She had neither mast nor figurehead. The launch was just to test her seaworthiness and to seal any leaks. There were no leaks and that was considered a good sign. We tied her to the jetty to allow the water to seep into the strakes. It was a good test of the sealant; animal hair soaked in pine tar. I went aboard with my two shipbuilders. They were proud of her. She was like a grandchild. All of their experience had gone into the design.

Sven explained what they had done, "She is narrower than any other ship we have made. You will not be able to man each oar with three men but that means she will be faster. She is slightly longer too. That will allow for more cargo. There is nothing afloat which will catch her."

"And have we a name yet?"

"Aye, jarl. We thought to name her *'Skuld'*." He turned and went to an object covered by a piece of old sail. Harold pulled back a cloth and I saw that the dragon had a woman's hair.

Sven said, "It was Skuld who foresaw your future. You are now living proof that the witch spoke true. It cannot hurt to name the vessel after the Norn."

I was not certain that it was true and I felt the hairs on the back of my neck prickle but I was in a dilemma. They had carved a witch into the dragon. When they had made her, they had sown the seed of her name and it would be just as dangerous to offend the Norn and reject the name. This was meant to be. "It is good. We shall so name her." When we sailed her, we would discover if she was unlucky or not.

We had heard nothing of the civil war. But the messages from both Rurik and my son were that the border was quiet and there were no warriors there. If we had so wished we could have enlarged our lands. We needed more men and it seems the gods listened to us. When Siggi returned from one of his Dorestad visits he brought with him twenty warriors. He stepped ashore and came to speak with me.

"Jarl Hrolf, I know that I have taken much upon myself by bringing these men to you but they were recommended to me. Ragnar son of Wolf Killer, grandson of the Dragonheart was there and he spoke for them. Their jarl was killed and they had no ship."

"Why did they not join with Ragnar?"

"They wish the sea and they seek land. The best land in the Land of the Wolf has gone. When they heard word that you were gathering a fleet they wished to join." He looked over his shoulder. "They have not had the best of jarls. They have swords and helmets, shields and cloaks but little else. None have mail. If you are unhappy then I will unload my cargo and sail back with them."

"No, Siggi, I would not do that. I trust Ragnar. He was but a child of six summers when last I saw him. He would not be foresworn. If he vouched for them… let them land and I will speak with them."

59

I entered my walls and waved over Sigtrygg Rolfsson, "How many men are there in the warrior hall at the moment?"

"Captain Alain is still on his patrols so there are only twenty, jarl. We could accommodate another thirty easily."

I gestured behind me, "There are twenty who may be joining us. I would have you and the others find out as much as you can about them. We need more men but we have had our fingers burned before by men joining us for the wrong reasons."

"You can rely on us."

I gave him some coins, "Go and buy a keg of ale from Brigid. We can make them welcome and the ale might loosen their tongues."

Our experience on Raven Wing Island had made us suspicious of strangers wishing to join us.

They stood before me looking as poorly equipped as any warriors I had seen for some time. Their shields had seen battles and needed repairs. Their helmets were equally old. I held my hand out and said, "Sword."

A number were proffered. I took one at random. It was free from rust and it had an edge. I put it across my knee and it bent. The man looked appalled. I smiled, "You shall have a better sword to replace it. Are the other blades as poor?"

They nodded, dumbly. I think they were embarrassed. A warrior was judged on the quality of his sword. They had tried to do the best with what they had been given but they were not good enough. I waved Sigtrygg forward, "Sigtrygg, when I am done with them take them to the armour store. Let them choose a better sword and helmet." Our battles had yielded many good weapons. My own warriors had used their coin to have their own swords made for them.

"Aye, jarl."

"I am happy for you to serve me but I demand an oath. Like Jarl Dragonheart, I am a great believer in oaths. To me they are binding. I have never been foresworn. However, I ask no man to make such a decision lightly. I leave for Kartreidh in seven days' time. You will come with me. If you change your mind in that time then Siggi will take you back to Dorestad and you may keep the helmet and the sword you will be given. Does that seem reasonable?"

There was one warrior older than the rest and he said, "Jarl, we will all swear now! We know your name and your reputation. That is enough for us."

"But not for me. We live by my code here. Sigtrygg and the other warriors will explain it to you. We live with Christians and we treat our slaves well."

"The Dragonheart and Ragnar son of Wolf Killer do the same, jarl!"

"And yet you did not choose to serve them. There are two sides to this coin. If we think you would not fit in then we will return you to Dorestad." I saw the light of realisation on his face. "Now you see?"

"Yes, jarl." He smiled, "You look young, Jarl Hrolf the Horseman, but you are wise. It is good. I doubt not that we will swear an oath and I hope that we can meet your high standards."

I put them from my mind as I threw myself into the preparations for our trip to visit my son. Father Michael and Æðelwald of Remisgat came to see me. Father Michael asked, "Have you given thought to the building a church at Benni's Ville, lord?"

"I do not object for Mathilde and her family are Christians. However, I will not make my men follow the White Christ. If they choose to follow your god then it will be their own choice. You know that I would not hesitate to have you slain if you disobeyed me."

Æðelwald of Remisgat nodded, "Aye lord. Let me go with you when you visit your son and let me ask him if I may build a church."

"You will build the church?"

"I would hope that the Christians there might help me but if needs be then I would do it alone."

"I admire your tenacity. You may come with us but you know the penalty for incurring my wrath?"

"I do lord."

My wife was both pleased with the presence of the priest and annoyed not to say angry with the threats I had made. "He is a priest! How can he harm the clan?"

"If he made women of my warriors then that would harm the clan. The White Christ is fine for women but I do not see many Vikings attending Father Michael's services."

"That is because they are afraid of offending you!"

"Good!"

My succinct answer silenced her. I met with Sigtrygg Rolfsson on the day before we left. "The new men: what is your opinion?"

"They are warriors, jarl, and they were badly led." He shrugged, "It happens. None appear to have any outstanding skills. I would think they can hold an oar and stand in a shield wall."

"Will they fit in with the clan? What do they wish?"

"I know what is in your mind jarl. Why did they not stay with Ragnar or the Dragonheart? I think that it is as simple as the land. The Land of the Wolf suits many men. I have never visited there and I do not know. It seems to me that men say the land is hard to farm. The Dragonheart does not raid as much as he used to and perhaps there were not enough slaves. These men want farms and families. The crew is not a young one."

"We let them stay?"

He looked worried and then he smiled, "A test for me eh, jarl? I would. If they let you down then it will be my fault."

61

"No, Sigtrygg it will not. You have done as I asked you. I will watch them when we are at Benni's Ville. The priest wishes to build a wooden church. They can build it. Which is their leader?"

"He is the older one who spoke to you, Finni Bennison."

"Good. While I am gone I would have our four drekar prepared for sea."

"Four?"

"Aye, we will see how *'Skuld'* sails. The new men will have their wish. They will have the opportunity to show me they are warriors and to become richer."

I took only Alain and his horsemen to guard the ten wagons and carts. We would easily do the journey in one day and there appeared to be no danger. That said, Alain and his men were vigilant. I learned that Æðelwald of Remisgat could not ride a horse. Many Saxons could not. He had to suffer the indignity of riding with the women in the wagons.

I led my horse and walked with Finni Bennison, "You have had the seven days. Do you still wish to take the oath?"

"We do, jarl. There was a good feeling in the warrior hall. We have sailed with other crews and there were ranks within the hall. There are none in yours." There was an earnest tone to his words, "We will not let you down jarl."

"When we reach Benni's Ville you will help to build a church of the White Christ."

He looked shocked, "I know you have a church at the Haugr but I thought that was for your wife."

"It is but there are Christians in this land and I would not try to make them follow our ways. They are Franks. For us, the old ways are in our blood. This keeps all of my people happy. Sigtrygg tells me that you want families. Most of the women we capture are Christians. Think on that Finni."

I let him walk with his comrades and I saw them debating. This was a test. I needed to be certain before we allowed another twenty men into our clan.

When we neared the new hall, I saw that my son had not been idle. The forest had been cleared further and there was a timber pile. The hall and the tower were complete. I knew that his new home could be seen from a long way away. Ragnvald had cleared trees along the trail we used. As we entered his gates I saw that he had built a stable block. There were white stones laid around the interior. Benni was building.

My son wisely greeted his mother first. His sisters flocked around Mathilde. I stood back to admire the tower. It was well made. It was ten paces square. The hall which was attached was thirty paces long. I saw that it was raised. The ground before it had been levelled and the spoil used to make the hall and the tower higher. It would be dry and, more importantly, it would be harder to attack.

Mary joined my daughters with Mathilde and they cackled and squealed. Ragnvald came over smiling, "You must excuse them the noise, father. They have just been told that I am to be a father. You will be a grandfather."

I clasped his arm, "That is good news! When do the women say that the child will be born?"

"Tvímánuður. He will be a boy. I can feel it in my bones."

I waved my arm around. "You have done well. Has there been trouble with your neighbours?"

"We visited but Guillaume of Rauville still fights for Charles and Louis. We left them alone and concentrated upon the building."

There was something in his tone which made me ask, "Do you intend to attack him?"

"I have spoken with Bertrand, Gilles and Rurik. The time seems right. The stronghold is guarded by a handful of men. We would attack in the night. It would make a good stronghold. Bertrand has men who wish land. I would put one of his men to command the stronghold. I would then take my riders and we would give the farmers the choice of serving us or leaving their farms. If you let Alain join my army then we would make the Land of the Horse greater."

I saw that he sought my approval. "You know that I raid the Franks up the Issicauna?" he nodded. "I will not be able to come to your aid if things go awry."

He smiled, "You will be helping me. We will not attack until your fleet has sailed. That way there will be no Frankish reinforcements forthcoming."

I nodded, "It is good."

"You have new men?"

"They came from the Land of the Wolf. I will have them swear an oath." I pointed to Æðelwald of Remisgat. "He and Father Michael have asked to build a church here for the followers of the White Christ. The priest you saved wishes to save the souls of you and your men."

He laughed, "We will not convert."

"Then you wish no church?"

"I did not say that. My wife would be happier with a church. She does not try to convert me but each night she says her prayers and on the day they call the Lord's day she and the other followers of the White Christ gather in the hall and pray together. I would be happier if there was a church and then I would not have to listen to their mumbling and chanting."

"My new men will help to build it. You had better get your master builder to lay out a church. I told the priests that it would be of wood and they were happy with that."

The news of the baby and the erection of the church was a cause for great celebration. We feasted well. The new men and Alain's men had to sleep in the open but that was no great hardship. The next day, while my new men were set the task of building the church, I went hunting with Alain and his horsemen. It was not for sport. We needed the meat for it was the time of the new grass and food was scarce. The animals had given birth to young and they would have to be protected until they were fattened enough to eat. The crops had just been sown.

Ragnvald was living from the supplies they had brought with them and the bounty of the sea. My other purpose was to ensure that the Franks were still in small numbers.

We used spears to hunt. Alain and his men were not as skilled with the bow as was I. This was better for it enabled us to learn to ride together and to think as one. I used the skills which Ulf Big Nose had helped develop. We tracked a herd of deer. The wind brought their musky smell to us and, using a long line, we were able to surround them. We killed neither young nor mothers. We took the old and the weaker stags. The herd would be strengthened. We did not kill indiscriminately. We took just eight beasts but we would eat well. Nothing would be wasted from the animals. Even their hooves would be rendered down to make glue.

On the way back, I took the road and we passed by the walls of Rauville. The last time I had been there was to deliver a warning, now I was there to assess their defences. The warriors who remained stared at us impotently as we rode along the road. I was intimidating them. The greybeard who commanded was wise enough not to rise to the bait. I saw that the only stone lay in the tower. It was even smaller than the ones at the Haugr. The wooden walls were low enough to be scaled using warriors standing on a shield and the ditch was without stakes. The gate was substantial but my son would have enough men to attack all four sides of the stronghold. The men I saw watching us would not be able to resist for long.

While Alain and his men butchered the beasts we had taken, I spoke with Ragnvald about what I had seen. "We sail at Harpa. That would seem to me the best time to attack the Franks. You would be able to take it and if Carentan's new lord has also gone to fight in the war then there would be no help coming."

"It is good." He pointed to Æðelwald of Remisgat who was stripped to the waist and labouring with a pick alongside my men. "He works harder than any. He truly believes that he can make us Christian."

"Just so long as he makes your women happy. And what of your men? Do they need women to make them happy? They were young men but, like you, they are getting older."

"That is another reason why I wish to attack Rauville and the lands thereabouts. There will be slaves."

"If they are women taken from close to here they may try to return home."

"Yet there are those like Seara the Breton who do not."

"Perhaps. Tadgh and Gurth still follow your banner?"

"Benni might be my builder but those two are my rocks. Each time we ride they are like twin shadows behind. Your rescue of them, it was *wyrd*."

"Then I am content. Come let us go and help Alain butcher the animals. The hunt has given me an appetite."

We stayed long enough to see the church built and the work in the warrior hall begun. My new men were hard workers if nothing else and before we left they had the supports and the roof beams in place. I saw my wife and Æðelwald of Remisgat in deep discussion. Mathilde was also taking a keen interest. As we were due to leave the next day I did not wish to leave with any uncertainties in the air.

"What is the problem here?"

My wife shook her head, "Nothing that you can deal with or even understand!"

"Perhaps I might surprise you eh? Try me."

She sighed, "Æðelwald here is concerned that we are building a church but we have no permission from the Pope."

"And what concern is this of the Pope? You wish a church and Æðelwald wishes to be a priest. I give permission. That is all there is to it."

Æðelwald of Remisgat shook his head, "It is not as simple as that lord. The Pope controls the Church. He is the head of the church."

"He is a man is he not?"

"Yes lord."

"I thought the head of your religion was this White Christ who died and was reborn. That is who you worship is it not or have I got your religion wrong?"

I saw the priest smile, "No lord, you have succinctly summed it up. We need the Pope to recognise our church."

"If it will cost her coin then we will not bother. I will not pay taxes to a king and I will certainly not pay to someone who offers no protection."

"I told you he would not understand. There is a church here and that is good. As for the rest, we will have to see what the future holds."

It was my turn to smile. "See wife, you are coming to believe in our religion. Urðr is the Norn who sees the future!"

Chapter 7

When we reached our home the ships which would join us had begun to arrive. There were two threttanessa in the anchorage. Our four ships were with them. I had never commanded so many ships before. I began to realise the enormity of what we had taken on. The first two captains, as one would expect with such a small drekar, were relatively young and inexperienced. They had both joined Thorghest in his war. Only the two captains had good byrnies. The others had either half vest like byrnies or leather ones studded with metal. Their ships were sound and their men were keen. Einar Bear Killer had taken the two captains to his hall and the men spread amongst my warrior halls. The ones who came later might have to sleep aboard their ships or camp.

My wife was ever the hostess and she invited the two captains, Einar, Alain, Erik Green Eye, Folki and Erik Long Hair to eat with us. My eldest daughter, Mary, thought it was for her benefit to have two such young Vikings at our table. I knew that my wife would be having a word with her when time allowed.

Bjorn Long Stride was a Viking from Orkneyjar. He and his crew had sailed with one of Klakke Blue Cheek's warriors, Ragnar Ragmunsson. He had been aboard a drekar which had survived the disaster at Hingston. With only a third of the crew, they had taken Bjorn and his inexperienced men to serve with them. Ragnar and his oar brothers had died in a battle with the Hibernians. I said to Bjorn, "Then the gods must have favoured you, Bjorn Long Stride, for they gave you a drekar."

"Aye, jarl but when we walked around your Haugr we saw that we are poor by comparison. Our weapons and armour are fine for half-naked Hibernians and the men of Strathclyde but the Franks and the Saxons are a different matter. We heard of a whole crew such as us who landed at Hamwic. They were all slaughtered and beheaded. Their drekar was burned."

I turned to Leif Blue Eyes, "And what is your tale?"

"My father was our jarl. We left our home in Norway when a plague took our families while we were raiding the Picts. There was just my father and me left from my family and he pined for my mother and my four sisters. The raids against the Picts had not yielded us much and so we joined Thorghest and

66

Magnus Axe Hand. My father chose to go berserk. He hurled himself into the battle with his hearth weru. They died."

I looked at him. There was an obvious question hanging like a cloud in the air. The others looked at him too. The only ones who did not see the question were my wife and daughters.

Leif swallowed the contents of his horn, "We would have all followed him had he not made us swear not to do so. Jarl Thorghest was saved by my father's sacrifice. He gave me a byrnie." He tapped the one he wore. "This was my father's. I will wear this in his honour."

I was content for both stories were common. When Vikings raided they often returned to a home raided by others or struck by disease. Men often chose a warrior's death by feigning madness or perhaps they were driven mad by the loss. I know that Mary had almost taken her own life when she despaired on Raven Wing Island. I saw her looking sadly at Leif Blue Eyes. She understood his father's pain.

"I will tell any other captains when they arrive the same as I tell you now. If you sail with me it is under my banner and you obey my orders. We will share whatever we take equally between the crews of all the ships."

Bjorn looked surprised, "But *'Dragon's Breath'* has a much bigger crew than mine. That does not seem fair. You should get a bigger share."

"We will all be taking the same risks, we share equally. My men will be happy about that."

Einar Bear Killer laughed, "Aye the Franks are rich. You will have mail for all your men! Mind you the swords are not as good as ours. If you want the best swords then fight the Saxons."

Leif said, "But they have burghs and are hard to attack."

Folki shook his head, "As do the Franks. Do not think that they will give up their treasures easily. We have taken much already. Jarl Hrolf will need to sail further up the river to find Franks who do not know us."

"Folki is right. That is why we need as many ships as we can. We will make a longphort which we can defend if they send their horsemen to attack us. However, the Franks are in disarray at the moment. Three brothers fight for the throne. If they have any sense they will put aside their differences and fight us! But I doubt that they will do so."

The next morning, I took Finni Bennison to *'Skuld'*. "This is the ship you will be rowing. I will have some others from the Haugr on board but yours will be the majority of the crew."

His eyes widened, "She is new and has not yet her figurehead." We would only put on the figurehead when we set sail.

I nodded, "Her story has yet to be written. You can put your past behind you, Finni Bennison. When we raid you and your men will decide how men remember you." I held his gaze, "Her name is *'Skuld'*, remember that. It was Skuld who sent me here to carve out this land for my clan."

"It is a great responsibility. Who will captain her?"

I smiled, "I will. I would see the mettle of you and your men."

I left him stumped for words. I had already had arguments with Einar, Beorn, Erik Green Eye, Folki and Erik Long Hair as well as Sven and Harold. They wanted me to sail with a crew I knew. I had silenced them. "This is the largest enterprise we have ever undertaken. Sven and Harold know better than any the value of the smallest part of each drekar. You can have the greatest ship afloat but if one of the strakes gives way then all will be doomed. *'Skuld'* is the smallest part of our machine. I would sail her. That is the end of the argument."

Two more ships arrived that day and the next morning another six. I planned to leave for the raid in three days regardless of how many ships I had under my command. I gathered the captains and my jarls in my hall. Alain had left already to join Bertrand and Gilles. They would follow my son's banner against Rauville and the other isolated strongholds. They would gather animals to increase their flocks and herds. We would strengthen ourselves at the expense of the Franks.

"We leave during the night two nights from now. I have sailed the river before and I will lead. The channel can be tricky and so you will all follow my drekar. It is the smallest. There are two small ports on the northern bank. By sailing at night, we can avoid discovery. The abbey of Jumièges is rich. It has been raided before but that was by just one drekar. There are a thousand monks there. It is one of the richest churches in Frankia. We raid there first. We make a longphort and then split up into raiding parties to gather what we can from the lands to the north and south of the river. We spend three days there and then return here."

Most nodded but two of them did not. Both were Danes. They had many rings on their fingers as well as battle bracelets. One had a necklace of human teeth around his neck. His name was Taki Toothpuller. The other who looked unhappy was Molti Regnisson.

"There are enough ships for us to take Rouen! There will be more treasure there."

"We have fourteen ships. That is not enough to capture such a formidable stronghold."

Molti laughed, "I thought we were joining a band of warriors and not women who were frightened of their own shadow!"

Einar Bear Killer jumped up and his sword went to his hand. I said, "Hold! This is a discussion, Einar, everyone is entitled to their own opinion." I forced a smile, "I am the leader of this raid. If you do not wish to follow my commands then you are free to leave."

They looked at each other and stood. Taki Toothpuller looked around at the others, "I can see that you are all Norse! We have brothers coming from Denmark! When they arrive, we will make our own fleet!"

I nodded, "Then find another anchorage. If you are not with me then you are not a friend. I only offer shelter and hospitality to friends." I saw Molti's hand slide down to his sword. My voice was heavy with menace when I said, "I am hospitable to a point. Anger me, Molti Regnisson, and you will see just what kind of warrior I am."

They both stormed out. I said, quietly to Folki, "Take some men and make sure they leave without causing mischief. Take men with bows."

After Folki had gone Tandi Spear Warrior said, "Have we enough ships now, jarl? I am happy to do as you suggest but there will be just twelve drekar."

"There are still a couple of days and three of my drekar can hold fifty warriors. We will have enough. Better a smaller number of warriors who can be relied upon."

It was some time before Folki returned, "It was as well you ordered us to follow. Molti thought to cause mischief. My men discouraged them with arrows. Molti will now be Molti the Lame and if he does not take out the arrow correctly then Molti One Leg!"

I took out my maps and showed them our route. I was glad I had not done so before. The two Danes were not trustworthy. The next morning we saw the sails of four drekar gingerly making their way into the harbour.

When they landed, I went to speak to them. I introduced myself and told them that I would be leading and would brook no dissent. Steinn the Wise, who was a Dane held out his arm for me to clasp. He grinned, "We met Taki Toothpuller. Had he been sailing with you then I would not for he is a treacherous snake. He persuaded ten other drekar to sail with him."

"Ten?" Einar could not believe the number.

Steinn shook his head. "There were more ships heading this way. We were all caught in a squall off the coast of Cent. More will come. Of that I am certain."

He was right. When all finally arrived, we had a fleet of twenty-two ships We heard, from their captains, of others who had chosen to follow the Toothpuller. That was their right. A warrior chose whom he would follow. What I was worried about was that they might warn the Franks that we were coming. We needed surprise. I had asked Sven the Helmsman to be at the steering board. As he had built *'Skuld'*, he had agreed. My mind was much easier. I led the way in my new drekar. She smelled new and her newly painted and fitted figurehead was distinctive. The Norn would protect us! I also had twelve experienced men from the Haugr to augment Finni's men.

Sven closed his eyes and sniffed the air, "We may find the wind changes before we reach the mouth of the river, Jarl Hrolf."

"The tide race?"

"Aye. If the wind is in the wrong direction then the mouth can become treacherous. I would have us sail slowly." He pointed at Finni Bennison. "And you have a new untried crew."

"Trust me they will show you. I can feel it."

Once we cleared the anchorage we ordered the oars out. It was as much to warm up the men for battle as anything. We had a wind with us but I wanted the men to sing.

"I have worked with Harold Fast Sailing on your own song for this ship. Let us see if we can make her fly." I began to sing and after three renditions they began to join in.

Skuld the Dark sails on shadows wings
Skuld the Dark is a ship that sings
With soft, gentle voice of a powerful witch
Her keel will glide through Frankia's ditch
With flowing hair and fiery breath
Skuld the Dark will bring forth death
Though small in size her heart is great
The Norn who decides on man's final fate
Skuld the Dark sails on shadows wings
Skuld the Dark is a sorcerous ship that sweetly sings
Skuld the Dark sails on shadows wings
Skuld the Dark is a sorcerous ship that sweetly sings
Skuld the Dark sails on shadows wings
Skuld the Dark is a sorcerous ship that sweetly sings
The witch's reach is long and her eyes can see through mist
Her teeth are sharp and grind your bones to grist
With soft, gentle voice of a powerful witch
Her keel will glide through Frankia's ditch
With flowing hair and fiery breath
Skuld the Dark will bring forth death
Though small in size her heart is great
The Norn who decides on man's final fate
Skuld the Dark sails on shadows wings
Skuld the Dark is a sorcerous ship that sweetly sings
Skuld the Dark sails on shadows wings
Skuld the Dark is a sorcerous ship that sweetly sings
The witch's reach is long and her eyes can see through mist
Her teeth are sharp and grind your bones to grist

The song was one to keep a gentle pace. It was not a song to row at speed. We did not need that. We had less than seventy miles to cover. We could do that in under three hours with the wind from our quarter. I saw Sven nodding. They had never rowed the drekar before but they were all together and, already, we were pulling away from '*Dragon's Breath*'.

"If they can fight too then they will be a formidable crew."

"And she is a fine ship, Sven. You and Harold have done well."

It was pitch black but our ship's boys had sharp eyes and anything which broke up the pattern of the waves was cause for them to stare even closer. "Drekar off the coast."

Leaving Sven at the steering board I ran to the prow and hauled myself up on the stay. The drekar was pitching and I had to balance myself and get into the rhythm of the ship. When I did I spied the ships. It was Molti and the other Danish ships. They were attempting to beat us to the abbey! They would reach the estuary first! I cursed the Danes. We might have to fight them and that would only benefit the Franks.

I went back to Sven, "It is the Danes! They are ahead of us."

Sven smiled, "And they have the tide to race. Unless they have sailed here before then they are in trouble."

All of my captains knew the mouth of the river well. We would head for the southern bank and avoid the shoals in the middle. With the tide against it was almost impossible to enter the river from the middle or the north. Even so, I was less confident than I had been. I was glad that I had ordered my men to follow in line astern. The first four were all drekar from the Haugr. We would guide them through. As Sven put the steering board over to head for the southern bank I saw that the Danes were sailing three abreast. The river was wide enough but they were heading for a sandbank. The coast was just a darker shadow and only distinguishable by the white flecked waves. My whole fleet was now in the hands of Sven. They would follow our stern. The new wood stood out against the sea.

I walked to the prow again and stood with Niels Erikson. He was the son of Erik One Hand whom we had rescued from the Moors. "What can your sharp eyes see, Niels?"

"I see the Danes, jarl but…"

"Yes?"

"One of them looks to have turned beam on. Why would they do that, jarl?"

I smacked the sheerstrake, "Because one of them has run aground." At the speed we were travelling, it soon became obvious that the Danes had grounded two of their ships on the sandbar. The others had been taken aback and were not moving. We now had the chance to get ahead of them. I turned and shouted, "Row! Men of the '*Skuld*'! Row and make her fly!"

Skuld the Dark sails on shadows wings

Ragnvald Hrolfsson

Skuld the Dark is a sorcerous ship that sweetly sings
Skuld the Dark sails on shadows wings
Skuld the Dark is a sorcerous ship that sweetly sings
Skuld the Dark sails on shadows wings
Skuld the Dark is a sorcerous ship that sweetly sings
Skuld the Dark sails on shadows wings
Skuld the Dark is a sorcerous ship that sweetly sings
The witch's reach is long and her eyes can see through mist
Her teeth are sharp and grind your bones to grist

The sudden burst of speed sped us towards the mouth of the river. We were close enough to the south bank to see the sand dunes but Sven knew his business and he was unerringly accurate.

"Down sail! Step the mast on the mast fish!"

As the sail was lowered and the mast lock removed to allow the mast to be laid on the mast fish I continued to stare at the Danes. They were throwing lines to haul off the two ships. It would take time. Of course, they would be watching us and they would identify the correct channel. They would follow! I left Niels to continue to look for danger and then hurried down the ship, "Well done! You are now the men of the *'Skuld'*! I look forward to watching you fight! This will be your last raid without mail!"

"Aye, jarl!"

The southern bank of the river had no settlements and but a few isolated houses. There were jetties which they used when they moved stone from the quarries along the river. They used barges. Had it been daylight we might have seen some tied up. The small anchorage was on the northern shore and was almost a mile away from us. They would neither see nor hear us. As soon as we entered the estuary then the motion became easier. The river was wide but there were few waves. We just had to fight the tide. The fact that we had outwitted Molti and Taki gave my new men more power. We surged along the river. The loops were very long and we could now sail in the centre of the river. We slowed the oars down. We were fighting the current. Sven could not use the sails and our men would have some miles to row. We had to pace them so that they did not reach there exhausted.

I stood with Sven at the steering board. We had raided this river many years ago. Jarl Gunnar had been alive then as had Ulf and Siggi. We had sailed down the river not knowing what we would find. Our raid had been speedy and we had not destroyed. We had taken treasure and fled. The Franks had pursued us. I hoped that this would be a different raid. With over six hundred men we had the opportunity to stay and, if needs be, to fight. I glanced astern. Would we be fighting Vikings?

72

Pinpricks of light along the river showed where people lived. We had not touched them the last time we had come but this visit would be different. Once we had secured the abbey my men would spread out to harvest the Franks. Niels Erikson brought me some ale. One of his tasks, as the new ship's boy, was to take ale to the rowers. A horn of ale every now and then revived the spirits and kept the mind fresh.

He handed me mine. "Have the rowers had theirs?"

"Aye, Jarl, the captain told me that your ale should be last." He looked fearfully at Sven who nodded and grinned.

"And he is right. I am just the jarl. I have an easy time of it." I drank some of the ale. His mother, Brigid, had made it. "This is good ale. Did you not wish to become a brewer like your father?"

"My father would be a warrior. He lost his arm and cannot but he still yearns to stand in a shield wall. He regrets that he can never have a warrior's death."

I shook my head, "It does not do to tempt the Norns, especially not on a ship named after one. Your father has earned the right not to fight. Along with Rurik One Ear, he saved the clan when we lived on Raven Wing Island."

"He told me how the three of you fought the Bretons and the Franks."

I nodded and remembered those days when I was so young and Dream Strider had been little more than a foal. "And how do you find the trip?"

"It is exciting. When I saw those ships founder on the sands I thought we were doomed."

Sven grunted, "I am no Dane! I know how to steer a drekar!"

"You know that you will have to defend the ship when we leave."

"I have my sling and my bow. My father gave me his old sword and I can use it. It is in my chest. They shall not have our ship, jarl. I am a Viking and I am my father's son."

I finished the horn and returned it to him. "Come home to your mother safe, Niels. That is my command!"

"Aye, jarl."

As he wandered down Sven said, "He is willing. Erik told me that he is handy with a sword. It is only a short one he uses and the boy has yet to grow into his man's body but if the Allfather is willing then he will take an oar. I will not see that. This will be my last voyage, jarl."

I turned and looked at him.

He shrugged, "I have been on the beach with Harold too long. Our days are our own. Some days we work on the drekar from sunrise to sunset and at others, we fiddle on with a scarf joint all day and then sit and talk of voyages. I think our next ship will take even longer. I am no longer young. It is time to sit on the beach and talk of the past."

"It is good for you are enjoying that which Siggi and Ulf did not. You are enjoying your old age. Do not berate yourself for that. It is your time to slow down. I am just grateful that I have your hand upon the steering board."

A short while later he pointed ahead. I could see a darker shape rising above the black snake that was the river. It was slightly lighter as dawn was almost upon us. "Unless I have lost all of my senses then that is Jumièges! We are almost at our destination."

As I remembered it the abbey lay on a high piece of ground less than a thousand paces from the river. When we had raided they had had few defences. I suspected that they might have more now. There was a road that headed east to Rouen. There they had a count. It was a mighty stronghold and even with a civil war, it would be garrisoned. Both sides would want their hands on Rouen and, at the same time, could not afford to offend the White Christ by allowing the abbey and its monks to be slaughtered or enslaved.

We were all wearing mail and, when we landed, we could get ashore quickly. I put on my cap and my mail hood. It had now become part of my ritual. I checked that I had a seax in my sealskin boot and another in my belt at my back. Bagsecg had made me two pieces of mail which I slipped on my hands. My palms were not covered but the backs were. They were light but they protected me from cuts to the back of the hand. If I lost my sword or shield then I still had a weapon; my fists!

The river was two hundred paces wide and the word was passed for the landward side of oars to stop rowing. The steerboard side edged us towards the northern bank when we were just twenty paces from it. Sven shouted for them to pull in oars and the current pushed us to the northern bank. Niels and the other ship's boys swarmed ashore to secure us to the bank. Sven had used all of his skill to find the best place to land. Already the sun was rising and I could see that he had found the closest place to the abbey, which rose a thousand paces away from us. '*Dragon's Breath*', *Cold Drake*' and '*Wild Boar*', each tied up to us in succession. We were a jetty that protruded eighty paces into the river. As each ship bumped next to us it was tied to us. We had both a bridge and a fighting platform. We rarely used the longphort but I knew we would need one now.

I stepped ashore and my men hurried after me. With my shield on my back, I looked down the river where the rest of my fleet loomed up out of the western dark. We would have a bridge five ships long and four ships deep. The crews of all twenty-two ships would be enough to defend the fortress.

Beorn Fast Feet and Rolf Arneson were the first ashore from '*Dragon's Breath*' and they joined me and Finni Bennison's men. I pointed up the hill and they nodded and all of them ran. Those twenty-two men would be our advance guard. They would try to gain access to the abbey to warn us of problems. Folki, Einar Bear Killer, Einar Asbjornson and Gudrun Witch Killer joined me with their men. The other drekar were disgorging their men. I donned my helmet. The bank would soon become crowded. As Thorbolt and Sigtrygg the Left-Handed joined me I unsheathed my sword, pointed up the hill and said, "Clan of the Horse! We go to war!"

Chapter 8

I began to run after Beorn and Rolf. They were a dark shadow moving up through the lightening land. The hill and the abbey made our side of the hill darker for we were in its lee. Above us, I suddenly heard the tolling of a bell. It was not the measured sound of a bell calling monks to worship. It was an urgent summons for help. It carried on the morning air and would be heard many miles away. We had been seen. It was inevitable. When we had raided before Ulf and I had sneaked close and slain the guards and sentries. They would have put measures in place to stop such a sneak attack. Rouen was twenty miles away. Even if they did not hear the bell others who lay between us and that citadel would and they would hurry to the aid of the abbey which had been endowed by their king. We had half a day to secure the abbey and then prepare for battle.

I heard the sounds of steel on steel. It hastened us. I drew my sword as I led my men up the slope. I left my shield around my back. I needed to have a clear sight of what lay ahead. It was still the half-light of dawn but I saw slain Franks and two of my men. Both had been wounded. That was the price you paid for not wearing mail. The gates were ajar and I saw Beorn Fast Feet, Rolf Arneson and Finni Bennison leading my men towards the huge church.

I waved to the right, "Thorbolt, take your men and sweep that way." Pointing to the left I shouted, "Sigtrygg, that way." I turned. "Gunnar Stoneface send the next crews in the three directions when they arrive."

"Aye, jarl.

I had no idea what defences they had put in place but I wanted my men spread out so that they could deal with whatever came their way. I led my men up towards the huge church. It was the largest building I had seen in this land. They had twin towers. One was still undergoing construction.

From ahead I heard Beorn yell, "Shield wall!"

My advance guard had hit trouble. As I swung my shield around I shouted, "Form a flying wedge!" I heard Einar Bear Killer repeat the order.

This would be an improvised formation. I would be the point and then the warriors would fit in behind: two, then three, four, five and so on. It was not ideal for you were not fighting alongside your usual shield brothers but it would have to do. We were approaching from the dark of night and so the Franks, who had been assigned to defend the church, did not see us. We were not making much noise. They had surrounded my men and their shield wall was circular. I did not break stride. I swung my sword overhand as my shield smashed into a Frank's back. My weight and that of the men behind knocked him to the ground. I heard the crunch of his skull as seal skin boots trampled him. My sword sliced through the helmet and head of another Frank. Finni Bennison skewered the other Frank who was between us.

We had done enough. The sheer weight of our mail and bodies had broken through the Franks' defence. I yelled, "Break shield wall!"

Knowing what was coming Rolf and Beorn stepped aside as I ran at the Franks who were facing them. The Franks had been fighting less than eighteen men and suddenly a steel giant of fifty warriors fell upon them. I do not think they had ever seen the like. It was at that moment that the sun chose to rise above the stone of the abbey church. It illuminated my warriors. The Franks wore open helmets and I saw the terror on their faces. A Viking fears no man. The Franks had never seen such ferocious warriors before. They involuntarily took a step back.

I saw a Leudes. He had a full byrnie with scale armour and a high crowned helmet. It had a plume in the top. He was drawing attention to himself. He held a smaller shield than me and I ran at him. I saw him raise his sword. He would swing at my head. I was already bringing my shield up as I brought my sword from behind me in a sweep towards his leg. A larger shield might have blocked the blow but the small shield of the Franks was not large enough. As his sword smashed into my shield, bending in the process, my sword hacked through his unprotected leg and half severed it. Our momentum knocked him to the ground. I did not know if he bled to death or was crushed by our feet but I knew, without looking, that he was dead.

The ground was flatter but I did not break stride. "Clan of the Horse! On!"

I saw priests trying to rush into the church where they would be able to close the doors. They were carrying treasures to save them from us. It was a mistake for it slowed them down. I saw two priests carrying a large chest trip and fall.

Behind me, my men began a chant.

Clan of the Horseman
Warriors strong
Clan of the Horseman
Our reach is long
Clan of the Horseman
Fight as one
Clan of the Horseman
Death will come

77

Clan of the Horseman
Warriors strong
Clan of the Horseman
Our reach is long
Clan of the Horseman
Fight as one
Clan of the Horseman
Death will come

I saw the two priests who had fallen stare in terror at the sight and sound of my men. They froze. I had seen rabbits do the same. In that hesitation, they were lost. They tried to pick up the chest and then saw that we would reach them. They ran. The doors were slowly closing. I heard them shout something. We were gaining on them and the ones inside should have closed the doors. Perhaps the two priests were important, I know not. Whatever the reason they delayed closing them. As the two priests reached them so did we. We burst through like a ram at a gate!

Inside was confusion. The church was packed with priests who were either hiding or desperately trying to escape us. Although they outnumbered us I did not fear them. However, it was possible that should they try to escape they might kill some of my men. We would need every man for the battle which I knew would come later. I shouted, in Frank, "Hold!" My men stopped, almost as one. They were my warriors. The other crews would be racing through the many buildings and they might not obey but my men were well trained. When my men stopped a strange silence fell upon the church. "If you surrender then I give my word that you shall live! I am Hrolf the Horseman of the Haugr."

I saw that they had an abbot. He was both older than most of the priests and better dressed. In addition, six priests stood around him holding candle holders like spears.

I pointed my sword at him. "Abbot, do not make me order your priests to be slaughtered it would be a waste. I swear that you shall live."

He pointed his crosier at me, "Aye but we will be slaves! Better death than a life as a slave."

"We will sell you back to your king. He would buy you would he not?"

I saw that I had set them a conundrum. Who was the king and should they believe me? I counted on the fact that the story of my abduction of the priests from Cantwareburh would have reached them. I guess it must have for the abbot shouted. "We surrender."

I turned, "Beorn, take charge here. Put half the men to guard the priests and the other half to strip the church and take the treasure down to the drekar."

"Aye, jarl."

"Have our wounded and dead taken there too. I will not leave men to be despoiled by our foes." I saw that Finni Bennison had a slight wound. "You and your men did well, Finni."

He nodded, "I lost six shield brothers." He shook his head, "If we had had mail…"

"And after this, you shall. Go back to the drekar with the wounded."

"No, jarl, this will not keep me from serving you."

I walked out into the morning light. I could hear, all around the sound of men fighting and men dying. The majority would be priests. The other jarls and captains were not my men. Thorbolt and Sigtrygg would spare priests. They knew their value. To most Vikings, they were just easy victims.

Niels Erikson ran up to me. I saw he had his father's sword in his hand. "Jarl, Sven sent me. The Danes came up the river. We thought that they were going to fight us. He had men man the sides and have arrows ready. We sent a couple of flights towards them and they continued upstream. Sven said you ought to know."

"Thank you. Go into the church and help any wounded you find back to the ship." I nodded towards his sword, "Today you take the first steps to becoming a warrior!"

He strode off proudly. I headed for the northern part of the monastery. They had but a single gate and a low wall. The gate was open. Priests, warriors and slaves had fled.

I found Ottkell, Last of the Bears there. He was a Dane. "They are easy to catch and to slay, jarl."

I shook my head, "Dead they are of no value. Alive, we can sell them as slaves or even back to their church."

He nodded, "I was told by Haaken One Eye that I would learn from you. He said that you may be young but you have an old head on your shoulders."

"Did many escape?"

"They were mainly slaves and a few warriors, but four priests escaped. The rest dropped to their knees and jabbered at me. I did not understand their words."

I realised that was my fault. I should have each wing commanded by one of my men who could speak the language. I was learning too.

"Have some men guard the gate and give warning of any who try to come to the relief of the priests. Then have the rest search the buildings. Destroy nothing. We can sell back their Holy Books. Search the floors for hidden doors. They like to bury treasure in crypts beneath their churches. We put all the treasure in the drekar and sail back to the Haugr to divide it up. My men and I know what is valuable and can be resold."

"Aye, jarl."

It was all over now. The monastery and its contents were ours. A stream of men began to head down the hill to load the drekar. All of our ships had their decks removed to facilitate the loading. This was where the longphort would prove invaluable. Tied together they were a stable platform.

I went back to the abbey. They had found the crypt and secured the treasures there. "Beorn, Erik Long Hair, Rolf, see if you can find four horses. I would ride afield and see if there is any danger."

"Aye, jarl."

What I did not know was how the attack on Rouen would affect our raid. I had planned on defeating whoever they sent against us and then raiding the countryside. If I waited for an attack that did not materialize then I would be wasting our most valuable resource: time.

Erik Long Hair, Einar Bear Killer and Sigtrygg the Left-Handed sought me out. "We have much treasure, jarl. I have never seen such a rich place."

"There will be more that is of value in the houses and towns which lie close by, Einar Bear Killer. The people who live there will service the abbey. They will have coin, pots, linens and other treasure. While the ships are being loaded take your three warbands and scour the land hereabouts. I will scout further afield. Molti and Taki have sailed upstream to Rouen. That may bring us trouble or relief. I know not which. Take all that you can. Have the wounded and dead taken back to the ships and prepare to defend these walls against Franks. This is not over yet."

I heard the sound of hooves. My three men brought four scrawny looking horses. They were so small that my feet almost reached the ground. They would do. We did not head north. There was a loop in the river and it enclosed the abbey. We headed northeast and followed the road. Even as we headed down I heard the sound of Thorbolt's men as they tramped down after us. I saw houses ahead. The people were hiding, hoping that the terror of the Northmen would pass. I saw, just a mile up the road, a larger settlement. There was no wall but there were men preparing a defence. I realised that the ones who had fled would have thought we were just there to raid the monastery. Had they known what awaited them they might have fled. It would have been wiser.

Behind me, I heard the shouts and screams as Thorbolt's men winkled out the residents. Thorbolt had enough men to continue behind us. We approached the armed men. Some had helmets. There were three of the guards from the church; I recognised their livery. The rest were just the townsfolk armed with spears, hunting bows and crude hand weapons. My shield was on my back. I nudged my horse forward.

"Jarl there are just four of us."

"Beorn, are you afraid of twenty men who could be knocked senseless by Brigid the Alewife?"

He laughed, "No, jarl!"

As we rode forward one of the bowmen released an arrow straight at me. I watched it coming but I could do nothing about it. It struck my mail. Bagsecg had made good mail. The links were small. The leather byrnie beneath was also tough. The arrow just stuck there and I continued forward. I saw fear in their faces. Another arrow was sent at me. This time I was ready and I batted it away with my mailed hand. I then roared, "Clan of the Horse!" I drew my sword and galloped towards them. With an arrow still embedded in my mail, I must have terrified them for they fled down the road. As they passed the houses others joined them. I reined in.

My men began to laugh. "This will make a good tale to lighten the long winter nights. I thought you were a dead man, jarl."

I pulled out the arrow. It had a barbed tip. There was no way it would have penetrated my mail. It would have been caught, even by an inferior byrnie. I turned in the saddle and shouted, "Thorbolt search this place, they fled quickly there may be goods inside, and then build a barricade. We shall fight any Franks who come from here."

I dug my heels into the flanks of the game little horse and pursued the ones who had fled. It was not bravado. I wanted them running all the way to Rouen if needs be. The story of a Viking who was struck by an arrow and lived to catch another would make us seem even more invincible. Rouen had been protected from Vikings. Since Folki and his brother had been driven from Ouistreham we were a distant memory. We were an annoyance on the coast. We were a passing plague that would move on to another land. Now we would be a real and present threat. When the road entered the heavily wooded area I stopped.

"Beorn you and Rolf stay here. I will send more men to you. Watch the road until this time tomorrow. If no one has come by then return for they will not be coming at all."

"Do you not need us to raid?"

"My men have done enough. We were the ones who drove the guards from the abbey and we took the greatest chances. I will let the other jarls raid further afield. It is the reason they came with us, is it not?" They nodded, "And if a priest should come do not take him prisoner but tell him that we hold the abbot and his monks as hostages. If they wish them alive then they pay!"

I rode back with Erik Long Hair. "A good raid, jarl."

"It will be a good raid when we are back in the Haugr and counting our treasure. Until then it is not. But I hope that it has enabled my son and his men to capture more places close by them. This is an opportunity sent by the gods. Had the two kings not died then I might have delayed expanding. The gods are on our side."

Thorbolt had a happy look on his face. "Many of those who fled here had come from the abbey. We found chests of goods they had taken. There is plenty of coin, fine vessels, furs, jewels, the candles they use in their churches. We also found much food and animals."

"Slaves?"

He shook his head. "Most were older or had the soft white hands of a clerk. I sent those back to the abbey to be herded with the others. I have kept the likely slaves here. I thought you could cast your eye over them."

"No, Thorbolt, you are a good judge. I leave it to you. Send six men up the road to wait with Rolf and Beorn. Send food and ale. They will watch there until the morrow. This is the main road from Rouen." I pointed to the signpost in the centre of the crossroads. "You and your men can stay here or come back to the abbey."

"We do not raid?"

"There is no need. I will speak with the other jarls. We will guard the priests and the longphort and they can raid. I want enough men here to bloody the nose of any Franks who venture forth from Rouen."

I dismounted and led the horse through the gate. When we reached the abbey, I saw that the wine had been broached. One of the men who served Hagnni Nisson was riding on the back of a priest and beating him with the flat of his sword. I pulled back my hand and struck him in the side of the head with my mailed mitten. He fell unconscious and his shield brothers turned on me. "If one hand goes to his sword then you shall die by the blood eagle! I am jarl!" I whipped my head around and pointed at Hagnni. "Control your men or take your drekar and leave! So long as I lead then the prisoners are treated well for they are valuable."

He nodded, "Arne is a fool who cannot hold his ale but to be fair we thought it over!"

"And I thought you came to me to raid." I swept my hand around. There are many villages close by with animals, treasure and slaves. Jarl Thorbolt has captured one a mile from here. Take your men and raid! By tomorrow we may be fighting Franks!"

He gestured for his men to pick up the bloody Arne, "I am sorry jarl. You are right. Come, you whoresons! Let us become rich men!" His words did not sound sincere but I had much to think about.

Leaving my horse at the abbey I walked the thousand paces to the longphort. I was pleased to see that Folki had organised some of our men as guards. If Molti and Taki had gone upstream then what was to stop them coming downstream to take our treasure?

"Any problems, Bergil?"

He shook his head. "Some of these warriors have never been on a proper raid before. They must have become used to the poor pickings of Hibernia. You would have thought they had liberated the Emperor's Treasure from Miklagård!"

I laughed but for some Vikings, especially the Rus of the Dnieper, a raid on Miklagård was seen as the ultimate treasure hunt. One day ships would sail down the rivers and the Emperor would discover that the Vikings were a threat to be taken seriously.

"We may be called upon to fight so make sure our men get rest."

He nodded, "Half of them are sleeping now. They are like veterans. Even the new ones who joined us, like Finni Bennison, know the value of food and rest."

I stepped aboard my drekar and found Sven speaking with Siggi on my old ship. "Problems, Sven?"

"The wind is turning. I believe it will be in our favour for another day or two but the clouds suggest that it will turn around and make our voyage to the sea harder if we overstay our welcome."

"I agree. I intend to sail this time tomorrow. I have men watching the road."

Sven pointed upstream, "And I would watch there, jarl. I have placed our best archers on '*Cold Drake*'. I fear an attack from the Danes."

"It is good that you watch." I turned to Erik Long Hair, "Go around the drekar and the other jarls. We leave this time tomorrow. Anyone not here gets left behind."

He grinned, "I will impress that upon them!"

Before I left I asked, "You have food?"

"We have plenty, jarl."

I returned to the abbey for the smell of cooking meat drew me there. As I walked up the track I saw that most of the warbands were heeding my advice and heading out to raid. After I had eaten I lay down in the cool of the church to rest. The Franks built well in stone. I knew that one day I would have to pay a Frank to build a stone hall for me. A longhouse was warm and it was cosy but it was also dirtier than one which used stone.

I was awoken when it was dark. "Jarl, Beorn Fast Feet sent me. The Franks come. They have camped a Roman mile from where he waits."

"Return, Leif Blue Eyes, and tell him and Jarl Thorbolt to bring their men back to the gates. We will meet them there on the morrow."

If I was Jarl Dragonheart I would have had my Ulfheonar await the Franks and ambush them. They were the masters of such attacks. We were the masters at ambushing with horses. I had neither horse nor Ulfheonar. I would have to make a shield wall and fight them beard to beard. I was heading down to the river when Niels Erikson found me. "Jarl, Sven the Helmsmen said that five Danish drekar sailed along the river. They did not stop and they looked to have been in a battle and just before sunset he saw smoke in the sky."

I did not know what that meant but I put it to the back of my mind. I had a battle to fight. "Tell him the Franks are coming. At dawn, I want all the ships turned around to face downstream. We may have to leave quickly."

By the time dawn had broken I had organised my men. I had the crews of my four ships drawn up before the abbey wall. Steinn the Wise had returned and I had him and his men watching the hostages. I told him to send any warriors who arrived back to help us at the gate. I did not expect any. This would be the Clan of the Horse holding the line. We waited. The wind still favoured us but I trusted my captain. If he said it would change then it would.

I had no scouts out. They could tell me nothing. The Franks would come down the main road. We had a wall against our back and behind it, I had every man who had no armour ready with a bow. The ones with armour were in a three-deep line with me in the middle. Every man had a spear. I thought that there was an irony in using the Franks' own spears to fight them. They were slightly longer than ours. I had, about me, my most trusted warriors. My jarls and captains were in the front rank. The Franks would have to send their very best men to defeat us.

I heard horses neigh. They were sending horsemen against us. That tactic would often work against other Vikings but we were horsemen and we knew how to fight horses. We were not afraid of them. The only tactic they could use which was effective would be to make their horses rear and our wall of spears would deter that.

We had taken them by surprise. I could see that as they appeared through the trees, a thousand paces from us. They looked to have a hundred horsemen and a hundred men from the local levy. I suspected that they thought that we would have fled. Their leader was dressed in fine armour. I took him for a count or some lord who was even greater in ranks. It glistened and shone in the morning light.

Einar Bear Killer shouted, "If that rider comes near me his armour is mine!"

The leader shouted something and bags were brought forth. His men took out Danish heads. I recognised Molti and Taki. Men held the heads by the hair and then threw them at us. They thought it would anger us. It did not for they were not our friends. It was a ruse that failed but it told me the fate of the Danes. The leader arrayed his men. The Franks did not couch their spears they thrust them overhand. As they prepared I shouted, "On my command, we make a shield wall."

My men shouted, "Aye, jarl!"

As we waited Folki and my men began a chant. They banged their spears against their shields in time.

Clan of the Horseman
Warriors strong
Clan of the Horseman
Our reach is long
Clan of the Horseman
Fight as one
Clan of the Horseman
Death will come

It was a simple chant but it seemed to inspire fear in our enemies. The Franks who were facing us had never seen the like before. We had warriors who were tattooed. Many had long plaited moustaches and hair which hung down below helmets. They had cloaks lined with seal fur, bear fur, or, as in my case, wolf fur. Our weapons were different. Many of my men had two handed axes which were deadly weapons. They could split a shield with one blow. They could outrange any sword and mail was no obstacle to them. The chanting, the banging and the singing added to the terror of the new warriors they were facing. I saw that some of the levy decided to leave the field. The leader shouted something. I worked out that it was, "Charge!"

They began to gallop towards us. They were travelling too fast. As a horseman, I could see that. They would not arrive in a line. I had a good eye for such things. I shouted, "Archers, when you are ready then release!"

The Franks did not use archers and they were in for a shock.

When the archers released I shouted, "Shield wall!"

A shield appeared above my head and a spear was rested upon my shoulder. All that I had to do was to put my shield before my left shoulder, step onto my left leg and brace my spear against my right foot. We had done this so many times before that it did not need any thought at all. The arrows began to pick off the horsemen. We were not using hunting bows; we were using war bows. We were not using hunting arrows; ours were narrow and could pierce mail. Less than half of the Franks wore mail. Their horses were unprotected. The thirty archers we had sent wave after wave of arrows. Horses and men fell. Still, they came.

"Brace!"

There came a point at which either horse or warrior waiting for the horse blinked and lost. We did not blink. I felt my arm jolted and then heard a crack as a horse ran into my spear and broke it. The horse died. As men on foot, we had a narrower frontage than the horses and while I speared a horse, Folki speared the rider. The smell and sound of dying horses made many of the other horses baulk. As they did so the men in the second and third rank thrust with their spears and men died. Had they had warriors on foot behind they might have succeeded but they had farmers and they stopped as the wall of horses fell apart and then fell back.

My men banged their shields in sheer joy. They had driven off horsemen.

Clan of the Horseman
Warriors strong
Clan of the Horseman
Our reach is long
Clan of the Horseman
Fight as one

Clan of the Horseman
Death will come

I watched as the enemy held a debate. Eventually, the rider with the fine mail and two others took off their helmets and rode towards us. They sheathed their swords and held their hands with palms uppermost.

"Is this a trick jarl?"

"I think not, Folki. Sigtrygg and Thorbolt sheath your swords and walk with me."

I slipped my shield around my back, sheathed my sword and took off my helmet. I let my mail hood fall to my shoulders. We met in the middle of the two armies.

I spoke first. We had won and I wanted to let him know that we had. "I am Jarl Hrolf the Horseman of the Haugr."

"I am Louis, son of Louis the Pious and brother to the King of France."

"You have left many men on the field."

He ignored the unspoken question. "What will it cost to rid this land of you?"

"To rid your land of us? That would be twelve thousand gold pieces. To save the lives of your priests will cost a further ten thousand gold pieces."

Louis looked at me and nodded. "How long do we have?"

"Rouen is two hours ride away. You have six hours from now. Any delay will result in the death of a priest."

His lips narrowed and he hissed, "You are barbarians. We slaughtered the men you sent to take Rouen and the rest fled with their tails between their legs. You will be also be driven into the sea when my brother and I have settled our dispute."

"The price is still twenty-two thousand gold pieces."

"You shall have your money but if any priest is harmed…"

I smiled, "You will still pay to be rid of us."

He turned his horse and left the field. As we walked back towards our men Sigtrygg said, "You have cowed a king!"

"He is not a king yet. There are two others who dispute it. He was a fool to attack us with the forces he did."

"Hrolf! Hrolf! Hrolf!" My men began chanting and banging their shields.

I took out my sword and raising it shouted, "Only the Clan of the Horse could have done what you did! You sail home as heroes!" As I sheathed my sword and began to pick my way through the dead I said, "Take the mail from the dead. The swords can be melted down by Bagsecg. Have our dead taken aboard our ships."

I found some of my jarls heading up from the church. I took off my helmet. "It is over. The Franks have agreed to pay us a ransom for the priests and to leave them alone. You can sail to my home now if you wish and I will follow with my drekar when the ransom is paid."

Steinn the Wise said, "You have shown great wisdom. I think many of us would have slain the priests. You give us a new way to war."

Just at that moment, the first of our dead were carried reverently down the hill. "There is still a price to pay."

"Should we wait for you? Another of Molti's drekar sailed down the river during the morning. They may wish to make mischief."

"I do not fear them. They were defeated by the Franks. I think they will sail home and choose more wisely next time. Taki and Molti are dead. I saw their heads and those of some of their other warriors. My helmsman tells me that the weather is changing. We do not want to be trapped on the river."

Steinn nodded, "I will do as you command. I will make sure that all the ships are at the Haugr when you return. You command and you will divide!"

I went into the church and sought out the abbot. "Louis' son, Louis, is paying a ransom for you, abbot. I told you that you would not be harmed."

He gave a rueful shake of his head and spread his arms out, "And what have you left us? This is an empty shell!"

"I thought you were priests who dedicated your lives to the glory of your White Christ. What do you need with gold, perfumes and candles? You have your lives. I would be grateful for that."

"You are a strange Viking. You speak our language as well as we do. You understand our beliefs and yet you are a barbarian."

"I was brought up in this land and I dispute the word barbarian. Your Louis took the heads of the Danes who attacked him and then rode his horses over them. We did not despoil your dead. They lie, even now, beyond your walls. Is that the act of a barbarian? Did we mistreat you? Were you not fed and given sustenance? Are those the acts of barbarians? Look into your own heart first, priest."

"Yet you come and you raid. Why?"

"You are rich and most of the men who follow me are not. If you would keep your gold then protect it better. There are many other men such as I lead. I have said I will leave but when my ships sail home they will tell others of your riches. I would rid yourselves of your gold." I pointed north. "There are islands off the coast of Britannia. On those islands are priests with monasteries. They do not follow your Pope and his commands. They wear crude habits and live off the land. No Viking raids those men. Ask yourself why."

He nodded, "You are a strange one. Do I have your permission to bury the dead?"

"Of course. I will come with you. I am interested in your practice."

As I watched the priests bury the dead of the Franks who had fallen I saw that their practice differed little from ours. They took them within their walls to a graveyard filled with crosses. They dug holes as we did and laid the men with their arms folded across them. We would have placed the warriors' swords in their hands. We had taken the swords but the priests did not ask for them. They mumbled words that I did not understand and I took them to be Latin.

By the time they had finished and, as the sun tipped past its zenith, the first of the gold arrived. The warrior who brought it said, "We did not have enough gold. There is the equivalent in silver."

His belligerent tone told me that he was not happy about paying off raiders.

"We will count it when we return to our home."

He pointed at me, "I would look for another home soon, Viking, for when we have one king we will join together and drive you back into the sea!"

I nodded, "You can try, Frank, but if today is a foretaste of the future, you will have to bleed heavily to do so."

"You were lucky!"

"No, we were better!"

The change of metal meant we had more chests to carry. It took time to load them for we did not want to be unbalanced. It meant that the weather was changing as we pushed off from the bank. We were at the rear. We had our masts and sails raised for we were no longer trying to hide.

Sven said, "I told the other captains that we would have to row until we reach the sea. Once there we can rest."

Folki said, "It is good jarl. We need to sing for we have had a great victory."

I nodded, "And as we have lost men I will take an oar!"

I joined my men and we sang.

> *The night was black no moon was there*
> *Death and danger hung in the air*
> *As Raven Wing closed with the shore*
> *The scouts crept closer as before*
> *Dressed like death with sharpened blades*
> *They moved like spirits through the glades*
> *The power of the raven grows and grows*
> *The power of the raven grows and grows*
> *With sentries slain they sought new foes*
> *A cry in the night fetched them woes*
> *The alarm was given the warriors ready*
> *Four scouts therewith hearts so steady*
> *Ulf and Arne thought their end was nigh*
> *When Hrolf the wild leapt from the sky*
> *Flying like the raven through the air*
> *He felled the Cymri, a raven slayer*
> *The power of the raven grows and grows*
> *The power of the raven grows and grows*

Ragnvald Hrolfsson

His courage clear he still fought on
Until the clan had battled and won
The power of the raven grows and grows
The power of the raven grows and grows
Raven Wing Goes to war
Hear our voices hear them roar
A song of death to all its foes
The power of the raven grows and grows.
The power of the raven grows and grows.
The power of the raven grows and grows.

This time we saw people in the fields as we rowed the few miles to the sea. Other drekar had sailed west before us but they stood and they pointed. The sight of our dragon prows and shields was now a warning of their future. Hitherto they had been spared but, like the people of Northumbria, they were going to fear the Vikings.

PART THREE

Chapter 9

This would be the first time I had led men without my father alongside me. Gilles, Bertrand and Alain were all older than I was. I had the horsemen they led as well as the horsemen Rurik One Ear had sent. It was a formidable force. I was not a fool. I had learned from my father. If he took their advice then so would I. We gathered at my new hall. I knew from my time at the Haugr that you left men to guard your home. I left ten of my warriors. Some were carrying wounds but all were reliable. I was leaving my wife and unborn child. My raid would be worthless if they were to perish while I was away. My priest had asked to come with us. I was tempted for he was a healer but I also knew that he could handle a sword. He would make eleven men to guard my home. He was not happy about my decision but I ruled and I let him know it.

I let him sit and listen to our plans. He needed to know how hard it would be to convert myself and my men. We were Vikings. We rode horses and we spoke the language of the Franks but we were Vikings at heart. My horse medallion protected me in battle and I would make a blót before we left. That was our way. I had learned from my father and the other warriors. Even now he was leading a mighty fleet to distract the Franks and to gain treasure. We would do our part and I would not let the clan down.

"My plan is to surround Rauville and to demand their surrender."

Bertrand nodded, "They will, of course, refuse."

"Of course. We then leave a force to stop anyone gaining entry to the stronghold and we ride to all the local farms and give them a choice. They can become part of our clan and swear fealty to me or they leave. There will be no third way. We continue to spread out doing the same until we come to Lessay and Périers. I have scouted them both out already. They each have a hall and a wooden wall but it is smaller than Rauville. There is a small monastery at Lessay."

Gilles asked, "How do we stay in touch with one another. We have almost a hundred horsemen. That is a formidable force but if we are split up then we are not."

I had thought this out already. Alain of Auxerre had spent a few days with me thrashing out the bare bones of the plan. "We use Rauville as our base. Each night we return there. I hope to weaken their resolve. We might even assault it."

Bertrand said, "That is not something to be undertaken lightly."

Alain smiled, "To Franks, it might be a difficult task but Ragnvald and his men are Vikings."

"Thank you, Alain of Auxerre, that is a great compliment. If there is a small garrison then we distract them and simply climb the wall. My father and his men have done that many times. We have archers."

Æðelwald of Remisgat ventured, "You make it sound remarkably easy, lord. They may well defend the walls with their lives."

"I would hope that they would but you should know better than most, Æðelwald of Remisgat, that when we are determined to take somewhere we normally succeed."

He gave me a rueful nod.

We had spare horses and plenty of arrows. We left at dawn. I wanted to intimidate the seneschal at Rauville. His lord was still away fighting in the civil war. We had made a few raids on his hunters and foresters. They had fled within the walls and so a state of siege was almost in place already. Since the war had begun the supplies had been trickling into the small town. I hoped that a show of force would make them more likely to surrender. My mother had made me a banner. It was almost identical to my father's save that the background was not blue but red. That had been my decision. I wanted it to stand out on a battlefield. I led with my men. I had a red cloak and six of my oathsworn did too. With our red shields, we were hard to miss. The rest of my men had the same shields but their cloaks were not the same. That would come.

Behind my men came the blue cloaks of Alain of Auxerre and his men. The rest of our column all had different colours but the main effect was of a red and blue army. The seneschal had men in the forests cutting wood and emptying traps of animals. As we rode down the road they fled. It suited me. The more mouths they had to feed the better. By the time we reached Rauville, the gates were barred and the walls manned.

As we approached, I turned to my lieutenant, Snorri Snorrison, "Count the men with helmets on the wall. I need to know the number of real defenders and not just those who man the walls."

"Aye, lord."

I stopped just fifty paces from the gates. I said nothing. I waited for my men to pass behind me and form a line fifty men long and two men deep. I waited. I raised my sword and every man banged his shield with his spear and shouted, "Clan of the Horse!" I wanted an effect and I had it.

I nudged my horse forward. "Who commands here?"

The older warrior whom my father had mentioned, the greybeard, said, "I am Guy of Lessay. I command."

"I am Ragnvald Hrolfsson. I command this valley. I am happy for you and your people to live but you will all swear fealty to me."

He laughed, "You have barely begun to shave, barbarian. Besides, I swore an oath to my lord to keep his town for him and I will not be foresworn."

"If you defend the walls then we will put every man to the sword and the women and children sold into slavery. This will be my town with you or without you."

"Our walls are high and we are determined to resist."

I raised my voice and spoke so that all could hear. "So be it. I have offered terms and they have been refused. Whatever happens, is on your heads!" I paused. "Those who still have them when we are finished." I turned, "Alain, secure the other gate. Make preparations for war!"

My warriors knew what to do. There would be a great sound of galloping and we would surround the walls. It was not a large place and our warriors would outnumber those able to defend the walls. I was trying to frighten the inhabitants. I had learned this from my father.

I dismounted and led my horse, Lightning, to the camp which my men were making. Snorri galloped up and threw himself from the saddle. "There are just twenty men whom I would call warriors, lord. The ones around the gate are the most experienced. At the back, I did not see a single helmet. If we attacked there then they would piss their breeks and run away."

I nodded. I was taking a risk but if we could secure this town then we would have a secure base and be able to raid at will. I knew it was what my father would have done. "Have my men prepare. Tell no one else. We will do this ourselves. I will not risk another."

"Aye, lord."

While he went to organise the men, I sought out Alain. Alain was there to watch me. I knew that. My father would not risk my life without a watcher. Alain was as trustworthy a warrior as I had yet to meet.

"Alain."

"Aye, lord."

"I intend to lead my men over the rear wall tonight and gain entry to the town." He nodded but I could not tell what he was thinking. "My men have ascertained that their warriors are all at the gate. If you and the others make a show of attacking the gate with arrows then we have a chance to climb the walls and surprise them."

He smiled, "That is an excellent plan and I can think of only one modification."

"Yes?"

"I will come with you and watch your back."

"I have my own men!"

"And I am your father's man. I will come with you." He had a steely look to him. "There is no argument." I knew when I was beaten. I nodded. "Good. I will tell the others."

We took no cloaks. While Bertrand and Gilles prepared to begin a half-hearted attack on the main gate we headed down the road and then backtracked through the woods to arrive at the side. The wooden wall was not high. Our men on the back gate would also start an assault when they heard a noise from the front. My four largest warriors would be our bridge. They stood, at the edge of the wood, waiting for my command. I peered at the walls. I saw a Frank head towards the north wall. As soon as he was twenty paces down the fighting platform I tapped my four men on the back. They ran and, on reaching the ditch, slithered in and then scrambled up the far side. When they rose to stand with their backs against the wall, I knew that the Franks had neglected their defences. The slope on the wall side should have been steeper and harder to climb.

The sentry turned to walk back down the wall and my men readied the two shields which would be our bridges into the settlement. I heard a cry from the front gate and then a bell was rung. The sentry on our wall peered into the woods. We were hidden and he saw nothing. He shouted something to someone on the north wall and then turned and ran to the main gate. That was our opportunity. We broke from the woods when the Frank disappeared and hurried across to the ditch. It was as deep as a man but with almost gentle slopes. An old man might have struggled to climb them but not Vikings. The shield was in place and, as I stepped onto it, the shield was raised above my two men. I sprang up. My fingers found purchase on the wooden wall and I pulled myself up and over. I drew my sword as Alain joined me. He pointed to the main gate and led off. I followed.

There was a noise at the main gate but no sound of clashing swords. Gilles and Bertrand were just showering the defenders with arrows. We found a ladder and descended. I saw Snorri and the rest of my men close behind. Our four warriors would be making their way around the edge of the wall to the main gate. It was as we reached the bottom of the ladder that we were seen. A woman came from a small hall and screamed, "Vikings!"

Snorri roared at her and she ran back inside. We hurried to the main gate. Faces were turned towards us as we ran to it. I saw a Frank pitch from the walls as an arrow struck him in the back. Guy of Lessay shouted, "They are inside the walls!" He led his men from the gate towards us. Alain of Auxerre did not hesitate. He ran directly at the leader of the Franks and I followed. Using his own shield to block the blow from the Frank, Alain brought his own sword in a sideways sweep. It hacked through the leg of the warrior. A younger Frank lunged at Alain's unprotected side. I brought my sword down on the blade and then swung my shield into the young Frank's face. As he tumbled backwards I slashed my sword, backhand, across his throat. He was dead before his body hit the ground.

I shouted, "Snorri, the gate!"

Alain had killed another Frank and the rest were hesitant about advancing towards him. He had killed the leader with one blow. I shouted, "Yield and you shall live!"

Two of the younger warriors, each with a good helmet and short mail shirt raised their swords and one shouted, "Never!" as they ran towards the two of us. They were young and they were reckless. Both were about my age but I had been fighting now for three or four years. I had been trained by my father. I blocked the blow from the sword with my shield. The sword rang and then bent a little. I saw the look of horror on the youth's face. I pulled his shield towards me and punched him in the face with the boss of my shield. I could tell that he did not expect that move. He spread his arms as he tried to regain his balance. I lunged at him with my sword. I struck below his mail shirt and my blade ripped up through his groin and into his body. He shuddered and shook as he died. Alain had disposed of his enemy and the rest threw down their weapons and dropped to their knees. I saw that the gates were open and the survivors of our attack were surrounded. We had taken Rauville.

It took until dawn for us to gather all of the people and bring them together so that I could speak with them. My men searched the houses for the coins and the treasure they had hidden. The men who had followed Guy of Lessay expected to be executed but I did not see the point. The ten warriors who had survived were stripped of their weapons and would be sent back to the Haugr as slaves later in the day. I stood on the fighting platform above the gate so that they could all see me. There were about sixty people all told. Their faces were filled with dread.

"I gave you the chance to avoid the bloodshed of last night. Your leader is dead. Perhaps his loyalty to Guillaume of Rauville blinded him to the possibility that he might lose. I give you all two choices. You can live here as you did before and swear fealty to me and my father, Hrolf of the Haugr, or you can leave now with just the clothes on your back. It is that simple. There is no third way. I give you until I have supped a horn of ale to make up your mind."

I descended to the open gate. Snorri handed me a horn and Olaf said, "I can see that you have inherited your father's ability to see into the hearts of your foes."

Snorri asked, "Will any stay?"

I shrugged, "I would. The alternative is to leave here and begin again with nothing. Look at those mothers. They are picturing their children starving. Some have lost husbands and fathers but if they stay they will still have the land and they can farm. Life will be hard for them but not as hard as if they began again. And those that had little before will stay in the hope of gaining favour with me. I am expecting more than half to stay."

In the end, only four families left; fourteen people in all. It struck me that it was strange that three of them had men who had not fought against us. I also guessed that they were related in some way. The one widow amongst them spat in my direction as they left. Snorri drew his hand back to strike her but I shook my head. "She is angry and unless I miss my guess that is the widow of Guy of Lessay."

We later had that confirmed by one of the townsfolk. Haaken the Bold asked, "Where will they go, do you think, lord?"

"If her husband came from Lessay then they will go there. This may be for the best. If they arrive and warn of what is coming their way then we have an ally in the town before we get there. That ally is fear."

Alain said, "On the other hand they may send to Carentan or Caen for more men."

"And that, Alain of Auxerre, is what my father hopes for it means it will draw men away from the river. This was meant to be. Bertrand, arrange sentries. Tomorrow we begin our raids. We now have walls should one of the brothers decide to attack us and we can make our lands bigger."

I examined my new stronghold. The buildings were mainly made of wood although the lord's hall had stone incorporated into it. It was not a warrior hall but made just for the lord and his family. His wife and children were now my hostages. He would return for them. It might take some time for him to discover that he had lost his home but he would and then he would return to demand them from me. There were not as many supplies as I might have hoped. Bertrand, Gilles and Alain walked with me. "We had better begin to gather them from the neighbouring farms. I will ride with Alain to Carentan on the morrow."

"You would tell them who we are? What if they try to retake this place?"

I smiled at Gilles. He was older than I was but he had not fought for many years. I had fought alongside my father more recently. It was what Hrolf the Horseman would have done. "I think that Carentan will have been stripped of men too. Besides I do not fear an attack from Carentan." I swept my arm towards the stables. "Are there any horses here? The Lord of Carentan will have taken his best warriors and his horses to fight for whichever brother he supports. I wish to make whoever holds the town to bar the gates and to eat their supplies so that, when we have secured the lands and farms around here then we can take Carentan."

Alain nodded, "You are your father's son, lord. I will organize the men."

95

"First we bury our dead and burn those of the enemy."

"We lost but one, Sven Bjornson."

"He was young."

Alain nodded, "Young and careless. He should not have died but he held his shield too low. His death will serve a purpose lord, it will teach the other young warriors a lesson. They think because you are young as they are that they will have the same success. It was a needless death."

"You are right Alain. Those who survive this campaign will become better warriors."

The wife of Guillaume of Rauville, Eloise, was older than I expected. Her two daughters were twelve and ten summers old. They clung fearfully to her but she stared defiantly at me "You would be wise to leave now, barbarian. When my husband and King Charles return they will merely punish you!"

I laughed. "The wind has changed, lady. It has swept a new lord to this land. My father is even now ravaging your lands. He and the rest of our men are raiding the Issicauna. The day of the Frank is coming to a close. Your Charles is no Charlemagne! You will be safe here and cared for but if you or your people cause us any trouble then you will be chained."

"My family is related to the king. He will not suffer this insult and besides, you are just a boy!"

I nodded. I was not insulted. "Aye, lady, and I am the boy who has taken your husband's home with the loss of but one warrior. Think on that!"

I took six of my men and all of Alain's the next day. I left the rest of mine to guard Rauville while Bertrand and Gilles took the neighbouring farms. The ones who fought or left would have their homes burned. As the two bands headed south it would spread the word. My men would point to the smoke to the north and it would be a clear message.

It was a long day. We rode south and east. When we rested at noon and ate a rider galloped along the road behind us. It was a single horse and we were not worried. It was Tandi Svensson whom I had left at Rauville. "What is it that brings you here?"

"I am sorry, lord, we have failed you."

"The hostages?"

"They are safe but a Frank managed to get into the town and speak with the Lady Eloise. We were careless. After you left the gate was not guarded as well as it might have been. He must have been waiting for you to leave and he took advantage of the open gate."

"And where is he now?"

"When we discovered him, he fought. He is dead."

"And you do not know what he told the lady?"

"No, lord."

"Then keep a close watch on them. I do not think that this can harm us. We know that a rider left before we took the walls but he cannot have reached Guillaume of Rauville yet. This message will just have been news for his wife."

"I am sorry, lord. We will be more vigilant."

As we continued our journey Alain said, "Perhaps Guillaume of Rauville was telling his wife that he will be returning?"

"Perhaps." The hostages were not safe at Rauville. I had left a handful of men there to watch it. When I reached Carentan I would make a decision about their future. I began to realise that being a leader was like trying to hold a clump of frogspawn. You needed quick reactions and eyes like a hawk.

Carentan was as I remembered it from the time I had scouted it with my father. That had been half a year ago. The town stood on a small hill. It was really just a high piece of ground. The road south headed towards the forest and the bridge. There was a ford further upstream and the river could be swum by horses. It was not wide and it was shallow. The Franks had cut back the forest so that they could not be surprised. That had been the result of my father and his men. They had learned to respect us. He had told me that his time on Raven Wing Island had taught him to be vigilant. We scouted, just the two of us, to see if they had improved their defences. They had. He had shown me the tricks which Ulf Big Nose had taught him. We were able to use the natural cover and spy their walls and ditches. The fresh soil spoil told us that they had cleaned the bottom of the ditch. The wood on the gate was new. It had not been finished off as well as the old gate but it had looked to be made of sturdier wood. It would withstand axes. As we had headed back to the Haugr he had taken the time to explain to me how he would take the stronghold.

"I would starve them out. They have a granary but it is not as large as ours. They have many people living in the town. The walls are wooden and could be stormed but it would cost men."

"They would burn."

"They would burn but they would be hard to set alight."

I did not often argue with my father but that day, I did, as we headed north and passed Gilles' horse farm. If we sent men at night then they could plant faggots soaked in seal oil. In the daylight, we could send fire arrows into them. Anyone who tried to douse the flames would be exposed to our archers."

He had remained silent and then made me happy by smiling, "That would work. You are almost ready to lead."

It was on that day that I finally found myself becoming a man for my father had respected one of my ideas. He was the one I wished to emulate. Now, as we reined our horses in beyond bow range, I examined the walls again to make sure that they had not changed anything. The main difference was that they had erected a second palisade inside the original walls. It meant that they had a double barrier against us. The new wall and the old one. My father had shown

97

them he knew of many ways to defeat their defences. I had sent Sihtric Karlsson with six men to ride around the walls. He had a good eye and knew what I needed from him. I heard Alain chuckle as he pointed to the wall. "They are wetting themselves, lord!"

I turned and saw men hurrying to the walls to repel what they saw as an attack. "It will do no harm for them to prepare their defences. We will be able to see how many men they have."

"It looks to me that they have but thirty men to guard the walls."

I could not see how he could know that. "How do you work that out?"

"There are twenty men before us, lord. They think this is where we will attack. They may have forty but I doubt it. If they had more men they would try to outnumber us on this wall." He pointed to the eight on the fighting platform above the gate. "There they have men with helmets and mail. If you look further along then you see their burghers. They have weapons and they may have fought but they are not warriors. That is why men such as the Lord of Carentan hire men such as me. He will have taken his best men to fight for Charles."

Taking off my helmet, I spurred my horse towards the walls, "Then let us see if they will make life easier for us!" I had my hands before me to show that we came in peace. Alain came with me.

As we neared the ditch a spear was thrown, badly, towards us. I almost laughed as it landed twenty paces from us. I nudged my horse towards the spear. It was an eight feet long ash shafted spear. I dismounted to pick it up. It was not intended for throwing. My act of bravado was deliberate. I wanted them to see I did not fear them. I climbed back on my horse and held the spear above my head. "Thank you for the weapon but we do not need it. We have plenty although this is a good weapon. A pity that whoever threw it is not a good warrior."

I saw one of the warriors glare at a young Frank whose head dropped. The warrior said, "What do you want, Viking? Our walls are strong and we have God on our side. I am Captain Henry of Argentan and I command here. I am sworn to keep this town safe for my lord."

I nodded, "And yet your lord is not there and his best men fight against other Franks! He has left a few old men and some hired swords. It is not an impressive defence." I stood in my stiraps and pointed towards Rauville. "When Guillaume of Rauville returns he will find that he has lost his home and his wife and daughters are my guests." I waited to let that sink in. I saw them talking amongst themselves.

"You lie!"

I shook my head, "I do not lie and what would the lie gain me?" I left them to debate again.

"What is that you wish?"

98

"My father is Hrolf the Horseman. He is lord of the land north of here. We agreed not to attack King Louis' land. King Louis is dead. My father would have Carentan as part of his land. I am here to enforce that decision."

I saw Sihtric approach. He nodded. He had left men in place. The Franks would not escape. They were trapped.

"You come here with a handful of horsemen and expect me to capitulate? I have fought for the King for more years than you have seen on this earth. I am not afraid of a barbarian who has barely begun to shave."

"Then I hope that you have plenty of food for we are going nowhere."

I turned my horse around and rode back to my men. I dismounted and we began to make a camp. Alain came to speak with me, "Captain Henry is a sword for hire. I fought alongside him once. He is no Captain. However, he is a fair hand with a sword."

Despite what the Frank had said they were worried for they did not attempt to sortie and to remove our threat. As I handed my horse to Sihtric, Alain said, "They have few horses and soon they will realise that the other gate is watched." Even as my men tied a line for the horses we heard a shout and a cry.

Sihtric laughed, "They have found that my men are on the other side and they are watching and that they have sharp eyes."

My men soon had a fire going and food cooking. We had a deer's hindquarter. The wind was blowing in the right direction and it was intended to waft over to the walls and it would make them hungry. They had not even begun to eat into their supplies but the smell of cooking meat would make them think they were hungrier than they actually were.

"When do we attack lord?"

I wiped the juices from my chin. "I want Bertrand and Gilles here. I need the valleys under my control. Until my father returns with his men, we must be both cautious and frugal with our men. Besides, it will just make them weaker. I want ten men on each gate. Rotate our men so that all share the duty. Include me!"

Alain grinned "Aye lord. I would have expected nothing less."

"And send our hostages back to the Haugr. My mother will be fretting over me and our prisoners will be safer there."

"Aye lord."

Chapter 10

Three days later I was with my men watching the walls. Smoke drifted from the south showing another farm that had refused to accept the rule of my father. Their owners had been driven off. Gilles and Bertrand had told me that they were both surprised by the refusal of half of the farmers. One or two had offered resistance rather than just fleeing. My men had discovered that the fleeing farmers headed for family living further south. I was intrigued by that. I had spoken with some of my hostages and by careful questions, I had discovered that many of the farms in the land which was now the Land of the Northman had been there for less than thirty years. They had taken them from Bretons who had once farmed there. Others had fled to Angia. I told Gilles and Bertrand to continue probing south.

Folki arrived with forty warriors. We saw them approaching on the road from Valognes. They were like a metal snake, sinuously sliding down the cobbles. We heard them chanting as they marched down the road.

The Clan of the Horse march to war
See their spears and hear them roar
The Clan of the Horse with bloody blades
Their roaring means you will be shades
Clan of the Horse Hrolf's best men
Clan of the Horse death comes again
Leading Vikings up the Frankish Water
They brought death they brought slaughter
Taking slaves, swords and gold
The Clan of the Horse were the most bold
Clan of the Horse Hrolf's best men
Clan of the Horse death comes again
Fear us Franks we are the best
Fighting us a fatal test
We come for land to make our own

Ragnvald Hrolfsson

To give young Vikings not yet grown
Clan of the Horse Hrolf's best men
Clan of the Horse death comes again
Clan of the Horse Hrolf's best men
Clan of the Horse death comes again

The words of the chant told me that the raid on the Issicauna had been successful. They had taken the churches along the river. I could not help grinning as Folki strode up to me with his arms wide. He had grown since he had joined us and was now a huge bear of a man. With plaited moustache and bones tied in his hair he looked fearsome and yet he was one of the gentlest men I had ever known. He had helped me become a better warrior. No horseman himself he had shown me how to use a sword and spear on foot and how to defeat a horseman. That was a valuable lesson.

He picked me up in a bear hug. "Your father sends his greetings! I can see that marriage has been good for you! One town was taken and another was about to fall!"

I held up my hand. "Do not tempt the Weird Sisters, Folki! They are still within!"

"Then they had better fear for Folki the Fearless is here!! He spied the food on the fire. "And we have marched all morning so if there is spare food here we will share it and in return tell the tale of how your father is becoming as famous and renowned as the Dragonheart."

"Then eat and be welcome!" I pointed to the walls. Folki's arrival had caused consternation. My men dressed and looked almost the same as the Franks but Folki and his band were true Vikings. Their chant would have alerted those in Carentan. He told me of the voyage north and the treachery of Molti and Taki. I clutched my horse amulet. "The gods repay treachery with death."

"Aye some escaped but they will keep away from the land of the Franks. Your father is still dividing the treasure. I was glad to be sent here to join you. The Haugr was filled with too many warriors. Your lady mother will be happier when they are gone."

"And was my father uninjured?"

He hesitated and then smiled. I sensed some deception. "A couple of scratches but he is hale. He had more problems after we arrived home and that is why he is not here at your side. He sent me instead. He will tell you more when he comes." I knew then that something had happened and my father had told Folki to remain silent. I would not press the matter. Folki was as loyal as they came and it would not be fair of me to delve deeper into his unsaid words. He lowered his voice. "He said, lord, that there is no rush for you to defeat the Franks. He comes with our army soon enough. He is pleased with what you have achieved already with so few men."

101

I nodded, "I know that we have done well but I think that with your men we can take Carentan." He frowned and I laughed, "I know that look, Folki! You think the whelp is biting off more than he can chew. I am not." I had thought this through as I had watched the walls. "Valognes was the border. Rauville is too insignificant and hidden away for it to be a stronghold. This, however, is a major site! Look at its position. It is close to the sea. The land around floods easily in winter making this an impenetrable fortress. Summer will be the only time we can take it. I do not think the defences are strong enough. With your men and the ones who watch then I believe we can assault it." I could see that he was not convinced. "Folki, I am not being arrogant. I would go to my home at Benni's Ville and be with my wife when my son is born. You know not how long my father will take to reach us. Let me tell you how I will take it and then you can decide if I am a foolish young whelp." I explained to him my plan.

Alain had remained silent. He approved of my plan and he wanted Folki to see it too. If Folki had shown me how to use weapons it was Alain who had shown me how to use horses. I was becoming a different warrior to my father. I would not be better but, thanks to him and his men I would be different.

When I had finished Folki used a piece of bone to clear out some meat caught in his teeth. "Aye, that will work. We need the wind in the right direction." He pointed. "Are those new granaries there?"

"One is a granary but I think the other is a stable. They managed to send one rider off when we attacked and so we know they have horses. I have not heard many horses but they are Franks. They will have stables. So far we have not seen reinforcements but Gilles and Bertrand have scouts out."

Alain stood and threw some grass in the air. "If the wind does not change in the next day then it would be a good time to attack."

Folki said, "I will rest my men. Tonight, we put the faggots in place." He rubbed his hands. "It will be good to fight more than priests!"

I knew that the men Alain and I led were good warriors. As horsemen, there were none better but my father had sent me the best of weapons to assault the walls; Vikings! The wind did not change and that night, with archers watching, I led twenty men each with a faggot. The bound wood was soaked with seal oil. During the night, it would seep into the wood at the bottom of the walls. We reached the ditch and watched. We knew the way the sentries patrolled the fighting platform. I had had men watching them to see their pattern. We had ropes to help us climb back out of the ditch.

The night was black. The Allfather sent clouds to hide the moon and to make us invisible. It was my plan and I was one of the ten who would descend the ditch and then ascend to the walls. We used the ropes to lower ourselves into the ditch. There were traps there. We did not have to watch the walls and so we could watch where we placed our feet. When we reached the other side six of the men cupped their hands and six of us, each holding a faggot, were boosted up the ditch. I placed mine to nestle against the new wood of the walls. I could still smell the resin. It would burn. Sihtric and I reached down for another faggot and crawled to the nearest gate tower. I could hear the sentries within talking to one another. If they looked down they might see us but my watching men had bows ready to send arrows into them before they could do so. When we had placed four faggots there we crawled back, climbed down into the ditch and made our way back to the ropes where we joined a relieved Folki and Alain. Once back at the camp we prepared for battle.

Folki and his men would assault. Alain and his horsemen would be at the other gate ready to enter should the Franks decide to flee. It would be my men who would send the fire arrows over. We had made forty of them. Our fire was already burning. We had kept one going night and day. All we had to do was wait. I knew that Folki and his men could have attacked the gate without this ruse but they would have lost men in doing so. A wall, even one defended by Frankish burghers, was never easy to take. Stones, spears and arrows would shower the attackers. Like my father, I valued the lives of our men too highly to waste them. I wanted the enemy to bleed.

It would have been better to attack at night. We would have less chance of losing men and we were the masters of the night but fire arrows were less accurate than ordinary ones and we needed precision. We had to hit the faggots. We would wait until dawn. Just as we knew their routine, the Franks knew ours. We did nothing different. As the first grey appeared in the east we rose and men made water; others dropped their breeks. The horses were taken to the stream to be watered. The fires were fed. There was the same easy banter around the fires. The Franks would see our camp coming to life. The difference was that when the sun had risen we would not eat. The Franks would be ready to change their watch and the night watch go to eat and we would strike then. We would attack when they thought the danger was over. Vikings normally attacked in the night or just before sunrise. The sun would be visible in the sky when the first arrow struck.

Alain and his horsemen did not return from the stream. They were already riding round to the other gate into the town. Folki and his men were forming up in the woods where they would be hidden. They were forming into a column, five men wide and eight men deep. They would be a human battering ram once the gate was weakened.

I nodded to my men. No orders were necessary. The fire arrows were laid close to the fire. I had the Saami bow my father had given me. It was a wonderful weapon. The wind was from the south and east. We were going to attack the wall to the west of the gate so that the wind would spread the flames towards the gate. I plunged the bound arrowhead into the fire and the oil-soaked hessian flamed. I pulled back my bow and felt the heat from the tip. It encouraged me to release. We were just a hundred paces from the walls. I watched my arrow arc and heard the shouts of alarm from the sentries as the fire arrows plunged from the sky.

Another fifteen arrows joined mine. Each hit a faggot but we kept releasing until all of our arrows were gone. Then we switched to ordinary arrows. The fire had caught but it was not out of control. It could be doused and so we sent arrows into each Frank who leaned over the walls to pour some of their precious water onto the flames. When three men had fallen to their deaths they gave up and I heard the order to fall back to the second wall.

The flames suddenly seemed to race up the walls. The wind was fresh and it fed the flames. The wind spread the flames to the gates and then some of them seemed to leap in the air and landed on the granary roof. The Franks did not use turf on their roofs as we did but hay. I saw the flames catch hold. The cries from inside told me of the consternation we were causing. There were no ladders ready for them to reach the roof of the granary. When I heard the sound of distressed horses then I knew that the fire had spread to the stables.

The gate was now an inferno. Folki led his men to the bridge over the ditch. They were safe from attack and the only danger was the fire itself. When one of the wooden towers collapsed then I knew that it would not be long. I laid down my bow and took up my shield and sword. Most of my men would be using spears but I preferred a sword. On a horse, I would use a spear but this would be close fighting. I had my short sword which was perfect for the confined spaces in which we would be fighting.

Folki suddenly shouted, "Clan of the Horse! Charge!"

They began to chant as they marched quickly across the bridge. Their shields were held before them to protect them from the fire but, in truth, the gates had fallen and they would hurry across the burning timbers. The wind was blowing the smoke into the town. The fire had already spread to the second gate. That was made of old dried wood. The burning granary and stables had destroyed part of the walls and gate already. The Franks had aided us by offsetting their two entrances.

> *Clan of the Horse Hrolf's best men*
> *Clan of the Horse death comes again*
> *Clan of the Horse Hrolf's best men*
> *Clan of the Horse death comes again*
> *Clan of the Horse Hrolf's best men*
> *Clan of the Horse death comes again*
> *Clan of the Horse Hrolf's best men*
> *Clan of the Horse death comes again*

The chant helped my men to keep in time. They hit the doors like a battering ram. With their shields held before them, they easily smashed through. We could see little for we were hurrying across the bridge. We did not have to worry about the burning timbers ahead of us for we could step and jump over them. We were not in a solid column. The men who faced Folki had never seen anything like us. We were nothing like their own warriors. I could not see the impact as Folki's men were before us and all I saw were the backs of the rear ranks but I heard it. There was a sound like thunder. A crash and a crack intermingled with the cries and screams of men who were dying. I had a simple helmet with a nasal protecting my nose and I had a good view around me. I heard horses screaming in the stables to my right.

"Sven, take some men and rescue the horses!" Horses were as valuable as gold to us. Not only that, but we were also horsemen and the thought of horses burning to death was something we could not bear. I stepped over a Frank who was still writhing. He had had his stomach laid open by a sword. Our blades were intended for ripping open flesh. Folki's men had now spread out and were doing what they did the best. They were killing. They moved in groups. They were shield and oar brothers. It was beautiful to watch. One would pull forward a shield while another slashed over the shield. They protected each other's backs. The Franks had no answer and they died. My sword was still unbloodied as we made our way to the centre of the town.

Folki and his men halted to reorganize. They had broken through the first line of the Frank's defences. Captain Henry had decided to make a stand before the lord's hall. It was, like the church, a stone building. I saw no women and children. They would be in the church. They believed that their God would protect them there. He would have no say in the matter. Their fate was in my hands.

Folki had the joy of battle upon his face. "I will eat well this night. Killing Franks always gives me an appetite." His brother and most of his clan had been slain by Franks and he hated them. "What will you have us do?"

I said, "I will try reason again. We have lost few men. If we can keep it thus then so much the better."

"These will not hurt us!" He had scorn in his voice and he was right but I did not know when the enemy might try to retake the town. I wanted every blade and spear that I could muster.

"Alain told me that this captain is a warrior for hire. You do not live to be a greybeard like him if you are not a good warrior." I took off my helmet and moved forward. "Captain Henry, you have done your duty and have been bested. Surrender and you shall live. I do not desire to slaughter you. If I don my helmet again then all of you will die."

"A fair offer, Viking, but we took coin to defend these walls. We may be swords for hire but we have honour. Besides, I have lived too long if I am defeated by someone who is as young as you. Even if I live what will I do? Better to die now. Perhaps I can take a couple of you with me and then men will sing a song of our last stand. I have spoken enough. Do your worst! I have fought less polite warriors. I thank you for your courtesy."

"As you wish." I donned my helmet. "A shield wall on me!" Folki gave me a sideways glance and then nodded. He stood on my right-hand side and Sihtric stood on my left. I brought my shield up and locked it with those of Folki and Sihtric. I laid my sword beneath my shield. It was as I did so that I wondered how Bagsecg was coming along with my new sword. Perhaps this would be the last time I would use my old one. If so, then I would use it well. The old warrior deserved a good death.

The Franks also locked their shields and we advanced. Although I preferred fighting from the back of a horse, I had been drilled by Folki on the right way to fight in a shield wall. We all stepped off on our right legs. Once started we moved as one. We had ten paces to go to strike the static line of warriors. Even so, with the success we had enjoyed and the smell of blood in our nostrils we struck the Franks as one. The greybeard had not forgotten how to fight. He punched with his shield as we clashed. I was ready. Bigger men than the captain had hit me with a shield before now. I put my weight behind my own shield and our two lines clashed.

I might have been the most inexperienced of the warriors fighting on our side but it had been many years since the Franks had fought this way. These men had been used to standing on a wall and fighting. Now they stood shoulder to shoulder and we began the killing. I had chosen to fight their best warrior and I was wary. You did not swing in a shield wall. If you did then you opened yourself up and risked a swift death. You used your weight and looked for an opening. The old Frank's sword slid across the top of his shield towards my head. He had thought me young and arrogant. I swiftly slid up my shield. His sword slipped along the side of my helmet. More importantly, our two bosses had caught and his shield slid up with mine. Sometimes in battle, when you take a risk the gods reward you. I pushed my sword forward towards the Frank. His shield had moved up and my sword found something soft. I pushed harder and was rewarded by a grunt of pain. The warrior tried to move backwards, out of the way, and I leaned my shield into him and continued probing with my sword. I felt something hard and I twisted. This time it was more than a grunt, it was a shout. And then my sword slid into his flesh faster. I had sliced into his leg. Turning the blade, I pulled it backwards. I felt it grate along the thigh bone and then it slurped noisily out.

He fell backwards. He was brave and he was tough. He did not want to but his left leg had no tendons left and would not support his weight. He was still a threat and I quickly stepped over his prone body. Even as he tried to bring up his own sword I put both hands on the hilt of my own sword and plunged it into his throat. "Go to your old comrades. You were a warrior." There was a soft sigh as the sword punctured his throat and then his eyes glazed over.

The combat had not lasted but a few moments and yet, in that time, the Franks had been defeated. Most of the hired swords died but half, the men from the town, had surrendered. My men beat their shields and chanted my name. It was the first time I had been so honoured and I was touched.

I raised my bloody sword and shouted, "Clan of the Horse!"

Folki's men collected the mail. I went, with Sihtric, to the other gate. It lay open and Alain of Auxerre was herding the Franks, who had tried to flee, back into the town.

"Is it over, lord?"

"It is. They fought to the end."

"Then we will bury them. They deserve that."

That was one of those moments when a single act changed the future. Had we desecrated the bodies then there might have been animosity and more resentment than we experienced. Alain and his men treated the bodies with reverence. The priest spoke over their bodies and calm was restored. Gilles and Bertrand had arrived from their foray as we were burying the dead.

Gilles looked at the burned and charred wood of the walls, "You have done well to take the town, lord, but, unlike Rauville, it is not defensible any longer."

Bertrand nodded, "It is not a criticism, lord, but we have cleared the farms north and west of here. South? There are Franks and the refugees will have fled there."

"They will know that we have assaulted Carentan. They sent a rider before we could do anything about it. The smoke which drew you here will bring retribution. The question is when? As my father has returned I will send a rider north to tell him our news. We hold what we have taken."

"And the burghers?"

"The same as with the others. We will give them the option of flight or fealty. It will make it easier. We burned the granary and food will be in short supply." Although I sounded confident I was somewhat out of my depth. This was the first time I had been in such a responsible position. Hitherto I had raided and returned to my home. Now I had five warbands to command as well as the two conquered towns and the farms and villages. My father had asked me to push south. I had done more than he had expected.

My father's captains proved to be invaluable. Folki, Gilles, Bertrand and, most of all, Alain of Auxerre, proved their loyalty over and over during the next few days. They took decisions and they gave me advice when I threatened to do something foolish. We had buried our own dead. I had suggested the churchyard. They told me that would anger the burghers and my men would be unhappy. We made a new cemetery by the river. I was going to begin rebuilding the walls so that we would have defences. Alain showed me how much work would be involved. I realised he was right. It would be quicker to throw up a temporary wall around our camp and leave Carentan open. We would still be able to defend the town and we would not have burghers to worry about. "Better we throw up a

107

palisade to protect our men and horses. Your father will need masons to repair what we have done."

And so, over the next six days, we toiled. Gilles and Bertrand had scouts out and every other man dug the ditch and erected the wooden wall. We were almost finished when a scout rode in. "Lord, the Franks come. They have an army. There are more than a hundred and fifty riders. They have raised the levy. I counted three hundred spears."

I nodded, suddenly calm, "And, where are they?"

"Half a day south of here."

"Then we have time to prepare. Gilles, send one of your sons to Valognes. Tell them that Ragnvald asks for help."

"Aye lord."

"Alain, what do you suggest?"

"The palisade is incomplete. We fight them before it. If we put Folki's men in the centre and our horsemen on the flanks then we can harry and harass them. If we have to break them we take them into the walls."

I nodded, "Let us do that. Every man who carries a wound goes to the complete section of the walls and there they can use arrows." I looked to Carentan, just thirty paces from our wooden camp. "And the burghers of Carentan?"

"They cannot bar gates to us for they have none and they have little food. They will watch. The ones who swore fealty will change sides if we lose and, if we win, will hurry out to bring us sustenance. It is the way of the sheep."

We prepared. We had gained horses in the battles we had fought and, with wounded men, we had spares. We tethered them inside the wooden walls we had thrown up. If we had to flee then some of Folki's warriors would survive. I then surveyed the land before us. It was low lying and boggy. The river flooded frequently. We were on a slight slope and the advancing Franks would be at a disadvantage. I would have Gilles and Bertrand on the left flank and Alain and myself on the right. With Folki holding the middle ground we would let the Franks come to us and charge their horsemen with ours to both slow up their attack and diminish their numbers.

We waited. We stood by our horses with our helmets on our saddles. Our spears were sharp and ready. We had not needed them before but now we were fighting horsemen. We had repaired mail and shields which had been damaged and our swords were honed.

Alain stood with me. He handed me a piece of dried deer meat. I took it and chewed. "You have done well young lordling. Even your father could not have done much better. You are a leader, like your father. Rurik One Ear and Erik One Hand have told me how he took on that role even when Siggi White Hair led the clan. No matter what happens today you can be proud of yourself." His words were to stop me from losing heart at the prospect of fighting a large army.

"And yet if we lose then Carentan and Rauville will revert to a Frankish lord and all that we have done will be in vain. Benni's Ville might fall too. All of my father's horsemen are here under my command. If they are lost then we lose the Land of the Northmen. It is a great responsibility. I feel the weight of the clan upon my shoulders. My unborn child may grow up a Frankish slave." I could talk this way with Alain. He had helped to raise me as a warrior. There would be few secrets between us.

"That is how your father began, as a slave. If it is meant to be then so be it but do not yield just yet. You have the better warriors here. The Franks have marched a long way to get here. They have the levy with them. The hundred and fifty horsemen are the ones we fear. We have ninety horsemen. If we can beat them then Folki can defeat the rest."

We saw their banners first when they emerged from the trees a mile to the south of us. It took them some time to move towards us as the road through the woods was not wide. They had learned from us. Others crossed the wooden bridge which spanned the river. Four scouts approached to within half a mile of us. I nodded and Snorri Snorrison galloped hard towards them with five of my men. Gilles bred fast strong horses and my men took the Franks by surprise. They were not expecting to be attacked. They hesitated and then tried to turn to flee. Two were just too slow. Snorri and Sihtric rammed their spears into the backs of the two of them and the riders fell from the saddle.

The result surprised even me. The mass of enemy horsemen suddenly began to charge up the slope towards us. My six men whipped their horses' heads around and galloped back to the safety of our lines. My men cheered and banged their shields as they returned with bloody spears. The enemy's charge was not ordered and was not led. The riders just took it upon themselves. It was a mass of horsemen hurtling towards a stationery line. I had to time this well or I could undo the opportunity sent to me by the gods. Because they were spread out some were ahead of the others. When the leading riders were two hundred paces from us I shouted, "Advance!" My horn was sounded and we walked a few paces before gathering speed. I had my shield held before me and my long spear resting on my horse's head.

I could feel Snorri's boot touching mine on one side and that of Michael of Liger on the other. It was reassuring. I kicked my horse in the flanks and he began to canter. It moved me, briefly, ahead of the others but they responded. As the rest of our long line copied me so we became a line with me at the point and then we struck the disorganized Franks. They outnumbered us but we hit them together. The first rider tried to spear me. In doing so he opened himself to a thrust from Michael of Liger and the Frank tumbled from his horse. The riderless horse was bundled out of the way by Günter of Swabia and it began to gallop back to the safety of the woods. The already fractured Franks now had to avoid other riderless horses. Many Franks, hitting our line piecemeal, had suffered the same fate as the first one. A horn sounded from the Frankish commander and the riders stopped and then turned to head down the slope.

We had done enough. I shouted, "Halt! Fall back!"

My own ox horn sounded and men cheered as we turned our horses to return the three hundred paces to our own lines. As we organized ourselves once more I saw that the enemy had left another eight dead men on the field. We had lost none. Alain, who was four riders away from me raised his spear in salute. "That will have them thinking. You have done well, lord. Their most eager riders fell. They will come more cautiously." He shook his head, "That was dangerous and reckless from the Franks. They have lost the advantage for they will now be tired after their uphill charge and, worse, their levy saw their nobles defeated."

"Aye." I was busy surveying the field. What I was worried about was being outflanked. If their leader was any good then he would use his superior numbers to make a long line and turn our flanks. We were two deep but I dared not risk making it a single rider deep.

They formed their own lines and faced us. Their respect for our archers was shown by the fact that they halted over three hundred paces from our own. Even our best archers could not touch them. As they formed a line I saw that Erik, the scout, had not exaggerated their numbers. They had fifty more riders than we did. Their men on foot, the levy, led by mounted Leudes, had four times more men than Folki led.

We waited. A horn sounded and I prepared myself to give an order to repel their attack. To my surprise, a single horseman took off his helmet and rode towards us. I took off my own and nudged my horse forward. Turning in my saddle I waved Alain forward too. He took off his own helmet. I did not want the envoy to see the ground before Folki and his men. It was seeded with the twisted spikes of metal the Romans called caltrops. We met the warrior a hundred and fifty paces from our lines.

"I am Stephen of Caen and I am here to ask for a parley. My lord, Count Eustace of Bruggas, wishes to speak with you."

I noticed that he spoke to Alain who pointed to me, "Ragnvald Hrolfsson commands here."

The Frank's eyes widened in surprise. Before he could speak and insult me I said, "We agree. He returns with one man, no more." He was going to say something else but thought better of it and, turning his horse, rode back. "What do you think it means, Captain?"

Alain shaded his eyes to look at the sky. "They may not wish to fight today. The afternoon moves on and this count will need all the daylight he can get. The Franks have learned to respect the Viking ability to fight even better in the night than they do in the day. Or it may be that he does not relish a fight."

That I could not understand. If our positions were reversed then we would have attacked immediately.

Ragnvald Hrolfsson

An older warrior riding a large horse and with good mail, headed towards us. Stephen of Caen rode with him. I saw them speaking together as they approached. The leader annoyed me as soon as he spoke. He seemed to sneer his words and they were laden with insults. "It seems we are to fight with boys this day." His eyes flickered to Alain, "And traitorous mercenaries, of course." Although I was angry I kept my face impassive as did Alain. Both he and my father had taught me that. Nothing would be gained by reacting to the insults. "There is no honour in fighting such men. If you leave now and return your hostages then we will be satisfied. Your home is to the north of Carentan! This is the land of King Charles!"

I smiled, "So Charles has defeated Lothair?"

A frown creased the Frank's face. He thought I was a barbarian who had no idea what was going on in the land of the Franks. "It is only a matter of time. It is lucky for you that the king is far from here. He would not be so kind. So," he waved his hand before him, "do you leave and return our hostages or do you die here and feed the carrion!"

"I think we will test our mettle against you, Eustace of Bruggas. Besides, the hostages are far from here. The delay in their ransom may mean that they are now in the slave market of Dyflin."

Stephen of Caen reacted, "If my sister is harmed then I swear I will gut you like a fish!"

The count was annoyed but said nothing.

"Stephen of Caen, if you wish to fight me here and now then we can settle this matter before the real battle begins."

He looked into my eyes as I stared at him. He had expected me to back down and I had done the opposite. Fear flickered in his face. He did not trust himself to defeat me in single combat. "You are lucky that we came to speak in peace. Watch yourself when we fight, Viking, for I will come for you."

"And you know where I will be. I will be waiting for you beneath my banner and then I can tell your sister how you died!"

We returned to our men and waited. As the sun began to dip I wondered why they were delaying. We saw a debate amongst their leaders and then they descended to the bottom of the slope and set up camp. Snorri saw them and began shouting, "They are afraid of us! Clan of the Horse! Clan of the Horse!"

My men took up the chant. I rode to meet with Gilles, Alain and Bertrand. "What do you think, Alain?"

"We are facing a warrior who knows his business. His horses charged and he lost men. He wants to be fully rested and he will have a better plan than he did today. We can return to our camp and eat. He will attack in the morning."

We left men to watch the enemy camp and then retired behind our own palisade. As we ate that night, I asked, "What did you mean, a better plan?"

111

"Bruggas is in the north. It is not far from Dorestad. This count did not know the land. I think he and Stephen of Caen will be having words. He was the warrior with local knowledge but, because we took his sister, he will have urged the count to attack quickly. The count did not know we had horsemen. If he comes from Bruggas then he knows Vikings but the ones he met will have fought on foot. Now I see why they charged so recklessly. The ones who did so will have been Stephen of Caen's men."

"And how will he make a better plan?"

"I think he will try to outflank us. He has the numbers to do so. Then he will use the advantage he has in numbers to send the levy to try to smash their way through Folki and his men."

Folki laughed, "And they are welcome to try. Snorri told me that they just have a helmet, shield and sword. Some of the shields are made of new green willow. I do not fear them."

Alain had a word of caution. "They can tie you and your men up so that when our horses are defeated his mounted men will end our resistance."

I shook my head, "That will not happen. We must eliminate Eustace of Bruggas. Stephen of Caen sounds reckless to me. We do not want an ordered attack in serried ranks. We want a headlong attack of wild men."

Alain smiled, "You grow each day, lord. And how do we kill Eustace?"

"Simple, we make a wedge of horses and plough through the middle of the line. If he tries to outflank us then he must use a two or three deep line. We attack in his centre."

"And how do we protect Folki?"

"Do not worry about me, horseman! They will be tired and I have my shield wall. They will batter themselves against me and my rocks!"

"I worry about all of my men, Folki. We use more caltrops on the flanks. We have enough nails from the burned sections of the walls of Carentan."

"If he sees us lining up like that then he will know what we are about."

"I know, Captain, and that is why we line up the same way tomorrow that we did today. The only difference will be that we will be in a four-deep line. When I sound the horn twice we attack. Gilles and Bertrand just add their men to the rear of our line. We will have nine men at the front and we break their line. We do not ride over the seeded ground before Folki. We ride diagonally across the field."

We spent some time making more caltrops. They were simple to make for the heat of the fire had twisted many of the nails already. Folki and his men also embedded in the ground before and beside them some of the broken and burned timbers. They sharpened them into points. They would stop horsemen from charging them.

Gilles shook his head. "It is too hot this night. The air feels heavy. The horses will sweat."

Bertrand nodded, "Aye but that will affect the Franks as much as us. I fear it will make sleep hard."

Folki laughed, "I could sleep in the branch of a tree, horseman. We have toiled hard and drunk well. If it is too hot then I will sleep naked!"

That night, as I struggled to get to sleep, I went over the events of the day. Stephen of Caen's reckless charge had given us a chance. The levy had seen their horsemen defeated. The ground had been churned up and would slow down the Franks. My father would be pleased. As I thought about my own father I wondered how fatherhood would affect me. I was not a fool. I knew I was not immortal and that I could die the next day. I took comfort from the fact that my father would bring up my unborn child. If the child was male then he would lead the clan. Surprisingly the thought of my death brought me sleep. I had left my seed and my blood would carry on. If I died with a sword in my hand then I would go to Valhalla and that was *wyrd*.

Chapter 11

We rose before dawn. We had a battle coming and men needed to prepare. We were confident. I wondered how many of the Franks were dropping their breeks and emptying their bowels out of fear? Their dead still littered the battlefield. The carrion had been picking at them and their sentries would have heard the foxes and rats squabbling over the dead flesh. My men were not afraid. They had done this many times. Most of the Franks were fighting Vikings for the first time. None of them would have fought so many mounted Vikings. We knew what to expect and they did not. After making water and drinking some ale I ate some dried fish. Food was not a priority for me. I then found my horse. He was my favourite, Steabba. He was a mixture of white, brown and black. My father preferred horses like Dream Strider which were either black or white. He liked the fact that they would not be seen at night. I liked Steabba because he was brave and he could run all day. He was not as tall as some of the other horses, Lightning was much faster, but Steabba was solid and reliable. I groomed him and spoke to him as I did so. The land of the Northmen grew wonderful apples and I had a bag of them. I gave one to him as I groomed him. That done, I saddled him and made sure that his girth was fitted correctly. Gilles and Alain had shown me how to do that. I liked to use longer reins than most men. It enabled me to use my shield more effectively. I had trained Steabba to respond to my knees and heels. He would not stop if I dropped my reins.

Once my horse was ready I prepared myself. Like my father I wore a mailed hood but, unlike him, I did not wear a leather cap beneath. I wore one lined with sheepskin. I went for comfort rather than protection but I knew why my father used a leather one. He had been close to death. I had seen his body after the battle and I had thought him dead. It was a miracle that he had survived. He was the most important man in the clan. Without him we were nothing. I chose an ash shafted spear and, with my shield on the saddle, led Steabba to the front line. We took a wide berth around the traps we had laid. As it was dark the enemy would not see us.

Others were there already, "Morning, lord. A good day for a battle." Haaken the Bold pointed to the south, where the enemy were camped. I could see that there were clouds gathering and the air felt heavy. "I smell a thunderstorm! With Thor on our side, the White Christ will be defeated."

I saw Alain frown. He was a Christian. I knew that he had a dilemma when my men spoke thus. It offended his religion. He fingered the cross he wore about his neck.

"Any help we can get then I will take."

None of us mounted although we all stood in our allotted position. Every warrior wore mail, some more than others. We did not wish to tire out our horses. It also disguised our numbers. I could hear the enemy as they, too, prepared for battle. I saw, to the east, the sky begin to lighten but the heavy clouds delayed dawn. That was good. Darkness suited us. Sihtric carried my banner and my horn. I turned to him. "Keep your horse as close behind me as possible. You are vital to the battle today!"

"Do not worry, lord. Any closer to you and you would think I was your wife!"

I mounted Steabba for I wanted to view the enemy deployment. Alain joined me and we rode towards their lines. We were well out of the range of the few hunting bows they had with them. The lightening sky revealed that Alain had been correct. They were using a long line of one hundred and forty horsemen. Alain nodded, "They must have had some reinforcements in the night. See, they now have another fifteen gathered around the count's banner." The count was beneath a huge and ancient tree.

"And the levy is in a block, fifty men wide and six men deep, behind their horsemen."

Unlike us, they were already mounted. As the light improved I saw that they had a further fifty men guarding the camp and possibly as a reserve. Having seen enough we turned our horses and rode back. We rode to Gilles and Bertrand first. "They will try to outflank us."

While Alain went to organize our men, I rode to Folki. "Was the horseman right?"

"He was. They have their levy fifty men wide."

"Then if they get close we will be surrounded too." He had but forty men with him. Ten men in four lines would be outnumbered by more than five to one. He saw my frown. "Do not worry, lord. Those odds do not frighten us. When our spears are blunt we will use our swords. When they become dull we use our seaxes and if there are any left... we use our teeth!"

By the time I reached Alain the enemy were arrayed. I saw Count Eustace and Stephen of Caen ride along their front. Their words were lost in the drumming of the hooves but I caught the words, *'barbarian'*, *'God'* and *'pagan'*. They were using the usual invectives. Then we heard the first rumble of thunder in the distance. The storm was coming. There was no lightning and I could not estimate the distance but a few drops of rain plopped onto Steabba's head.

115

Günter of Swabia laughed, "Thank you, Thor! That will put the shits up the Franks!"

I saw Count Eustace look up to the skies and decide that he ought to begin the battle before the storm arrived. He raised his sword and shouted a last invective.

"Mount!"

I prompted him by preparing my men. The count slipped through his ranks to wait before the levy with his reserve horsemen. His horn sounded and I saw that Stephen of Caen led his men. They did not gallop this time; they walked up the gentle slope. Then the rain began to fall harder and the thunder cracked again. This time I saw the lightning first. It was still some miles away but it was getting closer. I slid my shield onto my arm and rested my spear across my saddle. When we made our formation Snorri and Michael of Liger would flank me and Sihtric would sit in behind me. It would not be a true wedge but we would have a tip to drive through the first of their horsemen.

Suddenly the rain began to pour down and the lightning flashed in the sky. Folki and his men began to bang their shields and chant, "Thor! Thor!" Over and over. The Franks began to gallop. They were just three hundred paces from us. They were not moving as fast as they wished. Already the ground was becoming slick with rain.

"Sihtric, the signal!"

He sounded the horn twice and I dug my heels into Steabba. We began to canter down the slippery, slick, rain-soaked slope. I headed diagonally towards Stephen of Caen and the centre of their line. It would make it easier for Gilles and Bertrand to join us. Even as we cantered towards them I saw that the count had realised our intention and he was sounding the horn. Thor came to our aid and there was an almighty crack of thunder which drowned it out. I saw some of the Franks looking fearfully at the sky. They feared the storm but we knew it came from Thor and we would not be harmed. I did not turn around but I trusted my men. I dug my heels in to make Steabba go a little faster. The slope was with us and the Franks' horses were struggling for grip on the slope. I resisted the urge to gallop. It was better to hit their line together. I pulled back my arm and, holding my spear slightly behind me, aimed Steabba for Stephen of Caen.

The dawn had disappeared in a maelstrom of rain and dark clouds. The rain was now a deluge making it hard to see more than a few paces. I knew that Stephen of Caen feared me. I did not know why. Mixed with that fear was hatred; he wanted me dead. A warrior cannot fight well with such mixed emotions. You do not fear your enemy for if you do then you are dead. Their line had gaps. There were two horses' heads touching Steabba's rump. Three spears were there to strike at Stephen of Caen and the warrior next to him. Fear won over hatred and Stephen of Caen turned his horse to present his shield to me. I punched and my spear struck his shield. His turn had unbalanced his horse and both horse and rider fell over, crashing into the next warrior in the line. As Snorri speared the other horseman who had been next to Stephen of Caen we had created a huge hole through which we poured.

Ahead, I saw the levy stop and present shields. At the rear, I watched as a dozen men detached themselves and ran towards the woods. They were the first trickle of the torrent of deserters who would flee before we hit them. The count had a decision to make. Did he order a withdrawal or would he charge us? He was no coward and he led his fifteen men towards us. The rain made visibility poor and the ground slippery. I slowed Steabba. The last thing I needed was to tumble from my horse. The count and his men had not had the luxury of time and they were not in a line. The count saw an untried youth. He saw a Viking on a horse! Such a warrior was not to be feared. Just as we sought to kill him he saw my death as the path to victory for him.

He rode directly at me. His spear was aimed at my chest. I had my shield low down. It was a deception. My own spear was pointed at his horse's head. I intended to use it to guide my spear. I stood in my stiraps as I brought up my shield. My shield was now in position and could block the count's blow. I punched with my spear. The horse's head dropped as the spear came towards it. The count could not bring his shield over his middle to protect it. My spearhead had slid between the links of his mail as his spear crashed into the boss of my shield. It was a powerful blow and I struggled to avoid being knocked over. I sat down and twisted the spear. The spearhead tore into his side. He was a tough warrior and he managed to knock my spear aside. It made the hole larger. The thunder and lightning were all about us. The rain made visibility poor and my world was bounded by my men and those who fought to protect the count.

Whipping Steabba's head around I dropped the spear and drew my sword. The count tried to do the same but he was hampered by his wound. I swung my sword backhand towards him and my blade bit into his upper arm. He managed to draw his sword and, even with a wound in his right arm, swung it at Steabba's head. It was a vulnerable target and I barely turned it away from the blow. It was a clever move for I was forced to turn my shield side away from him. Folki had drilled into me more times than enough. *'An enemy is not defeated until he is dead! A wounded man can still kill you'*. He was right and the Frank used his left hand to rear his horse while standing in his stiraps. He was going to end it by bringing his sword down upon my head. My shield was on the wrong side. I did the only thing I could; I kicked Steabba hard and he lurched forward. Holding my sword up I used the momentum of my horse to drive the tip of my sword into the count's throat and then up into his skull. His dying hand was still on the downward stroke. His dead hand brought his blade down on my helmet. I was lucky. It was the flat of the blade. As I pulled out my sword, his dead body fell from his horse.

117

Ragnvald Hrolfsson

I looked around. My men were still fighting the last of the count's men. The rest of the horsemen had galloped towards Folki and his men. At such times you have to make a quick decision. The levy stood but I could see that more men had left the rear. I stood in my stiraps and pointed to the levy. "Gilles and Bertrand, charge the foot!"

Sihtric, behind me, said, "What about Folki?"

"They will have to hold. The battle is here. Folki will have to hold off the horsemen. We rout the levy and the battle is won."

I rode at a Frank who had wounded Charles, one of Alain's men. It was not honourable but then anyone who thought that battle was honourable had only read of such things. I swung my sword wide and brought it across his back, above the cantle of his saddle. I cut through his mail and into his spine. He threw his arms wide and fell from his horse.

"Thank you, lord!"

"Get to the palisade and tell Folki that he must hold."

"Aye, lord."

As Alain slew the last of the count's guards I reached down to pull a spear from a dead Frank's body. "Captain! Let us charge the levy!"

"Of course!"

Just at that moment, there was a flash and a crack. A bolt of lightning struck the tree beneath which the count had sheltered. Branches fell and there was a brief flurry of flames before the rain doused them. Every eye was drawn to it. We knew that it was Thor and it encouraged us. I know not what the Franks thought but I saw the effect.

When the tale was told, over fires and in the safety of the Haugr and Benni's Ville, the act seemed ridiculous. How less than fifty men charged almost four hundred warriors and the four hundred broke. It was the sight of the bodies of the count and his men which started it. That and the lightning struck tree. The Franks were Christians but they were superstitious. Old pagan memories surfaced. It was the riderless horses wandering around and it was the fact that the men with the spears were Northmen which told them that flight was preferable to standing.

I watched as Gilles and Bertrand leading fresh, untested men, charged with levelled spears at the foot. Even as the first twenty were speared the rest ran. A man on foot, fleeing, is the easiest target in the world. It is not like a wild boar or even a deer. Men do not turn and try to gouge or kick you, they flee. They throw away shields and spears for they are an encumbrance and they forget those who were next to them but a heartbeat earlier. They ran for the bridge and the woods. They hurled themselves into the river in an attempt to escape us. I pulled back my spear and skewered a Frank in the back. He wore no mail and my spear slid into soft flesh. I did not have to push hard and his dying body drew the spearhead from his flesh. I know not how many times I repeated this but when Steabba stumbled through exhaustion I knew we had come far enough.

118

When we reached the river, I turned to Sihtric. "Sound recall! We must go to the aid of Folki."

Turning I saw my men chasing the Franks who were still on our side of the river. The Franks had tried to evade by hiding behind the trees. We had just followed. I found the road and walked Steabba back. It would not aid Folki if my horse died before we got there. When we emerged from the trees I saw the Franks streaming towards us. There were fifty or so on horses and a half dozen fleeing on foot. I could hear Folki and his men as they banged their shields and chanted. They were singing the song of Fótr and Folki and my heart swelled with pride as I heard the words.

Fótr and Folki were brothers free
Seeking fortune they sailed the sea
The Norns brought them to the land of the horse
They sailed they thought a charmed course.
Clan of the Horseman
Warriors strong
Clan of the Horseman
Our reach is long
Clan of the Horseman
Fight as one
Clan of the Horseman
Death will come
Lying Frank and treacherous Dane
Proved to be Fótr's bane
They fought as men all shield brothers
None fled, none left the others
Clan of the Horseman
Warriors strong
Clan of the Horseman
Our reach is long
Clan of the Horseman
Fight as one
Clan of the Horseman
Death will come
And now Folki is the last of his line
Revenge is sweet like aged wine
The Franks have paid a fearful price
Their slain by Heart of Ice
Clan of the Horseman

Ragnvald Hrolfsson

Warriors strong
Clan of the Horseman
Our reach is long
Clan of the Horseman
Fight as one
Clan of the Horseman
Death will come

The horsemen who fled the field were able to evade us. They spread to the left and right of us. The horsemen would swim the river. Those on foot would have little chance. We now had the problem of ascending a slick and muddy field. It was also littered with bodies. Those on foot were caught. Most were slain but a few, perhaps four, surrendered. They would be enslaved but at least they would live.

By the time I reach Folki I saw that they were surrounded by a sea of bodies. There were at least ten dead horses. I dismounted and walked to him. I saw that his mail and helmet, as well as his face and hands, were covered in the gore of battle. I knew, from his grin, that the blood was not his.

"Thank you Folki. I had to make a decision."

He hugged me tightly, "It was the right one. The Franks who attacked us were weak. They had no leader and very little skill. I hope my brother was watching in Valhalla! Had we known how to fight them he might have still been alive."

"Aye. Did you lose many?"

"Three died but they died well." He pointed behind him to the walls. "The archers and the traps did the most damage. You are the one who deserves the honour, lord. Your father could not have done better."

Alain dismounted. He too was covered in Frankish blood. "He is right, lord. When we charged I wondered if this would be a glorious end for us all. The count was a cunning warrior. You did well to trick him and then defeat him in battle."

"The gods were with us. It was *wyrd*. Sihtric, have my men collect the spare horses and then have some of these horses butchered. We eat well tonight."

The rain had stopped but the ground was a muddy morass through which we waded. I remembered my father telling me of the journey north after he had rescued the Bretons, when the land around Carentan had been totally flooded, making the town an island. I could see now that we would soon be an island again. There were large pools of water forming by the river making it seem like a lake. The bridge was threatened and I saw the water lapping around its top.

As we ate I spoke with Bertrand. "Ask the people who live here about the floods. I would know if this is likely to get worse."

120

"I will but, as I recall, the land here has always flooded in the rains. The town, however, stays dry."

"Gilles, if you are able, take some men tomorrow and see how far the enemy went. I suspect they went all the way back to Caen but it is better to be sure."

"I will, lord. We have some fine horses now." He pointed to the twenty horses we had taken. He hesitated, "Lord, how long do we stay here?"

"You tire of war?"

He nodded, "You know I am no warrior. I am a horseman. I miss my wife and I miss my horses. We have done more than your father wished already."

I chewed on the horsemeat and gave it some thought. I missed my wife and I wanted to be there at the birth of my son but I had been given a task by my father. "Folki, does my father come hence?"

"He will be here, lord, before the end of the month."

"And then it will soon be Heyannir. The men will wish to be home and begin the harvest. Give us until the end of the month and then we can all go home."

Alain waved a hand around, "And who will stop the Franks from retaking this?"

I shrugged, "That will be my father's decision. I am certain that he will have given it some thought." I pointed to the east. "The sea is barely a mile away. The river is a little narrow for a drekar but a warrior could use this as his home and then the sea to raid. It is not like Valognes, landlocked. Where there is water there is a way to the sea."

Alain nodded, seemingly satisfied. "Lord, your own home is not far away. The men and your father would understand if you rode there to visit with your wife."

There was a chorus of 'ayes' from the others. I was tempted. In two months, I would be a father. It was but twenty miles. "I will see what the morrow brings." I had, in truth, decided to go home. It would only be one night that I would be away and I yearned to see my home. The battles and the conquests had kept me going but now that the end of my task was in sight I yearned for my family. I shook my head. I had wanted to be a warrior all my life and yet now that I had the chance to do just that I sought the comfort of my home.

When dawn broke it was to clear skies. The rain had gone. Thor had sent his storm to help us win the battle. The tree he had struck stood black and gaunt. Its burned branches looked like a hand asking for peace. Alain and Folki walked with me as I toured the field. Our own dead had been taken already and buried. There were too many Franks for us to bury. "We had better burn their bodies else they will attract vermin."

Folki pointed to the burned tree. "There would be a good place, jarl. Their spirits would not roam for that was the tree touched by the god himself."

121

I nodded, "You are right. And I take these clear skies as a sign that I can return home, even if it is just for one night. I shall take Sihtric with me and I leave you in command, Captain."

Folki nodded and then said, "Lord, with your permission I would like to take some men and seek the sea." I gave him a sideways look. He smiled, "You are wise beyond your years, jarl. Your words last night set me to thinking. My men died protecting the walls of Carentan. Perhaps the Weird Sisters willed it so. If I like the estuary then I might ask your father for permission to live here." He laughed, Perhaps I am getting lazy but it would not take much work to make this into a stronghold!"

I nodded, "Of course, Folki. Your brother and his men left the Haugr to seek a new home. It seems to me that this is meant to be."

"We will burn the bodies when we return."

Sihtric was happy to come with me and I left in good heart. We paused at Rauville. I had left Leif Sorenson in command. He had had a dull time and was envious of our victory. "Jarl, how long do I stay here?"

"Not long. When my father comes it may well be that he allows Folki to rule at Carentan. With us to the north then we would need no garrison here. The people might like to revert to their old ways."

"From what we have learned I do not think that Guillaume of Rauville will like that. He will try to retake his home."

"And he will need to pass Carentan to do so. Folki will be there."

I could have wept with joy when I saw my home. Æðelwald of Remisgat had not been idle. I saw Æðelwald stripped to the waist and toiling on his church. Benni was up the ladder working on the tower. The walls of my stronghold were finished and men stood on the fighting platform. I was seen and hands waved. As I rode through the gates my wife waddled towards me. Her face was a mixture of joy and anger.

"And it is about time! I had thought you had forgotten me!" She burst into tears and, throwing her arms around me, began to weep.

Æðelwald of Remisgat had descended the ladder and he smiled, "She has missed you, lord."

I nodded. I, too, was filled with all sorts of emotions. "The wait is almost over, wife. We have Carentan and my father will come to relieve me soon. I will soon be back here. I swear that I will be here by the beginning of Heyannir!"

She pulled back, "You are not staying now?"

"I stay one night. I am making us more secure here. Then I will not roam. This will be my home and I will be lord here. Benni has made us a home that is safe. We now have more horses and we have taken treasure too. You can begin to furnish the hall the way that you wish. It is but the shortest of times you will have to wait for me."

Ragnvald Hrolfsson

Slightly mollified, she nodded, "I confess that Benni has made a good job of the hall. We even have an upstairs. It is but a wooden staircase but it is warm and cosy." She took me on a tour of my home and that made me even happier for I heard the joy in her voice as she spoke of our unborn child and the others we would have. She had rooms planned for them. This was the difference between the Norse and the Franks. We were happy to share and live in one hall. I was half Frank and I understood. We would have our own space and privacy. It would be a good place to live.

I left the next day feeling genuinely sad. I tarried as long as I dared and then headed south to Carentan. I would send a messenger to my father. I wanted to go home.

Chapter 12

When we finally reached the Haugr we were the last of the drekar to arrive. We were heavily laden and I did not wish to risk our cargo. We had taken more treasure than any other raid that I could remember. I did not think that even the Dragonheart had had as much success. We were very low in the water. Sven the Helmsman was philosophical as we saw Bárekr's Haven. "I am pleased that I came on this last voyage with you, Jarl Hrolf. I have seen that Harold Fast Sailing and I have made a good ship and I have taken part in a raid which men will talk about when the world has changed into one we do not recognise."

"It is a good ship but I hope it will not be your last."

"No, for good as she is, I have seen ways we could make the next one better."

I, too, was philosophical. I was thinking of my son. I had given him power. I had let him lead the horsemen I had created. I was excited at what he might do with that power. He might make mistakes and some of those warriors might not return but I felt, in my heart, that he would come back a better warrior. The only cloud was that of the treacherous Danes. I knew that there were Danes who could be trusted. Some had been with us on the Issicauna but there appeared to be a greater number who would act in a dishonourable way. I would be more cautious in the future. The couple who had sailed with me, especially Steinn the Wise, seemed good warriors but I had been unhappy with Hagnni Nisson and his men. They had not been as reliable as others.

My little harbour looked crowded with all of the ships anchored there. The captains had made a longphort. Someone, probably my wife, had arranged for them to camp between the woods and the Haugr. Each crew had their own fire and camp. It made sense. Vikings liked to fight. Frequently it was just with fists but occasionally weapons could be used. It rarely ended in death for that would incur weregeld but, after a raid, men were lively. Outside the walls, it was less intimidating. I saw the jarls and captains as they advanced down to the shore to meet us. They had left us a berth close to the shore.

Sven chuckled. "What is funny, Sven the Helmsmen?"

Ragnvald Hrolfsson

"I am just anticipating the division of the treasure. It is usually easy for you make the decisions and the men all agree. You have other jarls and this may not be as easy."

"They agreed to sail under my command."

"Aye, jarl, and what they agreed and what they will do are two entirely different things. I am just pleased that I shall be safe on the island with the priest of the White Christ."

I nodded, "Folki, bring the treasure chests ashore and take them directly to my hall!"

"Aye, jarl!"

Hagnni Nisson had been the most truculent of the jarls. He had argued before we sailed and when we had been loading the ships. His men had abused the priests. He, too, was a Dane. It was no surprise when he greeted me, somewhat belligerently on the shore.

"We have been waiting for you, jarl! We have a treasure to divide." He pointed to Steinn the Wise, "He said we had to wait for you!"

"And that is right. Besides, had you left how would you have divided this?" I pointed to the chests.

Folki and his men appeared carrying the chests of ransom. Hagnni went to open one. Erik Long Hair smacked his hand away. "I know you are a Dane but are you also a stupid Dane? The jarl divides the treasure. The jarl was the one who secured this for us. Had you been in charge then the priests would have been slaughtered and we would have been poorer."

"No man touches me and lives." He glowered belligerently at Erik.

I took out my sword, Heart of Ice, and placed it at the throat of the Dane. "This is my land and Erik is my man. If you object then speak with me or leave without anything!"

"We shared in the hardship!"

Steinn the Wise burst out laughing, "I did not see you at the fore. You and your men have the slowest legs I have ever seen. The fighting was all but over when you arrived."

The other jarls all laughed and I saw that Hagnni was angry. "Come to my hall and we will begin the division." He still looked angry. My sword was still in my hand. "I am not the most patient of men, Hagnni. Draw your sword and I will slay you and then get on with the real business."

He looked around. If he touched his sword then he and all of his men would be slain. That much was obvious. He nodded, "Divide it up and then I will be gone."

"Good and if I organize another raid then do not ask to join. I am careful about the warriors with whom I fight. You are a nithing!"

When we reached my hall, my wife was there and she greeted me with a hug and a kiss. She put her lips close to my ears and said, "Thank God you have come. Some of these are little better than animals!"

I whispered, "I know but we are now secure. It will just be for a little while longer. They will be gone and life will get back to normal."

I was fair. All those who were true warriors said so. Hagnni was not happy but the rest were. I divided the treasure scrupulously. I had said each ship would have an equal share and they did. Bjorn Long Stride had one of the smaller drekar. It was larger than *'Skuld'* but had a smaller crew. Hagnni glared when the young jarl took the same share as Hagnni's crew. Every captain had more treasure and slaves than he had ever had. The treasure we shared was that which the fleet had taken. I knew that individuals had raided farms and taken slaves and booty. That was theirs. Bjorn Long Stride's men had worked hard and done well out of the raid. I would enjoy sailing with him again for he reminded me of Folki and Fótr when they had first come.

As men counted it Steinn the Wise came over to me. "You could have taken more for yourself, jarl."

"I know but I would raid Paris one day. I will need warriors such as you and your crew. Call it bait!"

He laughed, "You need no bait for me. I would sail anywhere with you. However, I would watch out for Hagnni. He is a snake. You did not see for you were busy fighting but he and his men held back. They are nithings!"

"And they will not sail with me again."

He nodded. We walked back to the camp. I could see that he wished to talk with me. "I spoke with Folki. He said you have sent your son and your horsemen to capture land from the Franks."

"Aye. He is a horseman and not a sailor."

"Yet he has seen but seventeen summers."

"Does age make a wiser warrior? Hagnni is thirty and five summers yet he is a rat. I am content that my son will lead well."

"You are wise. If you will permit it then I will visit again. I see profit in following the banner of the horse.

My wife had laid on a feast for the jarls. She was a hostess and knew what they would like. I drank little for I wanted to watch these men who might follow me again some time. That night, as my men feasted, I saw that Hagnni did not drink as much as the other jarls. He sat scowling. He had not been happy with the division. I was happy that they would be leaving the next day. I was anxious to ride and see my son.

When Mary and I were alone and she lay in my arms, she asked me about the raid. After I had told her she said, "The people are pleased with the goods you have brought but there is some disquiet over the sacking of the churches."

"You mean the Christians?" She nodded. "There are more pagans than Christians who live in the Haugr."

"Many of the children born to Vikings are now baptised and will grow as Christians."

"We did not harm the priests."

"It matters not. It is the principle."

"I am afraid so long as they are an easy target we will continue to take the riches from their churches."

"Our son has married a Christian."

"As did I but the warrior remains within. Have you heard from him?"

"He has taken a place called Rauville and he is advancing on Carentan."

I was impressed. I had expected him to take longer to overcome Rauville's defences. My faith in my young son had been rewarded. I had been a warrior who led others at his age. I kissed my wife goodnight and we cuddled until we both fell asleep. We could not have been asleep for long when I was woken by something. I sat up in bed. I am a deep sleeper but it takes time to fall into the dream-filled sleep I usually enjoyed. I was about to turn over when I heard a distant clash of metal. I leapt from my bed and, donning my kirtle, I grabbed Heart of Ice and raced to the gate.

"What is it, Lars?" The sentry was peering towards the camps.

"Trouble at the camps, jarl. There are men fighting."

"Summon my men and have them follow me."

My men opened the gate and I ran towards the camp. I could now see that a drekar was slipping her moorings. It was *'Black Drake'*, Hagnni's ship. By the time I reached the camp, I saw Steinn the Wise standing with a bloodied sword and two of the Dane's crew, dead at his feet.

"What happened?"

"That treacherous bastard, Nisson, waited until we were asleep. He slew Bjorn Long Stride and most of his crew and took their treasure. They slit their throats while they slept. I think they would have had us all but Ottkell, Last of the Bears, awoke and saw them. He has a bad wound to his leg."

"Get him to Father Michael."

Just then Siggi Far-Sighted came running along, "Jarl, come quick." There was urgency in his voice and I ran.

When I reached the end of the jetty I saw Harold Fast Sailing having his leg tended to while Sven the Helmsman was trying to hold in his guts. A ship's boy, Egil, cradled his head.

Sven looked up at me and gave a sad smile, "I will not build that ship for your son now, Hrolf. I am going to the Otherworld."

You do not lie to a dying man and I could see that his life was oozing away. I nodded, "You have ever been oathsworn, Sven."

He nodded, "Siggi White Hair was right about you. He said there was something in you which was greater than any warrior he had ever seen and that included the Dragonheart. It was a good day when you joined our clan." He winced as pain coursed through him, "I beg a favour, Hrolf."

"Anything."

"Let me go to the Otherworld holding Heart of Ice. The Allfather will surely grant me a place in his hall if I hold an enchanted sword." I took my sword and gave him the hilt. He smiled. "I feel its power, thank you I…"

Then his eyes closed and he was gone.

"Farewell, my friend. I will see you in Valhalla. Siggi and Ulf will be there waiting for you." I gently prised his fingers from my sword and stood. "What happened, Harold?"

"We heard a commotion and came out. The Danes were trying to set fire to *'Dragon's Breath'*. We stopped them but we paid the price."

Some of Steinn's men and the remnants of Bjorn Long Stride's crew arrived. Bjorn Fast Feet and Erik Green Eye arrived with more of my crew. "Siggi, get your men aboard **Dragon's Breath'**. We are going after him."

"Aye, jarl."

Harold tried to rise, "I will come too!"

I shook my head, "No you will not. You will be a hindrance. You are wounded. I have enough men here." I waved to the men who stood before me. "Tonight, we become one crew. Board my drekar and we will show this Dane that it does not do to cross the Clan of the Horse!"

"Aye!"

There were fifty of us aboard the drekar. The Dane had slightly fewer men. Steinn the Wise had slain two. The jarl was with his men and he took an oar. It took a longer time than I would have hoped to navigate the crowded longphort. Steinn was rowing close to the steering board, he said, "Do not worry jarl. You will catch him. *'Black Drake'* is a cow of a ship. He has not cleaned the weed from her keel. I should have known something was amiss. He, alone of the jarls, loaded his ship before the feast and left a deck watch."

I nodded, "Bjorn Long Stride had the smallest crew did he not?"

"He did and he was the youngest of the jarls. He and his crew drank too much. The eight who are left will be keen for vengeance."

"As are we all. Sven was one of the original crew of the *'Raven's Wing'*. There are few of us left now."

Once we had cleared the ships, and, with every oar double manned, we began to row. Bjorn Fast Feet chose the chant. It was an angry one and one which gave power to the oars. It was the song of another treacherous Dane, Black Axe. The other two warbands soon picked it up as we flew through the dark waters. We would travel faster than *'Black Drake'*, for Siggi knew the waters like the back of his hand.

128

Ragnvald Hrolfsson

The horseman came through darkest night
He rode towards the dawning light
With fiery steed and thrusting spear
Hrolf the Horseman brought great fear

Slaughtering all he breached their line
Of warriors slain there were nine
Hrolf the Horseman with gleaming blade
Hrolf the Horseman all enemies slayed

With mighty axe Black Teeth stood
Angry and filled with hot blood
Hrolf the Horseman with gleaming blade
Hrolf the Horseman all enemies slayed
Ice cold Hrolf with Heart of Ice
Swung his arm and made it slice
Hrolf the Horseman with gleaming blade
Hrolf the Horseman all enemies slayed

In two strokes the Jarl was felled
Hrolf's sword nobly held
Hrolf the Horseman with gleaming blade
Hrolf the Horseman all enemies slayed

Once we had cleared Bárekr's Haven we turned east and had the wind behind us. Steinn joined me at the steering board. "Where will they go, Steinn? You know him better than I do."

"He is a nithing and how do you fathom such a mind? But I think he will head for Dorestad. There they do not care who you are so long as you can pay. He would not risk Dyflin. It is too far and you are known there. He may be a fool and head for Wessex but, since your raid on Cantwareburh, I think he would have a poor welcome. If I were to put money on a destination then I would say Dorestad."

"Good." I turned to Siggi. "Can we beat him there?"

He gave a grim laugh, "To avenge Sven the Helmsman I will make this drekar fly!"

It was not bravado. He was a good sailor and knew his ship well. "Good. I will arm myself." My chest was not aboard but there were mail and helmets as well as shields. I found a byrnie. I had worn many types of mail in my time from the kind worn by Romans to the mail made by Bagsecg. The one I donned was an old one. It would suffice. There was a plain round helmet and that would do. I had Heart of Ice and so I took a seax from the arms chest. I was ready.

I walked to the prow. Sven had built this drekar on Raven Wing Island. Part of him was in the timbers. He had bled when he had made it. It was Sven who had carved the dragon. I stood with my hand on the dragon and closed my eyes. The words I spoke were inside my head but they were intended for Sven. He would hear me. '*Old friend, guide us safely to this Dane so that we may avenge you and the others. We will make a funeral pyre of his ship. It will not make up for your loss but it is all that we can do.*'

The prow suddenly rose in the air as a gust of wind propelled us forward. It was enough. Sven had heard as had Ran. The Dane was as good as dead.

I could not tell if the gap was closing for we could see nothing in the black night but I knew that, as the night wore on, we would be catching him. I cupped my hands and shouted to the lookout on the masthead. "A gold piece when you sight the Dane!"

It was Egil the Squirrel who answered, "I need no gold, jarl. Sven was a good sailor. I will seek our prey. You have my word."

Dawn seemed to take forever to come. Not long before it did break, I heard Egil's voice. "Jarl! I see a sail. It is to the northwest!"

I looked to Siggi. He nodded, "It has to be the Dane. Who else would risk sailing along this coast at night time? I know it well and I am wary."

He was right. The Dane was keeping far from the coast. That, too, made sense. The rocky coast had claimed many ships in its time. Siggi adjusted the steering board. I cupped my hand, "Make ready for war. We take no prisoners and when they are dead then we burn their ship! Hagnni Nisson will learn that we do not forgive and we do not forget!"

The crew all began banging the deck with their hands. It sounded like rolling thunder and that was good. Men took their weapons and sharpened them. Many donned red cochineal for their eyes and hands. Others groomed themselves. They combed and plaited their hair, beards and moustaches. Each man had his own preparations for war but when they fought, they would fight as one. That was our way. Taking the Saami bow from the chest by the steering board, I walked to the prow and stood with one hand on the dragon's head and the other on the stay. I could not see the ship yet. It was still too dark but I trusted Egil and his eyes. As the light in the east became brighter so I was able to make out the sail as it rose and fell on the horizon. We had him. He was close enough to see. I strung the bow and selected the best three arrows I could. I was impatient. I wanted the Dane brought to book sooner rather than later and anything I could do to make that happen then I would.

I could see what Steinn had meant. The drekar was not sliding through the water as she ought. I saw that they had spied us and were now using their oars. They were trying to outrun us. It was a mistake. The men would be tired when it came to a battle. Each moment made the sky lighter and the drekar clearer. Siggi used the wind well and we edged inexorably closer to her. We were to the landward side and the only place the Dane could go was west and he would not do that. He would not risk the edge of the world or the rocks of Syllingar. He was trying to make Dorestad before we caught him. It was a forlorn hope. Siggi would bring us astern of him so that we could board him over his steering board. As we closed with him I began to make faces out. I saw that there were just two men at the steering board. Hagnni and his helmsman. The rest were trying to escape the wrath of my crew. They were rowing as though their lives depended upon it. Murder was still a heinous crime. It was one thing to kill a warrior in battle but to sneak up on him while he was sleeping and slit his throat was something else. It was worsened by the fact that they were not at war. We were all, ostensibly, allies.

Hagnni kept turning around to gauge our approach. He had to know that we would catch him. If our positions were reversed then I would have turned and made a fight of it. This way he exhausted his men to no avail. I took an arrow and prepared it as the gap narrowed. His men were tiring. The stroke was ragged and that slowed the drekar making it turn a little eastward. The helmsman was having to fight both the sea and the rowers.

With the wind behind, I could loose an arrow further. At three hundred paces, I pulled back. It was sent in hope rather than expectation. Perhaps the wind fluked it closer than I expected or the gods helped us but whatever the reason it struck the sternpost and rest there. I saw the Dane look up in shock. We were drawing closer and I readied another arrow. This one landed on the deck just a pace in front of Hagnni. Egil cheered. "You almost had him, jarl!"

I saw the Danish captain grab a shield and use it to protect both him and the helmsman. It was a wasted gesture. Each gust of wind took us closer to the enemy despite his efforts to evade us. Soon my arrows would be plunging into his rowers and they would have neither warning nor protection. My next arrow disappeared close to the mast fish. Egil shouted with glee, "You have hit one of the rowers in the leg!"

That caused pandemonium amongst the crew. I saw the oars run in and men grabbed the shields which lined the drekar. Without their oars, we were racing quickly towards the *'Black Drake'*.

I loosed another arrow and then turned, "Prepare for battle!" I sent my last arrow, at a range of fifty paces. This one hit a warrior who was bending to retrieve his shield. His arm was pinned to the gunwale. Siggi had shortened the sail to slow us down. Beorn, Erik and Steinn appeared behind me with their shields and swords. I donned the unfamiliar helmet and shield. Hagnni was now organising his men. Fighting on a ship was not easy. I had done it before but I was not certain that the Dane had. Egil and the other ship's boys had now swarmed down the lines and were ready with ropes and grappling hooks. Their task would be to secure us to the Dane. I saw that the Dane was riding lower in the water. They had a great quantity of treasure on board. It would make boarding easier. We just had ballast and the crew. Our gunwale was higher.

I drew my sword and raised it high, "This is for Sven and the other murdered warriors. Bjorn Long Stride's men began chanting, "Clan of the Otter" and banging their shields. I would allow them the honour of leading the attack. They had shield brothers to avenge. There would be enough men for us all to blood our swords.

A few spears were thrown towards us. They were wasted. The wind was against and the drekar was pitching too much. Two struck in our hull. As we neared them I shouted, "You are mine, Hagnni Nisson. I will send you to Ran. You will never see Valhalla. You do not deserve it!"

He raised his sword, "I am not afraid of you! This day will see the death of the horseman!"

As the gap closed to a few paces the ropes were thrown. Siggi turned our drekar so that we suddenly rose above their stern. The sight of our dragon looming above them made the warriors flinch and they were unable to cut the ropes which now drew them towards us. Dálkr Ragnarson led Bjorn Long Stride's men and they leapt over the side and onto the deck of '*Black Drake*'. Steinn and I followed.

Neither side would give quarter. There would be only dead left aboard the drekar. Steinn landed before I did. He took the blow from the helmsman. The helmsman was a brave man for he had no shield. The hatchet stuck in the jarl's shield. I lunged forward and Heart of Ice gutted him. Hagnni moved away from the fighting. He was saving himself. Dálkr and his men were hacking and slashing their way through the Danes. They were almost like berserkers. They were paying the price for already three were dead.

"Clan of the Horse!" Leading my men, I held my shield before me and brought my sword from on high. Even as Dálkr fell to the swords of two Danes my blade smashed through the shoulder of one of his killers. The drekar was out of control for no one was at the helm and the wind was pushing us around. I had a wide stance but, as the *'Black Drake'* lurched, one of the Danes before me over swung his axe and toppled over. I brought my sword across his prostrate body and cut him to his spine. I looked up and saw that Hagnni was racing to the prow. I knew not why. He could not escape me. Perhaps he thought his men would kill me. That would not happen. Already the Danes were being assailed and assaulted on all sides. I ran down the larboard side which was empty. The fighting was all around the steering board and on the steerboard side. Hagnni had reached the prow and had nowhere left to run.

He turned to face me. He was silent. There was no insult. He intended to use the prow to protect his back. He would have the advantage of height. That suited me. I moved closer to him. The ship was now pitching fore and aft as well as side to side. Hagnni swung at my head. I flicked up the shield. The blow would have missed my head for he was slightly off balance when he struck at me. My shield caught the edge. It would not be as sharp now. I swung at his leg. He had no mail and no protection save his sealskin boots. My sword was sharp and I had anger in the blow. It bit through the sealskin and into his leg. Heart of Ice came away bloody.

"Trickster! Loki!"

He swung again and this time brought his sword from on high. He would not miss this time. I took the blow on the boss of my shield. It rang like a bell.

"That is your death knell, spawn of Svartalfheim!"

I lunged upwards and my blade slid between his legs and into his groin. I struck diagonally, slicing into his manhood and then his hip. With the wound in one leg and now this mortal wound he collapsed to the deck. As he lay there writing in pain I stamped on his hand. He released his sword. I picked it up and hurled it over the side.

"I said you would not go to Valhalla and you shall not." I turned and saw that the ship was now a charnel house. All of his crew lay dead. Just two of the Otters were left alive. I waved to them. "Come, you shall have the pleasure of throwing this fish bait into the sea."

The two of them walked up to him. One took out his seax and tore it across the Dane's eyes. The other took out his hand axe and chopped off the Dane's right hand. In the Otherworld, he would not be able to see and he would not be able to feed himself. Picking him up by the legs and arms they hurled him high over the gunwale and into the sea. Although he was dying even a drowning man tries to save himself. His byrnie took him down and then the stump of his wrist came up followed by his head. He surfaced just once more and then his body slipped beneath the waves. His death was greeted by silence. This was not a time to celebrate.

"Take the treasure he stole and anything else of value. Siggi, have fire prepared. We burn this hulk. She will sail no more."

My crew worked quickly. The timbers covering the hold were piled close to the mast to make them burn quicker. The chests, spare ropes, swords, byrnies, warriors' rings and jewels were all taken. Many of the dead were despoiled by warriors who wanted the dead to suffer in the next world too. This was a victory that left a bad taste in the mouth. There would be no saga to commemorate this. We would not speak of it again. The silence would be more eloquent than a saga. The seal oil the Dane had carried was spread around the decks and the dead. If any of the Danes were feigning then they would be burned alive. I was the last to return to our ship. Siggi's boys had prepared four pots. Inside was kindling and it was burning. Two were given to the Otters and the other two to Steinn and me. We hurled them high in the air as the ropes binding us were severed.

133

The four pots smashed on the oil-soaked decks. Fire is always dangerous on a ship and '*Black Drake*' was old. The flames took hold and raced up the mast. They ignited the sail and the wind took her away from us. The fire seemed to dance along her length and the prow was wreathed in flames. It made it look as though the dragon was breathing fire. As the sail burned so she slowed and bobbed up and down as the fire ate the drekar. Suddenly one of the crew rose, he was wreathed in flames. He might have been unconscious when we left or hiding, I know not. He stood at the steering board and hurled himself into the sea. His body sank quickly. We watched as the whole ship became an inferno and gradually settled into the water.

When she disappeared I turned, "Siggi, take us home!"

The men took to the oars for we were sailing into the wind. There was no song. The crew rowed silently each remembering our own dead, our murdered friends.

Chapter 13

We reached home in the late afternoon. I had just left without telling my wife. Folki and Einar Bear Killer had not known where I had gone. They were all watching anxiously as we returned. We first carried our dead ashore. They had not sunk with the *'Black Drake'*. They would be buried with honour along with the dead of Clan of the Otter. I had spoken with the two survivors on the way back. They wished to stay on with my clan.

"Jarl, we owe you much. You allowed us to regain honour which the clan had lost. Our jarl was young but he was a good leader. We would follow you now."

Good warriors were hard to come by and I accepted their offer.

Einar Bear Killer said, simply, "He is dead?"

"And his crew along with his ship. It is as though they were never upon this earth. I have learned my lesson. I will take only men I know when next I raid. I would rather sail with fewer men but men whom I can trust."

Folki pointed to a piece of canvas. "Harold said to wait for your return to bury Sven. He said that his friend would wish you there when he was buried."

"Then let us do it now along with the other heroes who died." I turned to Folki. "What happened to the dead Danes?"

"We chopped up their bodies. We will have fine crabs and lobster next year. They will feast well on Danish flesh."

"Good."

"After the burial, we feasted. That was our way. It was a celebration of the lives of our friends and we spoke, not of their deaths, but of their lives and what we would remember. Harold pointed to *'Skuld'* and *'Dragon's Breath'*. "My old friend lives in those drekar. We spoke of the one we will build for your son, jarl, and I promise you that all of Sven's ideas will be incorporated into her. She will be the best drekar in your fleet."

"That is good."

Folki asked, "I wonder how Ragnvald is managing?"

Einar Bear Killer burped, "He has Gilles, Bertrand and Alain with him. As horsemen, they are the equal of any Frank. Your son is a good horseman, jarl. He will do well."

"He is but that does not stop me worrying about him."

Folki swallowed some ale, "If you wish, jarl, I could take my warband and join him. If he has taken Rauville then he will need men to man the walls. We will not be raiding again this summer. It will stop my men from becoming lazy."

"I may come with you. The last news we had was that he was considering taking Carentan."

Folki shook his head, "That is a mighty mouthful for horsemen! Can he do it?"

"I hope so but I do not know."

I spoke with my wife that night. "As much as I want you there with him he would not thank you for your presence. He is a man now and a father or he will be soon. Let Folki go. He is one of your warriors and will protect our son. Our son will accept that. Folki trained him."

I knew that my wife was right. She invariably was. I kissed her. "You are right." I cuddled into her.

She said, quietly, "You are upset about Sven." I nodded, not trusting myself to speak. "It is to be expected. Sven was always kind. He was not like the rest of your bloodthirsty men. He had a skill which did not involve killing."

"I am most upset because he did not need to die. I chose badly when I picked the jarls to sail with me. Sven was going to spend the rest of his life making ships."

"Harold will do so and Sven will be there in spirit."

I did not say that my wife seemed to have taken some of our pagan beliefs. "I am going to make sure that this does not happen again. Tomorrow I will build a wall around the shipyard and harbour. It will not just be the Haugr that deters our foes. Your church and my shipbuilders will have equal protection."

Even though it was dark I knew my wife was smiling from her words. "That is good, husband. Father Michael said he needed a new project. The wall will also protect the church. The attack showed me how vulnerable my church is too."

I rose early and told Folki that he could go alone. He nodded, "If we start now we can be at Valognes by evening. It will be good to march again." I nodded. "I promise that your son will be safe. Whatever I can do that will I do."

I sought Father Michael and explained what I wanted. He nodded. "We have plenty of stone left from the church and the towers. It is not the best of stone but if we augment it with the sea's bounty it will suffice. How high?"

"The height of two men with a fighting platform."

"Then the top will have to be timber. Have your men cut it, lord, and we will begin today. Can I use the slaves?"

"Of course."

I gathered every able-bodied man to begin the work. We were interrupted constantly as the jarls left to sail home. They all came to thank me and swear that they would follow my banner any time I asked. All of them felt guilty about

Hagnni even though it was nothing to do with them. They had sailed with him and not prevented the tragedy. Some said that they owed me. I did not see it that way. A man makes his own decisions. You cannot blame another for one man's evil. I was touched by their words. It took away some of the bile I tasted.

I was stripped to the waist and toiling with Father Michael when I saw the horsemen approach. I recognised Erik and Bjorn, two of my son's men. They had a wagon with them and in it were a woman and two girls. I saw them arrive at my gate and one of the guards pointed over to me.

"You have visitors, lord."

"Aye. I had better make myself presentable." I took a pail of water and doused myself with it. Using my cloak to dry myself I walked towards the Haugr. I slipped on my kyrtle and wondered who the guest was. I met them halfway between the water and the Haugr.

Erik dismounted, "Jarl, your son sent us. We have hostages from Rauville. This is Guillaume of Rauville's wife, the Lady Eloise and her daughters."

I nodded. I knew from the tight-lipped expression that they were hostages and so I smiled. "Bjorn, take our guests to Lady Mary and ask her to find beds for them."

"Aye, jarl."

The Lady Eloise jabbed a finger in my direction. "You and your son are barbarians. When my husband and my brother hear of what you have done they will have the skin flayed from your back!"

"First, they have to defeat us, lady, and so far, you have not the leaders to do so. Take her away."

When they had gone Erik told me of my son's successes. "We met Folki at Valognes. He will go directly to Carentan."

"And my son expects the Franks to attack?"

"Your son is no fool, jarl. He is making a palisade behind which they can fight. Have we your permission to return immediately?"

"Of course. You do not wish to miss anything?"

He grinned, "Your son has the taste of victory in his mouth, jarl. We would be there to taste it with him!"

"Then you have my permission. Tell him that if he needs me he just has to ask."

"He knows that, jarl." There was a pause. "He fights a war from the back of a horse. That is where he excels."

"I know, Erik, I know. I thought I was the horseman but not compared with my son."

The two horsemen turned their horses around and headed back. They would be able to change their tired beasts at Gilles' farm. It spoke well of my son's leadership that they did not wish to stay and enjoy the comfort of a hall. They would rather endure the hardship of a camp and serve my son.

Ragnvald Hrolfsson

My hall was well apportioned and there was room for Lady Eloise and her daughters. I never learned their names. I knew that the eldest was close to becoming a woman but they just glared at me whenever they saw me. It was the Lady Eloise who drew my attention. She was a strong-minded woman and held forthright views. She was not intimidated by the presence of a Viking warlord. My wife tried to make the situation a pleasant one. She assigned two slaves to act as servants. She made sure that they ate well and she diligently enquired after their needs.

In response, Lady Eloise was civil with my wife. They dined with us that first night. I received glares and silence when I attempted conversation and after a few hateful glances, I ceased trying. Instead, I listened. I became the scout whom Ulf Big Nose had trained. I was in plain sight but I was forgotten. My wife asked about the family of Lady Eloise and her antecedents. Lady Mary had been the daughter of an important Frank. He had been slain by us in a raid when Mary had been enslaved.

"My father was Pepin, Count of Caen. He was the cousin of Louis the Pious. Royal blood courses through his veins and mine. He was a great leader. If he was still alive today he would have got the brothers in a chamber and knocked their heads together. This civil war is unnecessary."

It was on the tip of my tongue to ask her why her husband was fighting for Charles but I resisted. I was rewarded with the answer a little later when my wife asked who Lady Eloise thought was in the right.

"Lothair is Emperor. He should be happy with that. Charles is the true King of Middle Frankia and Louis, King of Bavaria. They should all be happy with their titles. My husband fights for his friend and rightful lord, Charles. It is obvious who is in the right for Louis supports his elder brother."

My wife was no fool. She caught my eye and then asked, "But if Lothair is Emperor then surely he rules all the lands."

For the first time, I sensed uncertainty in the Frankish lady. "The other rulers, such as Angilbert of Milan and others, now believe they can elect the Emperor. Lothair has bought the support of the rulers of many of the eastern portions of the Empire but King Louis gave Frankia to Charles. Lothair rebelled against his father."

I gave the subtlest of nods to my wife. I now knew all that I needed to know. This civil war would tear the Empire apart. I had been told that this was how the old Roman Empire had finally fallen. It had become rotten from within and crumbled.

Suddenly the Lady Eloise turned to me, "And what is the price of our freedom?"

She almost took me by surprise, "That is my son's decision. He captured you. I dare say when your husband learns that you have been taken then he will come to Rauville to recover you."

She laughed, "And when he does your son should be afraid for my husband leads the finest horsemen in the whole of the Empire. It is why he has not returned yet. He serves King Charles!" She gave me a sly look. "His return is imminent!"

That night I pondered her words. She sounded confident. My son had sent her for safekeeping. Perhaps he knew more than he had told me. I decided to take my men and join my son. I needed to speak with him. I would not be undermining his authority. Sometimes you are sent feelings and warnings. Sven had just crossed over to the Otherworld. Were the seeds of doubt in my mind sent by him? I would trust my feelings. That night a messenger came from Rurik. My son had sent to him for help. Perhaps the spirits had put the idea in my head. Whatever the reason I was glad that we had prepared.

Before I left I visited my smith. "I go to see my son. How goes his sword?"

He unwrapped a sheepskin. The blade had no pommel yet. It was just the blade and the tang. The guard was there but the decoration was not. He held it for me to see and I was impressed. The runes which were etched on the blade and the dragon were exquisite. "You have excelled yourself. When will it be finished?"

"The end of the month."

"Good for my son can wear it when his child is born."

My smith smiled, "Then the timing will be perfect. The blade and your grandchild will be the same age. It is *wyrd*."

It took time to organize my men. I sent word the next day and summoned Einar Bear Killer and Thorbolt. I spoke with Sigtrygg and asked him to watch the Haugr and continue building the harbour wall. We left after noon and headed towards Valognes. There I would speak with Rurik One Ear. Although no longer an active warrior he heard much.

I led ninety men. It was not a great force but it would suffice. Lady Eloise had some news which I did not. I was blind. Our land was so secure that no news came to us from the outside world. Dorestad and Dyflin were the only places from which we gleaned intelligence and they were far from the heart of the Empire. Perhaps Rurik could help.

I felt happier as we headed through the forest to Valognes. My old friend was pleased to see me. "I have been receiving messages from your son. He is doing well. I would hope that my sons prove to be as skilled when they are older."

"I know that I am lucky." I put my arm around Rurik's shoulders. He was wider now that he was older. He enjoyed a good life. I told him of the death of Sven the Helmsman.

He shook his head, "The Weird Sisters, Hrolf. They gave you Carentan and took an old comrade. I now regret not visiting with him more. And is Harold recovered?"

"He is and he is busy building a ship in memory of Sven."

"Then I will journey north and speak with him. I will take my sons. I will show them real Vikings!"

"What do you know of Charles and Lothair?"

He took me to a quiet corner of his hall, "I still have merchants who travel to the land of the Franks. I hear things. Charles and Louis are in Burgundy, close to Auxerre. There will be a battle for I have heard that Lothair has gathered many men to face his brothers."

"Then that may be the news that the Lady Eloise kept from me."

"The wife of Guillaume of Rauville?"

"The same."

"She is well connected, Hrolf, and dangerous. Guillaume of Rauville may have had a small manor but it was rumoured that he was to be given Carentan in exchange for his support."

Now I understood.

"Have you heard from my son lately?"

"He sent a message that he had defeated Eustace of Bruggas and Stephen of Caen. I think he was strengthening Carentan in case there was another attack." He smiled, "I think he yearns for his wife and unborn child. He sent another message, yesterday, asking for help. I sent what men I could. I have others who wish to fight but it took time to summon them."

I felt guilty. I had been so concerned with greater matters that I had forgotten the most important matter. I was going to have a grandchild and Ragnvald needed to be with his wife.

"Have you any men who could join us?"

"I have. There are twenty warriors who wish some glory and booty. As soon as we heard you were coming they pressed me to allow them to accompany you."

"Then all is well. We leave before dawn. I am anxious to reach my son. Since the death of Sven and the arrival of Lady Eloise I have had a bad feeling."

"Aye, you always did have that extra sense. It has saved the clan before now."

We headed down the main road to Carentan. Hitherto this might have risked conflict but with Rauville, Benni's Ville and Carentan in our hands we were more secure. We were halfway to Carentan when we were met by a rider. It was Gangráðr Galmrson.

"Jarl, I am lucky to have found you. My lord is being attacked. Guillaume of Rauville is approaching with many horsemen."

"Return and tell my son that we will be there. He should hold on. Tell him…" I shook my head, "my son does not need my advice. We will be there."

As he turned to gallop off I shouted, "Clan of the Horse, our shield brothers are in danger. We must run to war. Can you do it?"

"Aye, jarl!"

I dismounted as did my other jarls. It was not right that our men should run while we rode. We began the run. It was not the lung sucking run a warrior needs to ascend a defended hill. It was the easy lope that ate up the ground. We were travelling on a Roman Road and we made good time. The men sang as they ran. It helped to keep the time and ensured that our pace was not sapping energy. There were mile markers in places and we were able to see our progress. They counted down the Roman miles to Carentan. When we reached the one-mile mark we stopped.

"Prepare for war."

Shields were swung around and spears prepared. Those of us who had them, mounted our horses and we led the men at the same pace. As we emerged through the trees we heard the noise of battle. I saw that my son had built a palisaded camp beyond Carentan. I could see the blackened buildings of the town he had assaulted. The enemy soldiers were a sea of warriors. I saw their banners waving above the battle. The slope and the town itself were our allies.

"Einar and Thorbolt, take half of the men and go around the western side of the town. The rest with me. We will flank the Franks." I dismounted. I would be fighting in a shield wall. I took my spear. Fighting horsemen required a spear.

I had fifty men with me. There were Rurik's twenty warriors and the rest were men like Beorn Fast Feet and Erik Green Eye. They were dependable and, more importantly, they could think for themselves. We had half a mile to run. When a warrior fights in a battle, he has eyes before him. His comrades watch his back. The Franks had pressed around the flanks of my son's men. He had placed his horses on the flanks and they were fighting the Frankish horse. They were outnumbered. What we were about to do was almost suicidal. Men on foot were going to attack men on horses.

As we ran I shouted, "Wedge on me. Axes to the fore!"

The one advantage we had was that we had axes. They were the most effective weapons against a horse. Swung by a skilled axeman an axe could hack through the leg of a horse. That would be our tactic. It was Sigtrygg Rolfson and Gunnar Stone Face who were at my back. Both wielded the two-handed Danish axe. Both had been taken from the '*Black Drake*'. The Danes had good axes. They had black hearts but their blades were true.

As we neared them I saw my son's banner held by Sihtric. He was using his sword and guiding his horse with his knees. My son was standing in his stirrups and keeping three Franks at bay. I saw that his mail was covered in blood and gore. I hoped we had arrived in time.

"We run!"

The run was faster than a lope but we kept in time. I would have chanted but I wanted surprise. Even though we approached silently a couple of the warriors at the back turned and saw us when we were twenty paces from them. Four of them rode at us.

"Shields and spears!" A forest of spears appeared over our heads. The Franks were in for a shock. They thought we would move. We did not. I jammed my right foot against the shaft of the spear. At the same time, Gunnar and Sigtrygg swung their axes. The leading Frank found that his horse baulked at the hedgehog of spears. As my two axe men swung at the next two horses the leading Frank tried to rear his horse. I moved my spear forward and held my shield up. As the horse's hooves clattered against the shield, the horse's own weight impaled the beast on my spear. I dropped the spear as the horse fell and thrashed against two other dying horses.

Drawing my sword, I shouted, "Clan of the Horse!" I clambered over the dead horses, pausing only to drive my sword into the throat of the Frank who lay trapped beneath his dead horse. The Franks turned. We did not pause and we did not falter. This was the time for aggression. I swung my sword hard and hacked through the leg of the nearest warrior. My sword found the horse's flank and it reared in pain. As the rider fell he dragged the horse with him and they crashed into other warriors who were then prevented from getting to us. A sword flashed in the corner of my eye. I just managed to block it and then Erik Green Eye rammed his spear into the warrior. The horses were pressed into each other. The smell of blood and the screams of the dying horses made the horses of the Franks rear and try to back away from the whirling blades before them. The riders were too busy trying to control their animals to defend against us. We went for the easy blows. Unprotected legs were at the right height for a sword or axe swing. Spears could find the space under the arms.

I kept my shield up as I ploughed my way towards my son's banner. I hacked and I slashed. I heard a horn sound. The Franks were retreating. The only way they could go was towards the river. We did not relent in our attack and continued to cause as much damage to the enemy as we could. When I heard my son's horn sound the charge, I knew that we had won this part of the battle. My son and his men hurtled after the Franks as they headed for the forest and the river. There was little point in us following and so we went across the battlefield giving a warrior's death to the badly wounded Franks and ending the misery of horses which had been hacked and slashed by my men.

Folki and his men stood. I saw that he now had barely twenty-five men. He had fought well. The barrier of bodies was a testament to that. He took off his helmet as I approached, "A timely arrival, jarl. We could not have survived much longer."

"When did the attack begin?"

"They surprised us this morning. The ten men from Rurik were welcome but the enemy brought a mighty host. This was not the levy we defeated last time. This was Guillaume of Rauville and his men. There were almost two hundred horsemen. Knowing that he had sent to you for your help your son decided to fight a defensive battle. He charged the Franks at the top of the slope. When we defeated Eustace of Bruggas we were able to break their line. Ragnvald realised that was impossible for they had a much deeper line. We waited and our horsemen charged to stop the Franks from overwhelming us. It almost worked but then another hundred men appeared from the woods. We were close to breaking."

"I am sorry I did not come sooner."

Einar Bear Killer appeared with six prisoners, "Jarl I thought you would like to question these men."

"Aye."

"Whom do you serve?"

One of the men spat at me and said, "I do not speak to barbarians!"

Einar whipped out his seax and ripped it up into the warrior's guts. He twisted it and pulled out intestines. He pushed the man to the ground. He would take time to die.

I pointed to the youngest of the warriors. "There are many ways to die! Einar could take your manhood and make you bleed to death slowly. Answer me!"

An old warrior said, "I will answer you and then you can end my life for you are about to be punished by King Charles and God!"

"Charles has been crowned?"

"It is a matter of time, Viking. He and King Louis of Bavaria have defeated Lothair at Fontenoy. My master will be crowned."

"Charles is here?"

He shook his head. Count Guillaume of Carentan commands."

"Is this the same lord who ruled Rauville?"

"It is. King Charles rewarded him for his courage at the battle of Fontenoy. I commanded the king's men who were sent to rescue his family."

I nodded, "You have made a poor stab at it!" I turned, "Beorn Fast Feet. Take six men and escort these Franks to the bridge." The old warrior looked surprised. "You have answered me honestly and I will use you as our emissaries. Tell your count that he can have his family returned to him upon payment of a ransom."

"And what is the price?"

"Five hundred gold pieces and Carentan."

He laughed, "You might as well kill me now for he will not agree to that. He has just been given Carentan!"

I spoke slowly, "Then his wife and daughters will be taken to the slave market in Dyflin and sold. It is that simple."

"You are a cruel man. I will do as you ask."

"What is your name?"

"Bernard of Chinon."

"I will see you on the battlefield."

"And only one of us will leave."

"As the Allfather wills it!"

I saw him clutch his cross as he left. We kept their swords and helmets. Folki asked, "Is his wife worth the price, jarl?"

"She is well connected, Folki. Her father was cousin to the old king which means, I am guessing, that she is related to all three brothers."

"Then he will pay."

Einar shook his head, "We did not slay many of their men. They still outnumber us. What if they chose to go to the Haugr and take her by force."

I had not thought of that and the image of my home being besieged sent shivers racing through my blood. There was but one drekar crew to defend the walls. "Then we will have to bring him to battle. Let us wait to see what he says."

I saw my son leading his horse up the slope. His men were doing the same. The animals were all lathered. The men had bloody mail. Although I saw Alain, Gilles and Bertrand I saw that many of our men had fallen. We did not have as many horsemen as we once did. The Franks were like sand on a beach. They had vast numbers of men. They could afford to lose horsemen and we could not.

"We chased them back across the river. They are camped to the south of it."

I clasped my son's right arm, "I am truly proud of you, Ragnvald. You have done far more than we could have hoped."

He nodded, "Had you reached us sooner then more of my men would be alive."

Einar Bear Killer said, "Ragnvald! Your father has barely had time to spend one night under his own roof. Did Folki not tell you of the treachery of the Danes?"

Folki shook his head, "I did not want the young warrior distracted, Einar Bear Killer. He bore a great weight upon his shoulders. If I am in the wrong then the jarl can punish me."

I shook my head, "I am the one who is in the wrong. I should have come sooner. However, I think that this is the work of the Weird Sisters. Who could have known that Charles would have defeated his brother?"

Ragnvald looked up at me, "He is King of Frankia then?"

"It is what his men believe and he must have claimed the field. Why else would he allow one of his better lords to travel so many leagues? You did well to send his wife to the Haugr but we must tread carefully. Ragnvald, take your horsemen into Carentan. They need rest. We have lost too many to risk them. Einar Bear Killer has planted an unwelcome seed in my mind. What if this Frank tries to go to the Haugr and take her by force? Yours is the only force that could reach your mother before the enemy. I want you in reserve. We will defend this palisade if we have to."

They nodded and began to move off. Ragnvald stayed by me. "I am learning, father. Leadership is not as easy as men think. You have to think of many things at once. I was arrogant enough to believe I had the besting of the Franks. When

Count Eustace was defeated so easily I thought that this army would be equally easy to defeat. I was wrong."

"And that is how we learn, my son, from our mistakes. Sadly," I waved a hand at our dead who were already being taken from the field, "those lessons are paid for in men's blood."

"I have lost good warriors. I am down to my last eight oathsworn. The rest perished."

"Then you know how I feel for there are less than four warriors left now from those who left Raven Wing Island with me. I feel their spirits each time I fight and it makes me more determined to do well for their sake." I put my arm around him. "Whatever happens you will be with your wife in three days' time."

"Three days?"

"I cannot see this Frank taking longer than that to either fight us or race north to find his wife. You and your best men must be ready to ride if there is any sign that he intends to do this."

Ragnvald pointed to the bridge. "The bridge is the furthest point west. We need to watch there. It is a wooden bridge. If he tries to use horsemen we will hear him."

"You have not forgotten how to scout then. I will send Beorn Fast Feet to watch. He is the best of my scouts."

He nodded and trudged wearily away. In truth, I was tired. We had marched hard to reach Carentan. However, I had much to do. "Thorbolt, I want your men to deepen the ditch. Einar, take some of your men to the woods to the north of us and cut down stakes to protect us from a frontal attack."

"The men are tired, jarl."

"They can sleep when they are dead. A little work now will save lives and ensure a sound night's sleep." They nodded and headed off. I waved over Beorn Fast Feet, "I want you to keep watch on the bridge. If the Franks try to cross it I need to know. I fear they may try to go directly to our home."

"I will take Galdr with me. He is skilled."

"Good."

I went to the palisade which Ragnvald and his men had thrown up. It would not stand up to a determined attack but it would slow down an attacker and allow the archers to slaughter many of the enemy. It was why I sought to improve it. The count's horsemen could cover great distances but they were ill-equipped to take walls. I was counting on that.

Einar and his men were planting the stakes when an emissary rode up to speak with us. He was a well-equipped horseman. His scale armour byrnie was burnished as was his high helm with the red horsehair plume. He carried the helmet beneath his arm. He had a long sword. It was like the Roman spatha. Handy when used on a horse but useless in a shield wall. I guessed that he had seen Roman armour and mail and was trying to copy it. His shield was painted red with a golden cross upon it. "The Count of Carentan would speak with you."

I nodded, "We are going nowhere. Tell him to advance."

"The count does not trust barbarians. He says he will meet you halfway between the river and here. You may bring one man with you."

"Very well." As he turned away I said, "Erik Long Hair, go and find my son. Fetch us two horses which are not tired."

"Aye, jarl."

I took out my comb and began to groom myself. I then sharpened my sword. By the time I had finished Ragnvald had arrived and Erik had the two horses. "Fetch me my wolf cloak. Let us not disappoint the Franks who are expecting barbarians."

"Aye, jarl."

Alain of Auxerre had come with my son, "Lord, the count is there at the meeting point."

I looked over my shoulder. He was there with the young man. "Good." I pointed to my son's sword. "Bagsecg says your new blade will be ready before your son is born."

"How do you know it will be a boy? Are you a galdramenn, too?"

"I feel it in my bones."

"Lord, they are waiting."

"I know, Alain, and I intend them to wait a little longer." I shaded my eyes against the sun. "It will soon be dusk. I need night time to prepare for their attack on the morrow."

"You know they will attack?"

"Of course, for I will make sure that they have no option. He cannot have the ransom yet and he will be anxious to have his family returned to him. The only way he can do that is to defeat us and then send his horsemen to the Haugr. The longer he waits for us the angrier he will become and an angry man never makes wise decisions. Ragnvald, put an edge on your sword."

He grinned, "Aye, jarl!"

I carefully fixed my wolf cloak about my shoulders and made sure that I had a seax in my boot and in my belt. When Ragnvald sheathed his sword I said, "Let us ride but we will make it leisurely."

As we headed down to the meeting Ragnvald pointed to a blackened storm struck tree. We stopped so that I could see it. "At the height of the first battle Thor sent a thunderbolt down and it destroyed the tree. It put fear in the hearts of our foes."

It was *wyrd*. "Your mother thinks that you may become a Christian because you have married Mathilde."

He laughed, "And the sun may rise tonight instead of setting. I do not object to my wife's religion but it is nonsense. Turn the other cheek?" He shook his head. "And they do not respect nature. How can you live on this earth if you do not understand it?"

We meandered down to the count. His face was as black as the Thor struck tree. "You disrespect me!"

"How? We came bareheaded. Our hands are not near our weapons. I was speaking with my son. I am sure you would enjoy speaking with your children."

The young warrior said, "We do not need to talk, lord. Let me kill them both and be done with it."

I said nothing.

Count Guillaume smiled, "There will be time for that Matfrid. It is courtesy to speak and although these barbarians do not deserve such treatment we will show them that we are better than they are."

"If this meeting is just to insult us then we will return to our men. We have many of your horses to butcher and to eat." I began to pull my horse's head around.

"This is intolerable! Bernard of Chinon gave me your terms. They are unacceptable."

"Really? I thought your wife quite pretty in a homely sort of way. Is this how a Frank rids himself of an unwanted family? They allow them to be taken and sold as slaves."

"You would not dare."

"A Viking dare do anything he wishes for he does not answer to a king. If that is all, then, good evening."

As I turned the young warrior suddenly drew his sword and galloped at me. My back was to him and I knew that even as I turned my horse I would not be able to draw my weapon. Suddenly there was a blur as my son drew his own sword and parried the strike. My son has good hands and fast reflexes. He whipped out his seax and he flicked his sword at the young warrior as he slashed through the reins of the horse. His seax caught the animal on the jaw and it suddenly took off. Matfrid the Frank could not keep his saddle and he was unceremoniously dumped to the ground.

I shook my head, "The price has now doubled. You have two days to fetch it." Shaking my head, I said, "And you speak of honour! You know not the word. Ragnvald, take our new horse. Call it weregeld, Count, and think yourself lucky that we do not take your life as well."

My son grabbed the cut reins and led the horse back up the slope. The young warrior still lay unmoving. I did not think he was seriously hurt. He had just taken a knock.

"Tomorrow, Viking, you and your spawn will all die."

I turned in the saddle, "We all die, Count, it is the manner which is important. I will be content so long as I die with a sword in my hand. And you? How will you greet your god?"

Ragnvald Hrolfsson

As we neared our camp I said to my son, "Tomorrow it will be a shield wall which greets the count. A shield wall and arrows. I want you and your men mounted and ready to ride. If I sound the horn three times then you are to attack the Franks. If it is just once then send half of your men to your home and the rest to the Haugr."

"What of you?"

"We will stand come what may. The count will look for you. He will be wary. It will cross his mind that we are trying to trick him. He will be cautious in his approach and that is what I want. I need him to come slowly. I intend to have half of my men behind the palisade on the ditch we will build this night. I want to make the ground before the gate a killing ground. I will tempt him into the open gates."

"It is a bold plan and has many risks."

I shrugged, "Had I known how many men we were facing I would have brought Sigtrygg, Bárekr and Rurik. This is the best that I can manage."

As we neared Carentan my son said, "Folki would rule Carentan if you would let him. He wishes to have roots and we are close to the sea."

"That sounds like a perfect solution but we will say nothing until the battle is fought and won."

My captains and jarls were waiting. They had all seen what had occurred. Their faces showed their approval.

"I have given them two days to fetch the gold. They will not, of course. Tonight, I want pits digging before our stakes. The pits will be ankle breakers. A short stake will be in each one. The spoil will be taken inside to make a step. Half of our men, the ones without mail, will be inside the walls with bows. We will cover the pits with brushwood. Place the dead Franks between the pits. They will not wish to trample their own dead. I will leave the gates open. If my plan goes awry and they do not take the bait then we will fall back inside the palisade and make a shield wall. I will sound the horn three times and our horsemen will encircle the enemy."

Einar Bear Killer shook his head, "All this came from your mind, jarl? You are like Aiden of the Land of the Wolf."

"I am not but I take the compliment."

I joined my men as soon as it was dark and we dug. The wet earth helped us. That was the work of the gods. We found much brushwood in the woods to the north and when we replaced the turf on top of it, was hard to see where we had dug the pits. If they chose to ride north then our work would have been in vain but I was confident that, knowing the land as we did, our horsemen could easily reach the Haugr before the Franks.

I walked with Ragnvald, Einar, Thorbolt and Folki when the work had been done. We knew where to step. We walked close by the dead Franks. They were the safe path. "I am counting on the fact that they will be looking for your horsemen to spring the trap. If they are hidden in Carentan then he will not see them. He might wonder where you are but that uncertainty will work to our advantage. They will see the stakes, our shield wall and the spears. He may think the horsemen wait inside the palisade. When he is close enough he will charge with his horsemen. Our traps will only work for a short time but that will be time enough to break the spirit of the enemy."

Chapter 14

I left Folki in command and joined my son and his horsemen inside Carentan. I had never been inside the town and I wanted to see what it was like. I saw how my son had taken it. I hearkened back to our conversation all those moons ago. He had impressed me then. He had done well. The town was larger than Valognes and better built. It would need a great deal of work if it was to regain its former glory. There had been no lord here for a couple of years and it showed. I sat with Ragnvald, Alain, Gilles and Bertrand in what had been the home of the Lord of Carentan. If he won then that would be Guillaume of Carentan.

"I am sorry that you lost warriors."

Bertrand shrugged, "That is what warriors do. They fight. If they fight then they risk death."

Gilles looked pensive. "What is it, Gilles? You know you can speak openly in front of me. You were the first to follow my banner."

"I do not enjoy horses being slaughtered and, if I am to be honest, I do not enjoy fighting. I am not a very good Viking."

I could see that my son was shocked at Gilles words. "You are part of the Clan of the Horse. Not all are warriors. Erik One Arm and his wife Brigid make ale and we could not exist without that. Rurik One Ear does not fight yet he holds a vital town for us. Harold Fast Sailing will war no longer; he will make ships. And you, Gilles, you will breed horses so that those who wish to fight as warriors can do so."

I saw the relief on his face. "I am not a coward, lord!"

"I know. We each play our own part. Even the priests of the White Christ who serve us. They heal and they give their own kind of sustenance to those like my wife and Ragnvald's. Just fight for me tomorrow and when this is over you can return to your horses. I believe that the dawn will bring a battle and that will be an ending of sorts."

I was wrong. We rose before dawn and my archers filtered silently to stand on the new fighting step. Ragnvald and my horsemen prepared their horses and I stood with my warriors in a five-deep line before our gates. And, yet, the Franks did not come. We saw them moving to the river to water their horses and we saw men foraging in the woods but they did not come. I sent men to relieve Beorn Fast Feet. He had been the closest to the enemy.

"Two men tried to sneak through the woods last night, jarl. We slew one and the other returned to the camp."

"Rest for the day and then return tonight. I would have your sharp eyes there." I wondered what the Frank was up to. Did he have reinforcements coming? I thought I had annoyed him enough to make him attack. Obviously, I had not. By the time the sun was rising high towards noon, it was obvious that they were not coming and we stood down. We were vigilant but I was confident they would not come. I summoned Ragnvald and Alain of Auxerre, "Come let us ride."

I led them towards the east. The river was to our right and we rode just fifty paces from its north bank. There appeared to be many smaller streams crisscrossing the land. At times, we had to head further north to avoid the mud and salt pools. The river was shallow. I could see that when we drew near to it. When the rains my son had told me about had inundated the land then it would have been hard to cross but now we could have forded it almost anywhere. It reminded me of the land of the Isle of the Sheep save that this was even more desolate. When we passed the Frank camp I saw that they had their horses well to the south of their main camp. It was better grazing. The camp itself would have no grass left after the tramping of so many boots.

As we approached the sea I saw that there were no houses. The land was low lying and swampy. If Folki wished to use it as a harbour he would have some work to do. We stopped at the sea. Dunes marked its edge. The lack of white water told me that there were no rocks there. Perhaps the channel could be dredged. It would be a lot of work.

"Son, you have better eyes than we do. What can you see out to sea?" I thought I detected something on the horizon but I could not make it out.

"There is a ship. It is not a drekar. It rides higher in the water. It looks like a Frank. She is sailing north."

As I turned my horse to head back to our camp I saw a knot of riders to the south of the swampy river. They were watching us.

Ragnvald asked, "Did they follow us?"

I shook my head. "There was no one south of us. They were already here. The question is why? This count is being trickier than I expected. I thought I had done enough yesterday to make him attack. Perhaps we will have to try something different this night."

"Different?"

"Yes, Alain. We will try to be Ulfheonar. We will not be as good as Jarl Dragonheart and his men but we may be able to do enough to irritate them."

"What happens if he does not send the ransom?"

"Then I keep my word. I send a rider back to the Haugr and instruct Siggi Far-Sighted to take the knarr to Dyflin and sell them. If you make a threat then you must see it through."

When we reached the camp, I sent for my jarls. "I want the best men you have for knife work. I need men who can hide and move silently." I smiled at Einar Bear Killer. "That rules you out, Einar! I need men who can ride a horse without falling off!"

My men all laughed for Einar was a bull of a man. In a shield wall, there was none better. He nodded. He knew his limitations better than most.

"Send them to me at sunset."

I began to plan what I would do. There was a ladder against the wall of the palisade. I climbed it to look at the bridge and the Frank camp. They had a line of sentries before the bridge and along the river. They were taking no chances. I saw that, in places, the river was still wide after the rains. I knew that it would be shallow too. The woods were also guarded. When we had ridden east I had seen that they only had the river guarded for forty paces beyond the bridge. I had worked out that the bridge was there to help carts and wagons. A man or a horse could walk or swim across it. That was what we would do.

The men who had been selected arrived as the sun was setting in the west. I had chosen Einar Asbjornson, Erik Long Hair and Beorn Fast Feet from my men. I would have to have others watching for riders heading north. The other ten were all small, lithe warriors. These were the men who were not in the front rank of a shield wall for they were not the biggest of warriors but they had skills with blades. They would be perfect for what I intended.

"We take just seaxes. We wear no mail. I intend to slay their sentries and then make our way around their camp to their horse herd. We slip onto the back of the horses and drive them through the camp. If we can bring some back to our camp then so much the better but my aim is to annoy them and make them fear a night attack. The only risk I want you to take is to get to their horses. No matter how many horses we take it will be a victory. I want no heroes. No one will make a song of this." I smiled. "In truth, I would be embarrassed if this story got back to Jarl Dragonheart. He might think I was trying to be as his wolves and we are not."

Beorn said, "Jarl, you and Ulf Big Nose could have been Ulfheonar but we will try to be silent and return here. I would rather die with a sword in my hand than a seax!"

"Good then let us prepare. Use charcoal to darken your faces and hands. It will suffice."

I took two seaxes. One I tucked into my boot and the other in my belt. As soon as it was dark I led my men a mile to the east of our camp and headed down to the wetland around the river. Although the mud was thick it did not suck at our boots. Progress was slow. We had hours. Once we reached the river we began to wade. The sound of the water hid the noise of our crossing. It came up to my chin at one point but then it began to shallow again. Once on the semi-dry land again we moved cautiously, sniffing the air. The Franks would smell differently from us. It was the food they ate. We moved out of the water towards the horses.

My plan was to slay the guards around the horse herd and then stampede them. Charging horses could be as deadly as warriors with swords. We had travelled far enough west to be beyond their sentries. We could hear the sounds of the camp. Men were gambling, arguing, laughing. We crept close to the guards. Once we saw them we lay down. The nearest was twenty paces from us. We could see their position by their helmets. The distant fires reflected from the metal. We were in a long line but all of my men were watching me for the signal to strike. First, I had to establish how many there were. They were not making the cardinal mistake of standing close to each other and talking. There were six of them on our side and they were twenty paces apart. I pointed to two men and then at the guard who was on the extreme right. I worked my way down the line so that each Frank had two men who would take them. Erik Long Hair and I were the only two without men to strike. We would act as a reserve in case we had missed someone.

Once I saw that we were in position we began to crawl. The guards were not looking down. They were watching the herd and then turning to look towards Carentan. I saw Beorn Fast Feet and Azil Finnison as they closed with the centre guard. They waited until he turned to look at the herd and then rose like two wraiths. The three of them disappeared and then Azil rose with the Frank's helmet on his head. I looked down the line. Beorn and Azil had been fast but I saw shadows rise, men fall and then my men rise to take the place of the dead sentry. Once the sentries had been despatched I waved my men forward.

We now had six swords as well; they had been taken from the Franks. We headed to the centre of the herd. I led and I stroked the mane of one horse as I moved through them. My men followed me. Some men have an affinity for animals. I was one and horses seemed to like me. They moved away from us but slowly as though they were seeking more grass. I saw that some of the larger horses were tethered to stakes. They would be the horses of the nobles. They were the better horses. I pointed to the tethered horses and my men nodded. They would be easier to steal. We could cut the tether and then use that as makeshift reins.

I found a golden coloured horse. I stroked his mane and then breathed into his muzzle. He raised his head and seemed to nod. I reached down and, holding the rope, cut it free from its stake. I saw my men standing next to tethered horses. I slipped across the back of the golden coloured horse. He snorted. I lay flat along his neck while I watched my other men do the same. The three biggest warriors were me, Erik and Beorn. All the others were small. It made them harder to see. When we were all mounted I began to move towards the rear of the horses. There were more guards there and it was a risk but this way we could cause more confusion.

It was Beorn who was spotted. One of the guards saw him and shouted an alarm. Beorn slew him with the Frankish sword but the time for silence was gone. I shouted, "Clan of the Horse!" and began shouting and screaming loudly. It would frighten the horses and make the Franks think that there were more of us than there were. My men took up the shouts. I slapped the rump of my horse with the flat of my seax and he bounded north, towards the bridge. Our fourteen horses made the others move. The sound of our shouts and screams added to it. The fact that the remaining guards all ran after us helped to make the animals panic. Some of those which were still tethered tried to run and they pulled their stakes. As the wood whirled through the air the stakes struck other animals and made them panic even more. We had our stampede. There were over a hundred horses galloping through the Frank camp. I saw one warrior with a pulped mess where his skull had been. I saw others thrown to the ground.

I kept low. I dug my heels into the horse and I headed for the bridge. I saw that Azil was slightly behind me and I slowed up my horse. Azil was not a horseman. He could ride but I was a horseman. When he passed me, I saw that I was the last. That was as it should be. I watched Beorn swing his sword and hack through the chest of one of the guards on the bridge. The others hurled themselves into the water. Some of the horses leapt into the water. As I had suspected it was not deep. A warrior ran at me, as I neared the bridge. He had a spear. As he tried to lunge at me the gods came to my aid and a black stallion crashed into him. The hooves of my horse clattered over the bridge. Something whizzed over my back as someone threw a spear at me. Then I felt the squishy, soft, churned up ground.

"Drive the horses towards Carentan. Avoid our traps! Take as many as we can."

I glanced around and saw twelve other riders. We had lost one. I could not see who it was. We had fifty horses. Thirteen of them were the horses of nobles. The count would be angry. He would have his nobles complaining of the delay. I knew not why he had delayed but there would be a reason. Was he expecting more men? Had the ship my son had seen landed men north of us? Was a force coming to outflank us? I had more questions than answers but I had a small victory.

My son had my horsemen ready to calm the horses. The gentle, muddy slope had slowed them up as I had known it would. They were easily caught and with my twelve riders behind them, we drove them into Carentan.

"Who did we lose?"

"Azil. One of the Franks at the bridge struck him. The Frank died but Azil was speared."

I nodded. I had allowed him to go ahead of me. If I had been where he was would I have been killed?

I dismounted and, holding the rope, stroked the horse. "You are a fine animal. I shall name you Azil in honour of a brave warrior."

Ragnvald and Gilles joined me. Gilles examined him. "He has not been gelded, lord. I would breed from him if you would let me."

"Of course. His name is Azil. Take him tomorrow, Gilles. I would have you ride home. Leave your men for my son to command."

"Lord I know what I said to you earlier but I would do my duty here."

"You misunderstand me, Gilles. I need you to go to the Haugr. I fear that the Franks have something planned for my home. This suits us both. One warrior will not make a difference when we battle."

He nodded, "I am yours to command, lord."

Once again, we were in our positions before dawn. And this time the Franks did not disappoint. Our sentries had reported a heated argument in the Frank camp. As dawn broke we saw them preparing for war. Gilles had left almost as soon as I had given him permission. As I looked at the sun begin to climb I guessed that he would be almost home. He would spend a few hours with his wife before heading to the Haugr. I knew I should have sent word sooner but I had vacillated. Indecision was never the right decision. The men around me were buoyant. We had lost but one man and gained good horses. Their jarl had bloodied the Franks and angered them.

As the Franks arrayed we prepared to meet them. The delay had meant that the Frank's bodies were now swollen and bloated. The stench of death hung over the field. We would normally have disposed of them but they were an ally now and we would use whatever we could.

Our raid meant that some of the Franks would have to fight dismounted. They were not the nobles. They were the warriors without mail; the poorer ones. The nobles who had lost horses had confiscated the mounts from others. Their horsemen equalled my whole warband but that suited me. I saw warriors wearing the count's colours in the second rank but I could not see the count. Matfrid, the headstrong young warrior, was leading the warriors. He rode next to the banner of Guillaume of Carentan. They had to be related. Close by was Bernard of Chinon. He carried the banner of Charles the Bald. Both would be coming for me. There was bad blood between us.

The Franks were moving slowly up the slope. That made sense. Their horses had been running during the night and would not be as fresh as they might have wished. They would save the energy for a charge when they were two hundred paces from us. They would have fifty paces to get up to speed and then they would hit the traps. Eighty paces later they would hit the stakes and then they would find the spears and shields of my men.

I stepped from the line to face my men. "Today we are going to fight more than three times our number. I am not worried. Are you?"

They banged their shields and yelled, as one, "No, jarl!"

"They will charge and they will think that we will flinch. We are the Clan of the Horse and we do not flinch. We do not even blink! We will take whatever they throw at us and we will not move. Three blasts on the horn will summon my son and our horsemen. Your signal to attack will be two blasts! Clan of the Horse!"

"Clan of the Horse!" They began a cacophony of banging and cheering. They were ready for battle.

I stepped back between Folki and Erik Long Hair. Thorbolt and his men anchored one wing while Einar Bear Killer the other. The centre was made up of my men. Our spears were at our side and our shields rested on the ground. There was no hurry. The Franks were still advancing. My men would lift their shields and present their spears when I did. It intimidated the enemy. They would see us and wonder that we were not nervous.

The ground began to thunder as Matfrid and Bernard pointed their spears at us and their horn sounded once. They began to lope along the ground. When they reached two hundred paces I heard a shout from Bernard of Chinon. His words could not be made out for the horses were thundering. I lifted my shield and my spear. Folki and Erik locked the shields with mine. I placed my spear against my right foot and supported it with my left hand. Four spears appeared above my head. We did not raise the shields of the second and third rank. There were no archers facing us. The shields of those warriors were pressed into our backs and their spears protected us. Behind the palisade, Beorn Fast Feet and Erik Green Eye stood with my archers. They would be sending their arrows over the wooden wall blindly. Beorn would command them and direct them. They knew their range and not an arrow would be wasted.

The men in the fourth and fifth ranks began to chant and bang their spears against the shields. It was a rhythmic chant. It seemed almost hypnotic as though they were summoning the Franks onto our blades. It filled those of us in the front rank with pride. It was a reminder that our shield brothers were as one with us.

> *Clan of the Horseman*
> *Warriors strong*
> *Clan of the Horseman*
> *Our reach is long*
> *Clan of the Horseman*
> *Fight as one*
> *Clan of the Horseman*
> *Death will come*
> *Clan of the Horseman*

Ragnvald Hrolfsson

Warriors strong
Clan of the Horseman
Our reach is long
Clan of the Horseman
Fight as one
Clan of the Horseman
Death will come

I saw the young warrior, Matfrid, stand in his stiraps as he urged on his men. Bernard of Chinon, in contrast, had his lance couched and was watching the ground. Matfrid's exhortations worked against him for some of his younger warriors urged their horses on to reach us as quickly as they could. It was they who discovered the traps. One Frankish horse hit the first trap. There was a sickening crunch as the animal's legs were broken and the rider was pitched from the horse. His neck cracked and broke when he hit the ground. Another horse caught a trap and fell to the side. It hit another horse and that was knocked into a third one. I heard Bernard of Chinon shout, "Ride on the bodies! Ride on the bodies!"

That was easier said than done for the horses baulked at stepping on a man even though he was dead. The ones that did found a slippery bloated corpse. One erupted as the stomach gases were released sending guts into the air. Horses screamed to avoid them. All cohesion was gone. The warriors were too busy watching the ground to even see us and it was then, when they were a hundred and eighty paces from us, that Beorn unleashed the arrows. Fifteen men and horses fell with the first flight of arrows. None had their shields up and a plunging arrow could be deadly. As men began to raise shields so more went into the traps. Sadly for us, they were almost through the traps but now they had stakes and caltrops to negotiate. They were easier to see but the arrows still fell and I saw one young Frank raise his shield and look up only for his horse to swerve and avoid a stake. The warrior lost his balance and was pitched onto a stake where he briefly wriggled and then died.

"Ready!"

We had thinned their ranks but the leading riders were almost through the obstacles. Matfrid and Bernard both rode their horses at me. Once again, that suited me. They were coming for the centre of our line where we had the best warriors with the best mail and experience.

"Thrust." The front rank all lunged with their spears as the horses approached. It would not actually hurt any of the horses but it would make them stop and turn. We had discovered the technique when we had been training with Ragnvald and Alain's horsemen. Of course, even though the horses were stopped, it did not stop the riders from thrusting down at us with their own

157

spears. Their spears struck shields and when I thrust again my spear sank into the shoulder of Matfrid's horse. It reared and screamed. Erik Long Hair rammed his spear into the belly of the beast. It fell backwards. This time Matfrid managed to land half on his feet. He stumbled but he remained conscious.

Bernard of Chinon was a wily old warrior. He turned his horse so that his shield was to us and then, standing in his stiraps he lunged down at me. I fended off the spear with my own. The Frank's spear clattered off Folki's shield and then I punched with the boss of my shield. It hit his knee.

Suddenly I heard a roared challenge and Matfrid ran towards me with a sword raised. He used a dead horse as a springboard to throw his body into the air. I just had time to shout, "Shields!" before he stuck my shield. The men behind and to the side leaned into me. It must have been like jumping into a wall. He fell backwards and I rammed my spear into his middle. He was skewered. He twisted and turned in his death throes and tore my spear from my hand. I released it and reached for my sword. As I did so, Bernard of Chinon saw his chance. He thrust his spear towards my unguarded right side. I just had time to sweep my hand around and grab the shaft. He was a strong man and the spearhead ground into some of the mail links on my byrnie but it held. I pulled. He must have been unbalanced for he tumbled from his horse and landed at my feet. I swung the boss of my shield and it smacked into his face. His nose and mouth were a bloody mess and he lay unconscious.

I risked looking along the line. The Franks had not penetrated very far and we were holding. Arrows still fell amongst those advancing and all impetus had gone. The banner of Carentan and Charles the Bald lay with their riders.

Drawing my sword, I saw that it was time! "Sound the horn three times!" The horn sounded. I saw Franks pause in their fighting and pull their shields tighter. They expected us to attack them. We did not. I heard a cheer and then the sound of galloping hooves as Ragnvald, Bertrand and Alain of Auxerre led my horsemen to sweep around the rear of the Frank's line.

"Sound the horn twice!" As the horn sounded I said, "Erik Long Hair, guard my prisoner. He is worth more to us alive than dead."

"Aye, jarl!"

"Forward!"

> *Clan of the Horseman*
> *Warriors strong*
> *Clan of the Horseman*
> *Our reach is long*
> *Clan of the Horseman*
> *Fight as one*
> *Clan of the Horseman*
> *Death will come*

My men chanted as they stepped forward. The archers still sent goose fletched death into the warriors waiting to get at us. The ones closest to us were battered and bloodied and now the untouched warriors at the rear were assaulted by fresh warriors on fresh horses. I blocked a spear and hacked through the throat of a horse. The horse slid to the side and thrashed its legs before dying, pinning its rider to the ground. I plunged my sword into his neck. We moved towards the river. We were like beaters driving game towards hunters. Ragnvald and my horsemen slew all who tried to pass them. I heard a shout as Beorn led my archers into the fray. With seaxes and shields, they were able to finish off the wounded and disembowelled horses.

When I heard warriors cry, "Yield! We yield! For the love of God, mercy!" then I knew that we had won.

I relented and ordered the butchery to stop. Some men had to be restrained for the blood lust was upon them. I looked at my warriors. Their mail was besmirched with blood and their swords notched. I saw that some of my warriors had fallen but more had survived.

Ragnvald stood in his stiraps and shouted, "Hrolf the Horseman! Hrolf the Horseman! Hrolf the Horseman!" Over and over. We had won but where, I wondered, was the count? I had not seen him in the battle and I had not passed his body.

I shouted, "Alain, take some men and capture their camp. Find the count!"

"Aye, lord!"

We gathered the prisoners and put them into the palisade. Any who looked as though they were nobles were kept to one side. The rest, the ones to be enslaved, were bound, hand and foot. The enemy dead were stripped of their mail and their treasure while our own dead were laid reverently in neat lines. We would bury them when time allowed. I had Bernard of Chinon taken into Carentan. I would question him later.

I took off my helmet and sent one of the archers for a pail of water. My son rode up. "A great victory, father."

"It was." I saw him looking north and west. "You wish to go home?"

"My wife's time is drawing near. I would be there for her."

I nodded. "When Alain returns then you can take your men home. You have done more than I dreamed possible. We will send your share of the treasure."

I saw the relief on his face, "Thank you."

The pail of water arrived and I tipped it over my head. It ran red. Folki was doing the same, "Folki, my son said that you would be jarl here at Carentan?"

He looked embarrassed, "I said that I would like that but I know I am just a warrior and do not deserve that honour."

"Of course you deserve it and it is yours. If any other warriors wish to stay with you then that would be good." I saw some of those around nodding. The last

159

of the Otters had survived and they were speaking together. The men we had brought from Valognes also nodded. I saw the webs of the Weird Sisters. Folki would be starting anew but he would have warriors from three clans. I pointed east, "However, I am not sure that it would be a good port. The river is too shallow."

He smiled, "It will give me something to plan. Besides, jarl, I have walls to rebuild. Your son made a real mess of my home!"

The men all laughed. I turned as I saw Alain and his men driving pack animals and servants towards us. The beasts and the men were laden.

"The Franks had fled, lord, but they left their treasure. The count was not there. These men say he left yesterday morning. They did not know where he went save that he took his oathsworn warriors, all ten of them, a priest and a bishop. They went west and the servants believe that they took ship. I believe that they do not know where he went but if you wish I can..."

I shook my head. "We have Bernard of Chinon. He will tell us. My son, you may leave. When I have been to the Haugr I will come and see your new home!"

The enemy dead were piled together. We used the prisoners to move the bloated bodies from the first battle. Using seal oil, we set fire to them. It was not what they wanted but I had the people of Carentan to think about. I did not wish Folki to begin life as a lord and have the plague ruin it for him.

Before I spoke with Bernard I gathered the people of Carentan together.

"This is your new lord, Folki Kikisson. He rules here for me. He is a just man but all of you should know that if you feel that you have been badly treated by my man then you must come and speak with me at the Haugr. All of those who live in my land shall have the same justice. All that has changed is the name of your lord. You are no longer Franks, you are Northmen. You are my people." I turned to Folki, "Rule them wisely, my friend."

Bernard had been taken to the church and had been tended to by the priest. "You are here to gloat before you end my life?"

I shook my head, "No, but you can answer a question. Where has the count gone? Back to Paris or Fontenoy?"

He laughed, "No, Viking. He has gone to your home for his family. He took the Bishop of Reims with him. Bishop Ebbo is the Pope's representative."

"With a handful of men, he will not storm my walls. He will still be there when I return home."

"Viking, you are a good warrior but you know nothing of the games that lords can play. I wager my life that when you reach your home the count's family will not be there."

There was no lie in his eyes. I had been duped but how? How could he have spirited them away? "And who was this Matfrid?"

"He was the count's young brother. He said that he would defeat you while his brother found his family. You dishonoured him and he wanted vengeance."

Ragnvald Hrolfsson

"And you should have exercised your authority. You know my reputation! You are responsible for that young man's death and you will have to live with it." I turned and said, "Erik Long Hair, bind him. We will take him to the Haugr. I am not finished with him yet!"

Chapter 15

Although I was desperate to get home I had much to do and it was not until the next morning that we were ready to travel. I gave Bertrand half of the horses we had captured. He would share them with Ragnvald. My men were able to ride back. There were enough horses. We even had spares to carry the booty we had taken from the battlefield. We parted at Valognes. I only stayed long enough to tell Rurik what had happened. He was philosophical about it. "You were never one to play games, Hrolf. That is the way of the Franks and not you. If the prize has been snatched away then there will be others. Besides, this old Frank may be lying. Leave him with me and I shall make him talk."

"No, old friend. We will travel home."

When we met Gilles, as he was approaching his own home from the Haugr, he confirmed what the Frank had said. "I am sorry, lord. I got there too late. The count and his family were sailing away when I arrived."

"Was there a battle?"

"No, lord." He paused, "Better to hear it from your wife. She can explain better than I can." He knew Mary almost as well as I did. He had lived with us before we were married. I did not press the point.

Bernard made the mistake of laughing. I backhanded him so hard that he fell from his horse. There was a crack as his arm broke with the fall. It was his right arm. As he was helped back into his saddle I said, "And your days of fighting are over, old man, so keep your face straight and your mouth silent."

Alain said, "What can have happened?"

"I know not but the victory now tastes bitter. We lost men and for what?"

"You have often told me, lord, that there are some things which are planned by spirits. I do not believe in such things but I do believe the men who died did not die in vain. Folki now holds Carentan. Your son holds Rauville, Benni's Ville and Kartreidh. We have almost doubled the land we once had. That is a victory."

I knew that Alain was right and I also knew that I should wait until I spoke with my wife. Gilles would not lie. If the prisoners had been taken there would be an explanation. Perhaps they had paid the ransom. I brightened. That made sense. The count had sailed to the Haugr to retrieve his family and he had paid the ransom.

"I am sorry Alain of Auxerre. You are right to chide me so. I am a warrior and we must bear all that the Weird Sisters plan and plot."

As we neared my home I saw that the work on the new defences was still progressing. The wall around the church and shipyard was now visible. By the time Yule arrived, it would be finished. When I had spoken with my wife then I would see Harold Fast Sailing. I saw Father Michael leave his work and, after donning his kyrtle, hurry across to the Haugr. I thought nothing of it. Skutal Einarsson greeted me at the gate. He was a fisherman and, along with his brother, were amongst the most trusted of my men. His brother would be fishing for I had left the two of them in command of my walls.

"I tried to stop them, jarl, but your wife was adamant that the count and the holy men could take the prisoners."

My black mood descended once more. I forced a smile, "Worry not, Skutal. I am back now and I will make it right. You may return to your fishing."

He smiled and looked relieved, "Fishing and fighting are easier than dealing with Franks, jarl."

I think he meant my wife. "Alain, keep the Frank safe. I have not finished with him yet."

"And should I have his broken arm seen to?"

I turned and stared at Bernard of Chinon who looked pale and pained, "Not yet. I would have him suffer a little more. He serves the treacherous count. The pain will be a reminder that you do not cross a Viking." I handed my horse to Erik Long Hair. "Stable him and then my men can return to their families. I will not need them again. When I go to see my son, I will take just Alain and his men."

"Aye, jarl."

I forced myself to become calm. I knew that if I went in angry I would not be able to control myself. I breathed slowly and I smiled. When I entered I saw that there was just Father Michael sitting with my wife. "I am home." I waited and they both looked at each other. Perhaps they expected anger and were confused. I said quietly, "Gilles told me that you have let my hostages go. Where is the ransom?"

My wife came forward and held my hands, "Husband, there is no ransom. We returned them to their lord. We had to."

I cocked my head to the side, "You had to? The walls were breached? I see no fresh mounds of earth where the dead were buried and no burned palisades. They sneaked inside and took them?"

Father Michael said, "No, lord, we were forced to let them go. They brought the Bishop of Reims."

"I know." I flashed him an angry look. I was losing my temper. "If this is the work of your White Christ then I will tear down your church brick by brick and feed your flesh to the fishes!"

My wife stepped between us, "It was not just Father Michel! If you tear down the church then feed my flesh to the fishes too."

I glared at her, "Perhaps I will."

She recoiled, "I do not know you!"

"Then tell me why you disobeyed my orders instead of this dancing with words! I am a plain man and I need plain words!"

Father Michael shook his head, "No, lord, you are not. You are more than a barbaric warrior! The count arrived with the Bishop of Reims. They told me that we had to let the hostages go. If we did not then the Pope would excommunicate every Christian in the land of the Northman."

"Excommunicate?"

"We would not be able to go to heaven, husband. We would be without our souls."

"And words can do that? I do not understand your religion. You let them take the hostages because of words?"

"There was more, lord. My church was not sanctioned. Bishop Ebbo has blessed it. We are now recognised by the Pope and the Church."

I turned on him, "I regret that I ever allowed you to build your church. The hostages were more than coin. They were the guarantee that we would hold Carentan. You have doomed us to fight for the town we have bled for." I pointed at my wife, "You will be responsible for the deaths of more men."

I turned, "Where are you going, husband?"

"Until I have decided what I will do with you and your church I will sleep in the warrior hall!"

I left and went back towards the sea. I would speak with Harold Fast Sailing. He saw me coming and limped towards me. His wound was healing but he had not yet fully recovered. I wondered if he ever would for he was getting old now. He shook his head, "I am sorry jarl. We could do nothing about the hostages." He nodded his head towards the church. "Father Michael is a good man and a fine builder but the other holy man seemed to curse him. He used a spell." He clutched his horse amulet which I had given him.

"Excommunicate?"

"Aye, that is the one. As soon as he did Father Michael took him inside the gates. Skutal could do nothing about it."

"I blame no one save my wife and the priest."

"They are Christians, jarl, and under the spell of their wizard. You, better than most, know the power of wizards; even Christian ones."

"I will deal with it." I then told Harold what had happened. "I know this drekar was intended for my son but we will need another for Folki."

He pointed to *'Skuld'*, "She is a fine drekar, jarl, and you have *'Dragon's Breath'*."

"You are right. I will speak with Father Michael about the walls. In light of the visit by the Franks I want them higher."

"We will need more stone, jarl."

"I will get it. I know where there is much!" Already I was calculating how to pay back the Franks. "Where did they sail to when they left?"

"I heard some of the crew and I think they were sailing to Caen."

I nodded. That made sense. The Lady Eloise's father came from there. It was the strongest place left before Rouen. I did not think the count would risk Rouen or Paris. The new king might be there and he would have to admit to losing Carentan. That suited me. There were quarries south of the Issicauna. I would take my drekar and my knarr and take the stone. Last time we had paid for it. Now I would take it! I had been denied my ransom. They would learn that a Viking did not forgive.

I took off my mail and my kyrtle and plunged into the sea. I liked the feel of the water. It seemed to cleanse me within and without. Mary's actions had come as a shock to me. I had never thought that she would put her religion before my wishes. I wondered if I should destroy the church and forbid the worship of the White Christ? I sank to the bottom of the rocky pool and submerged myself. I often did this. I would hold my breath for as long as possible and then rise to the surface. I opened my eyes and saw the fishes fleeing hither and thither. I stayed there until I was about to burst and then rose like a breaching whale. I dismissed the idea of destroying the church. It would be foolish to try to do so. Almost a third of my people worshipped the White Christ. That would create an enemy within our walls and I could not have that. I needed another solution.

I lay on the stones. The sun was warm and dried my skin. I was tired. I had ridden hard over the past days. I had gone without sleep. Was it that lack of sleep that had made me so fractious? And yet I knew that I was in the right. Mary should not have gone against me. She had been disloyal. That was inexcusable. I slept and my dreams were filled with the knives of Franks in the night. I did not sleep well. When I awoke the sun had passed its zenith. No one had disturbed me. Word would have spread that the jarl was in a bad mood. It did not happen often.

I dressed and headed back. The sentries on the gates nodded and said, "Jarl."

I smiled, "The water has refreshed me!"

Word would spread that my mood was changing. My oldest friend was Erik One Hand and his wife, Brigid. They made ale and I sought them out. The salty sea water had made me thirsty.

"Jarl, we heard you were back." Erik's words were non-committal. He was not certain of my reaction.

"And you would have heard more I daresay. The Haugr is a small place. Ale, Brigid. A large horn. I need some ale."

She nodded and handed me one. I went to pay for it and she shook her head, "No, lord. Perhaps the ale will make you realise that you have a good wife. That is the payment!"

Before I could say anything, Erik said, "Woman, go about your business and do not insult the jarl again. I have but one hand yet I would use it on such a serpent tongued witch!"

She laughed, "Aye and you would get as good as you gave. I will go but you need to talk sense into our lord. He stands on the edge of a precipice!"

I liked Brigid. She was Hibernian and had something of the witch about her. Other jarls might have objected to her words but I did not mind her honesty. I needed the same from Erik. "Is she right, Erik? What is the word in the Haugr? All men drink here. I have obviously upset the women but what did the men think of my wife's actions?"

He poured himself a horn, "Like you, jarl, they could not understand it. She is the lady of the Haugr and she knew your wishes but she is Christian. The priest wizard seemed to terrify both your wife and Father Michael. She wept."

I drank deeply of the beer. Brigid brewed good ale. "It still remains, Erik, that she disobeyed me. The clan has lost because of her."

"Gold? You are worried about gold? That was never important to you."

"Carentan. His wife and daughters would be exchanged for gold and the town of Carentan."

He looked at me sideways. "Folki holds that town, does he not?"

"He does."

"I am sorry, jarl, why do you need a Frank's permission to keep a town we have captured. If he wishes it back then he takes it."

Erik was right. I was playing the Frank's games. It was they who used treaties and alliances. We fought and we took. What we took, we held. Of course, I had too much pride to return to my hall. I spent the night in the warrior hall and ate with the young warriors. It was better than I had expected. I learned much about their hopes and expectations. All of them had been born either in the Haugr or Raven Wing Island. This was the world they knew. All of them desired land but they still wished to raid. They spoke to me easily and I listened. When I went to sleep my mind was filled with their words and the words I would say to my wife.

I had forgotten what it was like to sleep in the same hall as young warriors. It was filled with noises in the night; belching, farting, snoring, grunting and mumbling. I determined to spend just one night there. When I reached my hall, I saw that my wife and daughters had chests and servants were packing them.

"What are you doing?"

"Isn't it obvious? We are leaving. I have spoken with Brigid and the other women. It seems that I have transgressed. I have not behaved as a thrall should and I have disobeyed you. There is a convent close to Reims. I will go there with the girls. I will become a nun and the girls will be cared for. You can take another wife. Perhaps your next one will obey you better than I did."

I grabbed her arm, "I forbid you to leave."

"Forbid? Hrolf, you spend so much time away from our home that I can walk out at any time. Besides you made it quite clear, yesterday, that you no longer wish to have me as your wife."

I turned, "Girls, leave us."

"But!"

"Leave!" I roared and they fled.

Mary gave me a thin-lipped smile, "I see that the barbarian is returned. I had thought you were changed but I can see that it was an illusion. Scratch the surface and the Viking emerges."

"The Viking is always there. You knew that when you married me."

"And perhaps I am now sick of the Viking in you. When you begin to enslave Frankish ladies, I have to wonder at the man beneath the mail."

"Is that what this is about? It is fine to capture poor women but the wives of nobles are somehow exempt?"

"I would not wish you to enslave anyone. The Lady Eloise is related to the king. She has the blood of Charlemagne running through her veins."

I laughed. I did not mean to but I did. "That means nothing. I fought her brother and he died quickly enough."

She held up a hand, "I have heard enough. I am going and taking our daughters with me."

"If you leave I will tear down your church!"

Suddenly she stopped, "You mean you are not going to do that already?"

"What made you think I would?"

"Well, your words, yesterday you said…." She shook her head, "I am confused. What are you going to do?"

"Do? I am going to sail to the land of the Franks and take the gold which I am owed in the form of stones and we are going to build higher walls to protect your precious church and my harbour. And I am going to punish this Count Guillaume and his wife. When that is done I will visit our son and witness the birth of my grandson."

She sat down on the chest. "I did not know. I thought…"

"You thought that I was a barbarian. I know, you told me. Well I am a barbarian and if you do not wish to live with me then go but our daughters stay! They are of my blood and I will determine whom they marry! I will not have them taken to Reims and be married to fat old Franks!"

She laughed, "Married?" She stood and kissed me. "You are a fool! You are a barbarian but I still love you. I will stay!"

The mood of the Haugr improved with our reconciliation. That night we sealed it as we coupled in the hall. It had been so long since we had done so I wondered if that was part of the reason for my temper. Then I began preparations for the raid. I sent word that I needed two crews for *'Skuld'* and *'Dragon's Breath'*. Despite the fact that it was coming to harvest time I filled both drekar. Harold told me that the ships were ready for sea.

As I was going over the charts with Siggi and Skutal, Father Michael sought me out. "Lord, I know that your wife and I disappointed you but you must understand why we did so."

"I know why! The wizard priest cursed you or threatened you with a curse."

"A curse?" He looked confused.

"This ex-communication nonsense. It sounds to me like a curse and not a very good one at that. Your heaven does not sound like a place I would like to be. Your god allows in any, even cowards and liars, so long as they repent. I would rather spend my days in Valhalla with warriors!"

"It is not a curse. I know our action cost you gold. We will repay you but now our church is a legal one. I even have the Bishop's permission for the church at Benni's Ville to be sanctioned."

"And you know why that is, do you not?" As I had lain listening to my young men filling the halls with noises and smells I had worked out the motives behind the count and bishop's visit. They had been sowing the seeds of discord. They were trying to drive a wedge between the Christians and the pagans. I had nearly fallen into that very clever trap.

"No, lord, why?"

"He thinks that the land will be his again soon. He wants me to build churches for him. Did you have a church before?" The priest shook his head. "This land will not revert to the rule of the Franks! I am going to get more stone. I want this wall higher and a tower building. Next time a Frank visits here he will not find it so easy to leave!"

We left on the next tide. I intended to sail, first to Caen where I would leave my message for the count, then we would sail west and land close to where the Franks quarried stone. They were now using the river to transport the stone to Rouen and Paris. Our prisoners at Carentan had told us that Charles the Bald was embarking on an ambitious building programme. There would be stone aplenty and there was a certain satisfaction in taking it from the next King of Frankia!

The night before we left Erik Long Hair came to see me. "Jarl, I have a favour to ask."

"Consider it given. You are oathsworn and I owe you much already."

He shook his head, "My son, Rollo, wishes to come with us on the raid. I have been putting him off for he is but twelve summers old."

"And that is nearly a man but he cannot take an oar, they are all taken."

"I know, jarl, and he cannot stand in a shield wall. I ask if he can carry your banner. As I recall your son did much upon his years."

"Aye he did and I nearly lost him. No one knows better than you the dangers of standing behind me with my banner."

He laughed, "That is true but I also know that I will be able to watch him there and he can learn from the rest of the hearth-weru. I would have him be the best warrior that he can be."

"Does he have mail?"

"He is too small yet. I hope that the experience will encourage him to become both stronger and bigger. He has a leather byrnie studded with metal. He has a metal helm and a short sword. He will not need a shield."

"If you are happy then so am I." It had been on the tip of my tongue to say you and your wife but Agnathia had died giving birth to his stillborn daughter. I saw now, another reason why he wished his son with him. The last few months he had been in the Haugr without mother or father.

"I will fetch him. I would have him swear an oath."

I heard hidden words beneath the words Erik spoke. I held his arm, "Erik, is there more?"

He nodded, "He has become wild without me to scold him. He is of an age where his thoughts are on girls and women. It is because he has no mother. Bagsecg found him with his granddaughter. He thrashed him but I fear he might do the same again. He needs to be a warrior and learn the discipline of the warrior."

"Then, knowing that, I will accept his oath but he must keep it, Erik."

"Aye, I know."

He returned with the youth. I saw that he was tall but he had not filled out very much. I suspected he had not adhered to his sword training with his father out of the way. "Rollo, you would sail with me?"

The youth glanced at his father. "I do not ask your father, I ask you! You are of this clan and almost a man. You have not the frame of a warrior but unless you have other plans then your future is in the shield wall."

"I am too small for the shield wall, jarl. My father said that."

"You are. I am in need of someone to carry my banner. Could you do that?"

His face brightened, "There would be great honour in that."

"There would also be great danger. Ask your father. The banner follows me and I go where there is the most danger. You could die."

I saw then that he was a clever youth. "I could, jarl, but if I am not killed then think of the honour I would gain!"

"You will have to swear an oath." I took Heart of Ice from its scabbard, "On this sword. The oath is binding. If you break it you would be banished from this land. Are you willing to swear?"

I saw him hesitate and then he nodded, "I will."

I held the hilt towards him. "Then swear." He touched the hilt and his face looked as though he had touched something which burned. His eyes widened and he stared at me. I nodded. "There is power in the sword and that power is not of this earth."

"I swear that I will be Jarl Hrolf the Horseman's man until death. If I am foresworn may I wander the otherworld for all eternity, without sight and without hope."

I took the sword. "It is good. Now fetch your chest. Until we reach our destination you will work with the other boys and be part of the crew. You will work as you have never worked before!"

His face fell. I think he had thought he would be with me at the steering board. After he had gone Erik said, "Thank you, jarl. No matter what happens on this voyage I am satisfied. My son will either come back a man or he will not come back."

"It is in the hands of the Weird Sisters and the gods. Let us hope that they have tormented you enough with the death of Agnathia and your daughter."

Chapter 16

Our three ships did not leave until the middle of the afternoon. I wanted to reach Caen after dark. I had chosen my thirty warriors carefully. They were my best warriors and the ones who could slip ashore with me and bring terror to Caen. I was back aboard *'Dragon's Breath'*. She was double oared. I had seventy-two warriors as my crew. We would row down the Orne and thirty-one would land at Caen. It was Folki I missed. He and his brother had assaulted Caen and they knew it better than any. However, he had told me about it so many times that I felt I knew the place.

With wooden walls and four gates, it was vulnerable. We would not be breaching the sea gate. Instead, we would be landed downstream and make our way, in the darkness, to the west gate. I had archers with me and Saami bows. My aim was to breach the gates and set alight the town. I did not want to burden myself with slaves or treasure. I wanted the Franks to fear me. I wanted them to know that I could gain entry to any of their strongholds and I could bring terror to their lives. *'Skuld'* and *'Kara'* would land at Ouistreham and do the same. That small port had been devastated first by the Franks themselves and then by me and my men in an act of revenge. It would be a beacon to guide my drekar back out to sea.

We sang for the first part of the voyage. The wind would help us once we reached the Orne but until then it was an awkward and uncooperative wind.

Skuld the Dark sails on shadows wings
Skuld the Dark is a ship that sings
With soft, gentle voice of a powerful witch
Her keel will glide through Frankia's ditch
With flowing hair and fiery breath
Skuld the Dark will bring forth death
Though small in size her heart is great
The Norn who decides on man's final fate
Skuld the Dark sails on shadows wings
Skuld the Dark is a sorcerous ship that sweetly sings

Skuld the Dark sails on shadows wings
Skuld the Dark is a sorcerous ship that sweetly sings
Skuld the Dark sails on shadows wings
Skuld the Dark is a sorcerous ship that sweetly sings
The witch's reach is long and her eyes can see through mist
Her teeth are sharp and grind your bones to grist
With soft, gentle voice of a powerful witch
Her keel will glide through Frankia's ditch
With flowing hair and fiery breath
Skuld the Dark will bring forth death
Though small in size her heart is great
The Norn who decides on man's final fate
Skuld the Dark sails on shadows wings
Skuld the Dark is a sorcerous ship that sweetly sings
Skuld the Dark sails on shadows wings
Skuld the Dark is a sorcerous ship that sweetly sings
The witch's reach is long and her eyes can see through mist
Her teeth are sharp and grind your bones to grist

The crew of the *'Skuld'* heard our lusty voices and joined in. It seemed to echo across the empty dusky seas. There were no Franks to spy our passage. Rurik and his men had raided them too often and we passed deserted houses. As we passed the mouth of the river which led to Carentan I wondered how Folki and his men were doing.

Rollo Eriksson was kept busy by Siggi Far-Sighted. He was up and down the stays and shrouds like a sea squirrel. Siggi was trying to coax all the speed he could from the drekar. We stopped singing not long after we passed the mouth of the Isigny. The chant had served its purpose and we now had the rhythm. I had my hands and face covered in charcoal. My helmet was an old one which was also black. With my wolf cloak, I would be hard to see. The men I had chosen were similarly attired. We did not carry spears. Instead, we had hand axes and short swords. As we neared Ouistreham *'Skuld'* put on a spurt to overtake us. Skutal and his crew would want to silence the outpost at the mouth of the Orne.

It was now dark and I was amazed that she had disappeared so quickly. Her white sail should have been visible but the night was so dark that it could not be seen. Siggi must have been reading my mind for he said, "We should have a black sail made, jarl. We raid more at night than during the day and, in the day, it would appear more terrifying."

"We have the winter to make one. It is a good idea. Perhaps we could use a white horse on the black background. What say you?"

172

"That would be good."

The ships' boys warned us of the river's mouth but we had an idea of our position for the wind began to push us down it and we had the race against the river too.

"In oars!" The wind would take us the rest of the way.

The men could now begin to get ready. As we passed the small settlement of Ouistreham we heard the clash of metal as Thorbolt led his men to take the outpost. The fact that no beacon flared told us that they had managed to do so without being seen.

My thirty men did not need their shields. We had, instead, four ladders we had constructed. They were crude and they were rough but they would get us over the walls and into Caen. The Franks in Caen relied on the river for protection. The ditches to landward were not deep enough and they had few towers. I was relying on the accuracy of my archers and the speed of my men to achieve our objective. It was a bold plan but Einar Bear Killer and Erik Long Hair were both confident of success. It was a risk sailing down the river with a sail but as we had found it hard to see our consort's so I hoped that we would be difficult to see. We intended to land just half a mile from the walls. Siggi would lower the sails and the crew who were remaining on board would scull us to shore. The landing party waited by the steerboard side. Everything would be done in silence. Rollo would not be coming ashore. He and the ship's boys would be needed to help Siggi sail the drekar close to the walls and pick us up once we had fired the town.

We saw no one as we gently edged towards the trees. We would not be tying up. Lars and Gunnar Stone Face would leap ashore with ropes and use their strength to hold us there while we disembarked. As soon as we touched the shore the two of them landed and, wrapping their ropes around two trees, pulled the drekar tight to the shore. The ladders were taken ashore and then the rest of us. As I leapt to the ground the two ropes were released and the sail raised once more. We would race the drekar to Caen. Even if she were seen the Franks would expect an attack from the river and not from the land.

We ran down the river path. The eight men carrying the ladders were in the middle and I led with Beorn Fast Feet. I had my short sword out as we ran. We passed four huts. They appeared to be empty for there was no sign of any animals and no smell of wood smoke. I was grateful. Discovery now would ruin my plans. We slowed when we saw the walls of Caen loom up. There were huts on our side of the ditch and I could smell smoke. They were inhabited. We moved cautiously down the track which had grown from the path. It was wide enough for six men. I had just passed one of the huts when I heard a soft sigh. I looked behind me and saw that Erik Green Eye had slit the throat of a man who had left his hut. We had to hurry.

Ragnvald Hrolfsson

I saw that they had one wooden tower on the corner. I tapped Beorn Fast Feet on the shoulder and he and the four other archers loped off. They would eliminate any sentries. The rest of us edged towards the ditch. I saw a white face look over. There was a temptation to pull back but that would have been a mistake. With blackened faces, we were invisible but a sudden movement would have been seen. Suddenly the figure seemed to stand stock still. Then I saw the arrow in his throat. His hands went to the arrow and the movement tipped him over the wall and into the ditch.

There were other sentries but they were not on this section of the wall. We ran and slid down the ditch. The Frank was still lying in the bottom of the ditch trying to remove the arrow. Einar knelt down and slit his throat. We clambered up the side of the ditch. It was like the one at Carentan, too shallow to be effective. We placed the ladders against the wall and with a man bracing each one I joined Einar Bear Killer, Erik Long Hair and Gunnar Stoneface in racing up them. I had just reached the top when I saw the three sentries in the tower all struck by arrows. They disappeared. I both hoped and assumed that they were dead.

I ran towards the wooden staircase which led down to the town. There were burning brands placed at strategic corners and as I passed one I grabbed it. We would head towards the river gate. There was a flash of light as a door opened. Erik Long Hair did not hesitate. He and Gunnar ran to the light and, with their short swords, slew the two men who had just emerged. I heard the horses and knew that the men had come from the stable. I gestured for Einar to lead the rest of the men to the sea gate. I pointed to Erik Long Hair and he entered the stable. I saw Beorn and my archers arrive. They would be our rear guard.

The door the men had used was a side door. There was a pair of double doors further along. Erik had already opened them. The horses could smell us and they were moving about nervously. Taking my seax I began to slash the ropes which tethered them. As soon as Erik joined me I took the brand and went to the hay bales. I plunged it into them. Then we both flapped our arms and shouted. The horses bolted through the gates. The Franks would know we were here but the fire, once started, would be hard to put out. The wood and the hay in the stable were perfect for starting a fire.

The two of us ran out and we heard the sound of weapons clashing. It was soon drowned out by the sound of the horses as they fled the flames. The fire took hold quickly. We had barely reached the next house when the fire reached the roof. With my archers watching my back, Erik and I went into the houses on either side of the main road. A man stepped towards me wielding a sword. I rammed the brand in his face and then slid my sword into his gut. I heard screams. I shouted, "Get out while you can!" They had a fire burning already and a pile of logs next to it. I used my sword to drag the coals out and then I dropped a wooden chair onto it. The chair was old and flames ignited it. The family rushed past me and out of the door. That suited us for we needed the confusion.

Once outside I saw that the town was ablaze. I yelled, "Back to the drekar!"

I prayed that Einar and the others would have opened the sea gates and I hoped that when we arrived the '***Dragon's Breath***' would be waiting in the river for us! The guards in the town had now awoken to the fact that there were raiders in their town. They had a dilemma. Half of the town was on fire and we were running through the town as were the burghers. They knew that we were Vikings only when our swords slashed and stabbed them. As we turned a corner I saw that Einar had managed to open the gates and others had set fire to the wall. There were armed men trying to get at them. My archers, along with Erik and I, were the last of our men. Shouting, "Clan of the Horse!" we fell upon the undefended backs of the men who were trying to get to Einar Bear Killer. I drew my seax as well as my sword and used the two of them to hack and rip the Franks before us.

I saw Lars Ragnarson fall and two of my men picked him and ran through the gate and over the bridge. I could not see, through the flames and the drifting smoke, my ship. I shouted, "Back to the ship!" I turned and ducked as a two-handed sword was swung at my head. I hacked sideways with my sword and felt it bite into the Frank's thighs. As I dropped I ripped my seax across his throat. Turning, I saw that the death had made the enemy halt. I faced them and, raising my sword shouted, "I am Hrolf the Horseman. Tell your new king and his count that I have not finished with them yet. Lock your doors and guard your women! We will be back." I roared and lunged with my sword at the eight men who faced me. They took a step back. I laughed and ran back across the bridge to the drekar. A flurry of arrows sped into the open gate and I saw Franks fall. The walls were now truly ablaze as we headed downstream and my men chanted my name and banged their shields. I joined Siggi at the steering board and saw the three cloak covered bodies that were our dead.

He pointed downstream. I could see flames, "Thorbolt has given us our beacon!"

"Good, then the first part of our revenge is complete."

I looked at the walls of Caen. They were ablaze. The fire had spread quickly. They might be able to put it out but they would have to rebuild. They might even have to start again. Guillaume of Carentan would learn his lesson. I hoped that we would have made the Franks look within their borders so that we could raid their river. Having been along the river when I had led the raid on the monastery I was familiar with the waters and the lack of defences. The width of the river made defences difficult to create. The danger would be if they had a large number of ships. I was not leading a fleet this time. I had two drekar and a knarr. I glanced astern and saw that the fire had taken hold. The flames leapt high into the air. Our raid might not have cost them many lives, I doubted if we had slain more than twenty men altogether, but the effect would have been more devastating. I had also managed to spread dissension. The merchants of Caen and the prosperous families would know who to blame. Count Guillaume and Lady Eloise might not be seen as the victims any longer.

'Skuld' and *'Kara'* were waiting for us half a mile from the mouth of the river. Their oars were out for the short voyage to the river. The settlement was a glowing pile of ashes. It would have to be rebuilt. The Franks would remember the Vikings for many years to come. Even if we did not raid for a year or more they would be watching to sea for the dragon ships and the wrath of the Northmen. I took off my mail byrnie and laid my sword in my chest. I did not think I would need them again. I could not imagine quarrymen fighting very hard to retain their stones!

Einar Bear Killer was in an ebullient mood. He moved down the drekar exhorting the men, "That showed the bastard Franks. Thirty men and we ripped the guts out of their town! Wait until we return with a fleet. Caen will be like Carentan! It will be one of the jarl's towns. Now get to your oars! You whoresons are going to have to work some more!"

The men might have been tired but they all found a new energy. It came from the taste of victory which was the finest of foods. Even I felt exhilarated. Racing through a town of enemies and emerging unscathed made you feel like a hero from one of the tales of the gods. Rollo handed me an ale skin, "Here, jarl. One day I will follow you with a sword."

"Good, then watch the others and when you take an oar and men talk of how they did what they did then listen. You share oars with the finest of crews. I am a lucky man, Rollo. I have warriors around me."

Siggi shouted, "And now, young Rollo, I need you to race up the stays and to let out another reef. You have good eyes. Take masthead lookout."

As he raced off Siggi said, "This might be the making of him, jarl."

"What do you know?" I was unsure if the tale of Bagsecg's daughter was common knowledge.

"Since his mother died he has been a wild one. Erik has spoken of his son many times when we have shared a watch. Bringing up a child is not the work for a warrior. Left alone he found others who were equally wild. We raid often, jarl, and the young are frequently left alone. This will be good for him. I have seen a change already and it has been but two days."

I looked down the boat. I had been blind and not seen the problems I was creating. We had had bad Vikings before but they had come from outside. When we had lived on Raven Wing Island we had been beset by enemies and our young had not had the opportunity to become restless and irresponsible. They were normally standing a watch and fighting off enemies. They were becoming warriors rather than looking for relief from idleness. We were too successful. Our land was safe. The border towns might be in danger but the last attack on any of

176

our towns had been Valognes and that had been many years ago. I needed to put
something in place to keep the young men occupied. Often the Weird Sisters spin
and the web is hard to see. Sometimes an idea is planted by the gods and it takes
time to grow. This time I saw the answer and it was as clear as the moon which
rose in the sky.

"Of course!"

"What, jarl?"

I had not realised I had spoken aloud. "Nothing Siggi I am just thinking."

He laughed, "And that is good, jarl, for your thoughts mean the clan
prospers."

We were heading east and I turned to look astern. The Haugr and my land
were hidden but I looked there as I formulated my plan. I had horsemen. Every
one of my towns had horsemen. Horses and riders needed servants and slaves to
look after the horses, saddles, mail and weapons. Those slaves could be used on
the fields. We had young boys who would serve as the servant of a horseman.
The horseman would be responsible for training them to be warriors. It would
mean we had a greater number of warriors who could fight from a horse and yet
still raid on a drekar. It was what I had done with Ragnvald and the success of his
campaign in Carentan showed me that it would work. Why had I not seen it?
Why had it taken Erik Long Hair's wild son to make me see something as
obvious as that? I knew the answer. It was the Norns. They had hidden it from
me and now revealed it. I was part of their plan and I moved at their command.

Working out the details occupied me until the sun came up and we saw the
mouth of the river ahead. The last time we had sailed up it had been at night. We
had the luxury of daylight. The channel was clearer and the dangers more
obvious. The river was stronger than the Orne and Siggi had to keep the men at
the oars. They did not have to row hard for the wind was still with us. Coming
downstream, when we had completed our task, would be easier for we would
have the current of the powerful river to aid us.

I cupped my hands and shouted, "Lookouts, we seek either barges or stones
by the river. Look on the southern bank!"

I heard a chorus of, 'Aye, jarl' as they all answered. We made our way
upstream. I saw that they were building a watchtower half a mile up the river.
They had built the stone base and were adding the wood. I saw the workers point
while others grabbed weapons. One man leapt onto the back of a horse and
galloped off. It did not worry me. In fact, it pleased me. If the alarm was raised
then they would not see just three ships, they would see another fleet. They
would go inside their walls and slam the gates shut. They would have their
horsemen ready to catch us as we headed for their monasteries and churches.
Stones could not be moved quickly. Our only danger would be the time it took us
to load the stones.

The river twisted and turned. The quarries were some way upriver. The morning drew on and I knew that the men were tiring. "Einar, have half the men rest. It will not do to exhaust the whole crew!"

"Aye, jarl."

I turned and saw that our consorts were some way behind us. The knarr was keeping pace with *'Skuld'* but the drekar had a much smaller crew than we had. We negotiated another two bends in the river and *'Skuld'* drew closer to us.

"Jarl! Five hundred paces ahead. There is a jetty and there are stones."

"Are there barges?"

"No, jarl."

"Siggi, head for the jetty."

"Aye, jarl."

I walked to the prow and saw the jetty. There was not enough stone. It was, however, dressed. I saw that they had made a road through the forest. The trees surrounded the jetty. That was good. We would be hidden from view.

I shouted, "Rest while we are here. We will not be staying long." I saw the men at the jetty fleeing. They were expecting someone. It was just not us! "Siggi, tie up at the far end. We will leave *'Kara'* to load and we will head further east."

"Aye, jarl."

As soon as we tied up I leapt over the side and went to examine the stones. There were too many for the knarr alone. As Skutal brought *'Skuld'* next to the jetty I had a sudden idea. Thorbolt and his crew would be tired. At least half of my crew had rested.

"I want the stones loaded on *'Skuld'*. Do not overload her. Thorbolt, have your men cut down trees to make a raft. Load the rest of the stones on the raft. You can tow the raft back."

"Aye, jarl."

Beorn Fast Feet said, "Did Siggi White Hair not do this at Raven Wing Island?"

I nodded, "He did. The timbers for this drekar were fetched that way."

I walked to *'Skuld'*. "Skutal, load the raft and then turn the ships to face downstream. Wait here for us."

"Aye, jarl."

"Thorbolt, if the Franks come then anchor, in the middle of the river and await us."

"Aye, jarl."

"Siggi, we sail!"

My men took to the oars and we laboured upstream. The twists, turns and bends in the river meant that the best way to see a long way ahead was from the masthead. Our lookouts had a good view far into the distance. The barges which plied the river used oars and short sails. They were flat bottomed and could tip if hey had a large sail that was caught by a sudden gust of wind. That gave us an advantage.

"Jarl, I see three barges ahead. They are loading at a jetty two bends up."

I turned to Siggi. We can catch them! Einar, we have the barges in sight. They are loading. They are less than a mile ahead. Double crew and row for all you are worth."

"Aye, jarl. Let us see how many of you are worthy to sail Jarl Hrolf's drekar. Get to your oars."

"Sven, keep a sharp eye on the barges. Let me know if they attempt to flee."

"Aye, jarl."

I turned to Siggi, "If they leave can we catch them?"

"So long as this wind holds then aye. Even if it falls our oars will be faster than the horses they use to pull them."

"Then let us hope that the gods continue to favour us."

As we were turning to begin the second bend Sven shouted, "I think they have seen us, jarl. They have stopped loading stone. I think they are preparing to sail."

"War speed, Einar!"

Clan of the Horseman
Warriors strong
Clan of the Horseman
Our reach is long
Clan of the Horseman
Fight as one
Clan of the Horseman
Death will come
Clan of the Horseman
Warriors strong
Clan of the Horseman
Our reach is long
Clan of the Horseman
Fight as one
Clan of the Horseman
Death will come

Our favourite and fastest chant made *'Dragon's Breath'* leap forward as though she was a horse slapped in the rump. I walked to the prow with my Saami bow. I was the only one who was unoccupied. Racing around the bend I saw the three barges as they poled themselves into the middle of the river. Their small sails billowed but they were not moving as fast as we were. Even as I walked to the front I took in that there was still a large pile of stones on the jetty and that two of the barges rode lower in the water than the third. I also noticed that they had left the three pairs of large horses they used to pull the barges by the side of the river. We had frightened them.

We were overtaking them rapidly. I loosed an arrow at the rearmost barge. It was riding higher in the water. A sudden gust moved the arrow off target but it still struck close to the steering board. The effect was amazing. The six crew threw themselves over the side and began to swim to the shore.

"Rollo, Sven, when we pass the barge jump aboard her and turn her around! Take her back to the jetty. We have more stone to collect."

If they were worried about my order they did not show it. They both slid down the backstay and, grabbing a seax each, went to the steerboard side. Siggi shouted, "In oars!" Putting the steering board over we bumped into the lifeless barge and my two young warriors leapt aboard. We ground down the side and, as soon as we were clear Siggi shouted, "Out oars."

We would now catch the other two. Their captains saw that and they headed towards the northern shore. I could see houses. There were Franks there.

> *Clan of the Horseman*
> *Warriors strong*
> *Clan of the Horseman*
> *Our reach is long*
> *Clan of the Horseman*
> *Fight as one*
> *Clan of the Horseman*
> *Death will come*

The brief rest and the sudden spurt meant we were just one length behind the barges as they struck the shore. Siggi shouted, "In oars."

"Beorn Fast Feet and Gunnar Stone Face, take a couple of men and turn the barges around. I want us tied in line astern."

"You would tow them, jarl?"

"Yes, Siggi. I do not want us to become separated. When we reach *'Skuld'* and *'Kara'* they can take over the tows. You know better than any that we cannot risk their sails on the open water."

"Aye, jarl, but they will be almost a dead weight."

"Only when we are at sea. If we have to take a day to sail them home it will be worth it. This stone will make your ships and your families safer."

As we bumped into them my men leapt aboard and Siggi set about turning the drekar around. I saw that the bargemen were running towards a small town on the riverbank half a mile away. I could see them waving their arms and shouting. I was not worried. Even if they summoned help we would be on the south bank before they could reach us. Then I spied a spiral of smoke. They had a beacon. As Siggi turned us around I peered south. By the time we were turned around and we were level with the barges I saw another spiral of smoke a mile away. They had built watchtowers to warn them of Vikings. I had not expected this and it would make our journey home more difficult. The Norns had spun again. What would the Franks do?

Chapter 17

Riders came galloping from the town but we already had the two barges astern of us. The crew had to row. We lowered the three sails for the wind would not help us. We relied on the current and the strength of my men. By the time we reached the jetty, Rollo and Sven had tied up the barge.

"Get the rest of the stone loaded and then we leave."

"There is too much stone here for us to take, jarl."

I nodded, "I know, Siggi, we fill the barge and leave. We have three barges and a knarr filled with stone. That will suffice. We have the sea's bounty for the infill."

I could tell, from the time it took to load the barge, that my men were weary. I had the men fed before we left. We had gone almost a whole day without sleep and we had rowed many miles. My men were tough but this was asking much of them. We left in the middle of the afternoon. Rollo and Sven were given command of the barge which would be attached to us. The other two were tied astern. When my men were given the order to row, it seemed to take forever to begin to make headway. Once in the main current, it became easier and I had Einar slow down the beat until we were just keeping way. I saw that my men had loaded the knarr and they were looking anxiously at us.

I jumped ashore. "You will each tow a barge. I do not trust them sailing alone on the seas."

Sigurd Einarsson said, "Jarl, *'Kara'* is smaller even than *'Skuld'*. Will we manage to tow her?"

Siggi said, "When we hit the sea we will have the wind and the barge's sail will make it easier and the jarl has said that we can sail home slowly."

Thorbolt said, "What of the raft we have built? We have loaded her."

"It is a small raft. Tie it to your barge. Tell your crew that if it slows you down they are to cut the line."

"Aye, jarl."

The two barges were untied from us and tied to the sterns of the other two ships. The raft was attached to the barge behind *'Skuld'*. If enemies threatened then we would fight them. Skutal said, "Jarl, what do the beacons mean?"

"It means that the Weird Sisters have given enough, their webs are now there to entrap us. They mean to take away some of what we have gained. The Franks will spring a trap. We will have to fight our way out. When we leave '*Skuld*' and '*Dragon's Breath*' will sail side by side. I want '*Kara*' protected. Half the two drekar's crews will row and the other half will be ready to fight. Thorbolt, have your bows ready. Let us make the Franks be the ones to die. I will put my drekar in harm's way to allow you to escape if I must." I went to the six ship's boys who would be aboard the barges. "It may be that we are attacked. Take bows with you and prepare to defend what we have taken. There is a possibility that you may be cast adrift. Do not fear if that happens. We will come back for you. You will sail west."

"But if it is night..." I could see that my newest ship's boy was worried.

I smiled, "Do not fear, Rollo, the barges have a shallow draft. You may ground but we can pull you off. Can you do this or should I put warriors aboard?"

They all shook their heads and as one shouted, "No, jarl! We are Clan of the Horse!"

I sent Erik Long Hair and some men to collect the six horses. We loaded them on the knarr. One was a stallion. We could use him to breed. They were much bigger horses than the ones we used. They were also slower and stronger. Gilles had the skills and the knowledge to breed a bigger and faster horse than the ones we rode. Finally, I had others prepare kindling. I would fire the jetty. I hoped to draw the Franks to the jetty.

It was late afternoon as we prepared to leave. One of Sigurd's ship's boys was given the task of lighting the fire on the jetty and then jumping aboard the barge. Its low freeboard made that easy. With the flames sending a plume of smoke into the sky we left. Then we set off down the river. We had two miles to cover. I estimated that, with the current and the men rowing, we would reach the sea before dark. The question in my mind remained unanswered. What trap had the Franks made?

We were answered when we approached the last bend. The masthead lookout told us. "Jarl. There are six Franks in the river. They are under sail and holding against the current. They are in line abreast."

I nodded to Siggi, "At least now we know their plan. I want you to sail as though we are going to hug the south bank and then turn to sail between the middle two ships."

"And Skutal?"

"I will tell him the same."

I went to the landward side and, cupping my hands, told Skutal what he was to do. Finally, I went to the stern, "Sven, pass a message to Sigurd. We are going to pretend to head to the south bank and then Skutal and I will attack their middle ships. He is to follow through the hole we make." They nodded. "You two need to be ready with your bows."

Satisfied that I had done all that I could I went with the other archers to the steering board side. I wanted to make the two centre Frank's ships into charnel houses. They would be heavily crewed. Only a fool tried to take on a drekar with equal numbers. You wanted to outnumber your foe. I guessed that there would be few actual warriors aboard. We would be fighting farmers and sailors. We would be fighting family men. I had family men but mine were Vikings! If they died they would go to Valhalla. The family men of the Franks did not have that to look forward to. They believed that if they died without confessing they would be floating in nothingness for all eternity. It made a man seek life over death.

As we turned the last bend before the sea I saw the six ships. Here the river was over five hundred paces wide and the six ships went from bank to bank. They thought they had me.

"Now, Siggi!"

Siggi put the steering board over as did Skutal who had been watching us closely. Our ships seemed to move as one. The current was now stronger. The river was moving faster now and the six ships had to react quickly. They had the wind with them but their sudden turn to the south meant they could no longer keep their tight formation. Their crews were not as well trained as ours. They had ships that were different and they moved at different speeds. It made for holes where they needed none. Some crews were slower than others. My captains had the advantage that they all knew what they were doing. The southernmost Frank saw the bank of the river and the shallows approaching rapidly and the captain shortened sail. The next one in line did the same.

"Now, Siggi!"

As the steering board turned steerboard the enemy were taken aback. The two middle ones suddenly had sails that were billowing. They began flapping as they tried to turn. I drew back with my bow and then released. It was to gauge the range. My bow could send an arrow the furthest. It struck the mast.

I turned to my men and shouted, "Release!" I had thirty men with bows and the arrows darkened the sky as they flew towards the Franks who were, obligingly, racing towards us. A couple of arrows fell short but most struck home. We kept releasing as the range shortened. Victory was in sight. I saw that the Frank had lost many men and the helmsman was trying to evade us. It is at such times that Norns intervene or perhaps their webs were always meant to lead to this point. Aboard the Frank, the helmsman and the sailor next to him were struck by arrows. As they fell they pushed the steering board over and the Frank turned to ram us. It was lucky for us that the sail was not billowing. They struck us for they were far too close when they turned. Our mast and their stays became entangled.

As another of the Franks turned to attack our stern I shouted, "Cut us loose!"

184

Ragnvald Hrolfsson

I dropped my bow and, grabbing a short sword and taking out my seax, leapt aboard the Frank. Men followed me for I was the jarl and warriors do not let a jarl put his life at risk. As I landed I drove my sword across the middle of a surprised Frank. I saw that our arrows had killed many of the crew. I slashed and hacked with seax and sword to clear a path to the stay. Taking a hand axe from a dead Frank I chopped through the stay. As our ship's boys cut us loose from the Frank, Erik Green Eye chopped through the other stay as Beorn Fast Feet hacked the shroud.

"Jarl, we are free!" I swept the short sword in a wide arc and, jamming the seax in my boot, prepared to jump back. The gap was not yet wide and my men had all managed to regain our drekar. Just then there was a creak, a groan and then a crack. The stays and shrouds parted. The mast began to fall. It was pulled to the larboard side. As it crashed into the sea the whole of the ship rose and fell. I could not keep my balance and I was pitched into the river. I had the presence of mind to release the sword as I sank beneath the waves. I seemed to be underwater for an age. It was fortunate that I had often subjected myself to such immersions at the Haugr. I allowed myself to sink down and I held my breath. When I stopped descending I began to let the air out as I rose. When I eventually surfaced I saw that *'Dragon's Breath'* was now beyond my reach. The current and the oars, not to mention the sail, had taken her out to sea.

"Jarl! The rope!" I looked up and saw that Rollo, aboard the barge, had thrown a rope. I grabbed it, gratefully, and he and Sven pulled me towards the barge. I turned my head to the left and saw a Frank. It was heading for the barge. *'Kara'* had managed to pass my drekar and both she and *'Skuld'* were ahead of us. My own drekar could not turn. I saw my men hauling on the rope to draw us closer. The Frank would reach us first.

As I was pulled aboard the barge I said, "Take your bows and try to hit those on the Frankish ship. They mean to take this barge." I reached into my boot and took out my seax. It was all that we had. I could see that the Frankish ship we had boarded was now drifting towards the northern shore and that my other two ships were clear of danger but there was one ship and she was coming for us. I contemplated cutting the line and letting the barge ram the Frank but that would mean the end of two young warriors. I could not do that. I would have to hope that my men could row us out of danger.

The two boys started loosing arrows. They were not full-grown and their first few arrows fell short but, as the Frank closed, so their arrows found their marks and I watched as one eager Frank fell overboard. They were gaining. I went to the steering board. It had been tied so that it steered in a straight line. Whichever way the drekar went so did the barge. Using my seax I cut the tether and pushed the steering board hard over. We started to drift in front of the ship. I must have caused a drag on the drekar for the Frankish ship closed with us. Suddenly I saw the bow of the Frank as it loomed above me. I pushed the steering board hard over the other way and we were whipped out of the path of the ship which was now parallel with us. I returned the steering board to the centre and we began to draw clear. Beorn Fast Feet now had our archers sending arrows into the Frank and I could see the open sea. The flat-bottomed barge began to pitch. The captain of the ship was a brave man. I saw that the prow had a carved woman holding a cross. He was a Christian. He turned his bows towards us and, as he did so, six men stood on the prow. Once again it came close to us. I dared not risk turning the steering board again for I feared the effect of the drag. As two of the waiting warriors were struck with arrows the other four all leapt on board the barge.

"Use your seaxes!" The men had swords and daggers. We had seaxes. It was an uneven contest. I would sell my life dearly. I attacked. I used the pitching barge to my advantage. I went with the motion of the barge and as I neared the first two I tucked my head between my legs and, rolling, tumbled below the swinging swords and daggers. I ripped my seax up into the groin of one of the Franks and pushed hard until my hand entered his body. I twisted and pulled, shoving his body away. He fell into the second Frank. Before the second warrior could recover I leapt upon him. I used my left hand to hold down his sword hand and brought my seax over towards his eye. He blocked it with his own dagger. I was lying on top of him and so I brought my knee up between his legs. As his head came up, involuntarily, I headbutted him. I felt his grip relax and I whipped my seax across his throat.

I turned and saw that Rollo was down. He was bleeding. Sven Svensson had Rollo's seax but he was facing two men. Keeping his body between the two Franks and his friend, he was protecting Rollo's body with his own. He was a boy but that day he became a warrior. I ran down the barge and hurled myself, like a spear at the two of them. One turned and swung his sword wildly at me. He missed. My seax struck his upper left arm. I tore it out sideways and he screamed in pain. I used my left hand to ram my fingers into his eyes and gouge them. He screamed again and brought his right arm up to protect himself. I whipped the wickedly sharp blade across his middle. As I rose I saw Sven have his head taken by the swinging sword of the Frank. Even as the Frank turned three arrows struck him in the back. He fell forward with a surprised look on his face.

Looking towards the land I saw that the Franks had given up. I went to Rollo. He had a wound to his head and had lost the lobe and half of one ear but he opened his eyes, "Sven?"

I shook my head, "He stood firm protecting you, Rollo, but he paid with his life. He was brave."

He looked distraught, "We spoke of how, when we returned to the Haugr, we would have tales to tell and when you came aboard the story grew. I can never tell that story now."

"You must. If you do not then Sven's life was in vain. He died with a blade in his hand. He will have a place of honour at Odin's table. Tell the story and

Sven will live again. And the story will be of Sven the Brave and Rollo One Ear. Rurik will have to share that name." I went to the Frank I had killed and I took his sword. "Here, this is now your sword. You may have better ones in your time but this one will always be dear to you for it came from the battle where your friend died. Name it and hold that name dear."

"I will call it Frank's Bane for that is what I shall be. I will be the enemy of the Franks and they shall feel its edge. When my father told me, I would be sailing to war I did not know if I wished it. I do now. I will be the greatest warrior I can be."

I smiled for I saw now that my vision to train young warriors with my horsemen would work. *Wyrd*.

We pulled in to the shore so that Rollo could have his hurts tended and two other ship's boys were put aboard. Erik Long Hair looked relieved, "I thought I had lost my jarl and my son. I wondered how I had offended the gods."

"It was meant to be, Erik. Your son became a man and Sven had a good death."

"His mother will not think so. She is a Frank."

"She is young enough for more children."

That was our way. It was not the way of the Franks and that was one of the differences. We took the opportunity of spreading out the six horses we had captured. We had been lucky so far but I knew that it would not last. Einar Bear Killer and Erik Green Eye sat with me as we headed slowly west. "I too thought we had lost you, jarl. You were under the water for the longest time and then when the Frank tried to board you I could not see how a man and two boys, armed only with seaxes, could overcome four fresh warriors."

"Erik, they were Franks and we were Vikings. Sven knew that when he died he would go to Valhalla. The Christians did not fight hard enough."

I told them of my idea to train young warriors.

Einar Bear Killer frowned, "But why should they serve horsemen, jarl? Why not all warriors?"

"Because one day, Einar, the Northmen of this land will be known as much for their skills on horses as they are for their skills in a drekar and in a shield wall. We will not neglect the shield wall but only our horsemen are warriors all the time. You will tend your fields and raise your family. Alain and his men are dedicated to protecting our people. I think my son, Ragnvald, will also be known more as a horseman too."

It was a long slow voyage and we had the opportunity to talk through all of the problems which might arise. It was the middle of the night when we arrived back. We did not unload the stones, just the horses. Families waited to greet their men and there was sadness at those who had failed to return. There was equal joy for the rest.

187

I saw that Mary was relieved. I hoped that our life was back to normal but I did not know.

The next day, as we unloaded the barges and the knarr I was amazed at how much stone we had brought. We had enough for two towers. Father Michael shook his head, "You have surely taken more from the count than he withheld from you."

"And that is what the Franks need to learn, Father Michael. Do us harm and it will be repaid tenfold. I had thought just to hold what we have. Now I see that we can take this land. We have doubled our lands already. By the time my son has more children, we will have doubled it again!"

Epilogue

Mary and the girls were with me when we visited Ragnvald for the birth of his son. That event came after I had finished all the work I had begun. Since I had organized the raid on the Issicauna so much seemed to have happened and my life had changed. I knew that the birth of my first grandchild would be a momentous occasion. Before we left I travelled my land. I had taken the barge horses to Gilles so that he could breed from them. I had also spent time with Bertrand and Alain and my plans to train young warriors. We had come up with the name shield bearer. They liked the idea. Erik Long Hair and Erik Green Eye agreed to be the ones who selected the young warriors to train with Alain and Bertrand. First, they would undergo a moon of training in skills with the sword, spear and shield. When they satisfied my two warriors they would be sent to spend two years with a horseman. They would learn to ride and to carry the horseman's shield as well as bringing him a spare spear or a horse if he should need it. They would be responsible for the horses. That would be the least glamorous part of the job but it would teach them. They would also learn how to repair mail. Bagsecg agreed to do that. I chose the first ones to be assessed myself. Rollo One Ear was one of the first. He deserved it and, as I told him, if he was to carry my banner then he needed great skills.

Bagsecg had finished Ragnvald's sword. I had thought Heart of Ice was the finest of blades but Ragnvald's was superior. Bagsecg had fitted the parts from Hengist's sword and then etched runes along the blade. They said, '*Bagsecg made me. I come from the past and reach to the future. Enemies of the clan, fear me.*'

"It is a fine sword, Bagsecg."

He nodded and handed me a scabbard. "I felt guilty having taken so long to make the blade and so I took the time to make a scabbard. He might want to make his own but this one will do for a while."

We took servants, slaves, gifts and horses. It felt like a royal progress. Mary was determined that her first grandchild would be greeted as though a royal prince! When we arrived, I noticed a change in Ragnvald. He was different. He looked older and yet I had seen him less than a month ago. He spoke to me with more ease than he had before but, most important of all, I saw how his men, some many years his senior deferred to him. I had made the right decision in sending him to take Carentan. I could have sent Folki, Bertrand or Einar. Had I done so then we would still have our southern border at Valognes.

When he greeted me, I told him of our raid and he nodded. "It is good that you have hurt the count. This is not over."

I took out the sword. "And here is your new blade."

He slid it out of the scabbard, "This is a mighty sword."

"And you must name it."

"Did not Bagsecg do so?"

"He left that for you."

He lifted it up and a flash of light caught it and made it glint. "I think that Sól has named it for me. I will call it Sun's Vengeance!"

At the time I thought it just a good name but now I see that the Norns had a hand in its naming. They made the sunbeam flash. It was a prophetic name. That was in the future and that was hidden by the webs of the Norns.

His builder, Benni the Builder, had made a second hall. My son had asked for it before he left for Carentan. It was for his mother and me or for Mathilde's parents. He was a thoughtful son and I knew that I was lucky. It was too easy to make mistakes when bringing up children. Father Michael had come with us for he wished to see the new church. Benni had made a fine church for Æðelwald of Remisgat. It was built of stone. Admittedly it was not dressed stone but it had a small bell tower and when time allowed Æðelwald of Remisgat told me that he would find the funds for a bell. Father Michael, under the authority of the Bishop of Reims, ordained the young Saxon. He was a priest now and had the weight of the church behind him.

As we walked my son's new walls I felt that my world was well. We had overcome adversity and emerged triumphantly. My son and I had defeated all that the Franks had sent against us. I did not fear them. We had strong walls and towns manned by the finest of warriors. The world was in harmony. It is at such times that a warrior, especially a Norse warrior, should fear the Norns. I thought that they had played with me enough and sought a different plaything. I was wrong.

When Mathilde went into labour, the men left. That was what we did. Ragnvald had organised some fine ale and we sat in the warrior hall and drank. Father Michael and Father Æðelwald were with us. Æðelwald of Remisgat was drinking sparingly and enduring the taunts of some of my son's hearth weru. When my daughter came and asked for Father Æðelwald, we thought nothing of it but Erik Long Hair who had come with us frowned and clutched his amulet.

"What is wrong Erik?"

My son had drunk a good quantity of ale but he was not drunk.

"A man should not be there at the birth. It is not right. These are women's secrets. The Mother would not approve."

Ragnvald Hrolfsson

I had not thought of it before but I knew that this was unusual. Father Michael said, "He is a priest. Your wife, lord, needs the strength of Christ to help her."

Erik shook his head, "But if it is a boy then he will be tainted."

For the first time, the Norse in the hall all stopped drinking. He was right. If there was a man in the birthing room then it should be a warrior and not a priest. However, none of us would dare to breach the birthing room. We continued drinking but there was an oppressive atmosphere. I felt the Norns were spinning. I began to pray to the Allfather that it would be a girl. The labour was long and it was loud but, eventually, my wife came in, followed by Æðelwald of Remisgat, with a bloody baby in a swaddling cloth.

My wife glowed, "My son, you are a father. He has the right number of toes, fingers, ears eyes and all else that he needs to be a man."

She handed the child to Ragnvald. I saw the two priests make the sign of the cross and I did not like it. Ragnvald kissed his son on the head. I saw that his lips came away bloody. He held him up. "I give the world Ragnvald Ragnvaldsson. He will be jarl of the Clan of the Horse and he will conquer Frankia!"

It was too bold a statement to make but he could not unsay it and so I kept silent. He turned to me and showed me the child, "Father, here is your first grandchild."

I looked at my grandson. He had not been cleaned properly but on his forehead, he had a spot of blood and it looked like a cross. Worse than that, when he looked at me his eyes held mine. I had seen many newborn babes and none had ever done that. He was silent and his mouth appeared to have a cruel smile. I was aware of eyes on me and so I smiled and said, "Welcome, Ragnvald Ragnvaldsson, to the Clan of the Horse." Everyone cheered but I felt a chill in my heart. Erik Long Hair was right. I knew then that the Norns had not finished with me. I now had a son, Ragnvald Hrolfsson and a grandson, Ragnvald Ragnvaldsson. My blood would go on but I felt a fear in my heart that I could not explain. Everyone else looked overjoyed but I had a dread. I prayed that it was the ale but, in my heart, I knew it was not so. My work had not finished, it had just begun!

The End

Ragnvald Hrolfsson
Norse Calendar

Gormánuður October 14th - November 13th
Ýlir November 14th - December 13th
Mörsugur December 14th - January 12th
Þorri - January 13th - February 11th
Gói - February 12th - March 13th
Einmánuður - March 14th - April 13th
Harpa April 14th - May 13th
Skerpla - May 14th - June 12th
Sólmánuður - June 13th - July 12th
Heyannir - July 13th - August 14th
Tvímánuður - August 15th - September 14th
Haustmánuður September 15th-October 13th

Glossary

Ækre -acre (Norse) The amount of land a pair of oxen could plough in one day

Addelam- Deal (Kent)

Afon Hafron- River Severn in Welsh

Alt Clut- Dumbarton Castle on the Clyde

Andecavis- Angers in Anjou

Angia- Jersey (Channel Islands)

An Oriant- Lorient, Brittany

Áth Truim- Trim, County Meath (Ireland)

Baille - a ward (an enclosed area inside a wall)

Balley Chashtal -Castleton (Isle of Man)

Bárekr's Haven – Barfleur, Normandy

Bebbanburgh- Bamburgh Castle, Northumbria. Also, known as Din Guardi in the ancient tongue

Beck- a stream

Blót – a blood sacrifice made by a jarl

Blue Sea/Middle Sea- The Mediterranean

Bondi- Viking farmers who fight

Bourde- Bordeaux

Byrnie- a mail or leather shirt reaching down to the knees

Caerlleon- Welsh for Chester

Caestir - Chester (old English)

Cantwareburh- Canterbury

Casnewydd –Newport, Wales

Cent- Kent

Cetham -Chatham Kent

Chape- the tip of a scabbard

Charlemagne- Holy Roman Emperor at the end of the 8th and beginning of the 9th centuries

Cherestanc- Garstang (Lancashire)

Ċiriċeburh- Cherbourg

Condado Portucalense- the County of Portugal

Constrasta-Valença (Northern Portugal)

Corn Walum or Om Walum- Cornwall

Cymri- Welsh

Cymru- Wales

Cyninges-tūn – Coniston. It means the estate of the king (Cumbria)

Dùn Èideann –Edinburgh (Gaelic)

Din Guardi- Bamburgh castle

Drekar- a Dragon ship (a Viking warship)

Duboglassio –Douglas, Isle of Man

Dyrøy –Jura (Inner Hebrides)

Dyflin- Old Norse for Dublin

Ein-mánuðr- middle of March to the middle of April

Eopwinesfleot -Ebbsfleet

Eoforwic- Saxon for York

Fáfnir - a dwarf turned into a dragon (Norse mythology)

Faro Bregancio- Corunna (Spain)

Ferneberga -Farnborough (Hampshire)

Fey- having second sight

Firkin- a barrel containing eight gallons (usually beer)

Fret-a sea mist

Frankia- France and part of Germany

Fyrd-the Saxon levy

Gaill- Irish for foreigners

Galdramenn- wizard

Glaesum –amber

Gleawecastre- Gloucester

Gói- the end of February to the middle of March

Greenway- ancient roads- they used turf rather than stone

Grenewic- Greenwich

Gyllingas - Gillingham Kent

Haestas- Hastings

Haestingaceaster -Hastings

Hamwic -Southampton

Hantone- Littlehampton

Haughs/ Haugr - small hills in Norse (As in Tarn Hows) or a hump- normally a mound of earth

Hearth-weru- Jarl's bodyguard/oathsworn

Heels- when a ship leans to one side under the pressure of the wind

Hel - Queen of Niflheim, the Norse underworld.

Herkumbl- a mark on the front of a helmet denoting the clan of a Viking warrior

Here Wic- Harwich

Hetaereiarch – Byzantine general

Hí- Iona (Gaelic)

Hjáp - Shap- Cumbria (Norse for stone circle)

Hoggs or Hogging- when the pressure of the wind causes the stern or the bow to droop

Hrams-a – Ramsey, Isle of Man

Hrofecester-Rochester Kent

Hywel ap Rhodri Molwynog- King of Gwynedd 814-825

Icaunis- a British river god

Ishbiliyya- Seville

Issicauna- Gaulish for the lower Seine

Itouna- River Eden Cumbria

Jarl- Norse earl or lord

Joro-goddess of the earth

Jǫtunn -Norse god or goddess

Kartreidh -Carteret in Normandy

Kjerringa - Old Woman- the solid block in which the mast rested

Knarr- a merchant ship or a coastal vessel

Kyrtle-woven top

Ragnvald Hrolfsson

Laugardagr-Saturday (Norse for washing day)
Leathes Water- Thirlmere
Ljoðhús- Lewis
Legacaestir- Anglo Saxon for Chester
Leudes- Imperial officer (a local leader in the Carolingian Empire. They became Counts a century after this.)
Liger- Loire
Lochlannach – Irish for Northerners (Vikings)
Lothuwistoft- Lowestoft
Louis the Pious- King of the Franks and son of Charlemagne
Lundenwic - London
Maen hir – standing stone (menhir)
Maeresea- River Mersey
Mammceaster- Manchester
Manau/Mann – The Isle of Man(n) (Saxon)
Marcia Hispanic- Spanish Marches (the land around Barcelona)
Mast fish- two large racks on a ship for the mast
Midden - a place where they dumped human waste
Miklagård - Constantinople
Njoror- God of the sea
Nithing- A man without honour (Saxon)
Odin - The "All Father" God of war, also associated with wisdom, poetry, and magic (The ruler of the gods).
Olissipo- Lisbon
Orkneyjar-Orkney
Portucale- Porto
Portesmūða -Portsmouth
Penrhudd – Penrith Cumbria
Pillars of Hercules- Straits of Gibraltar
Qādis- Cadiz
Ran- Goddess of the sea
Remisgat Ramsgate
Roof rock- slate
Rinaz –The Rhine
Sabrina- Latin and Celtic for the River Severn. Also, the name of a female Celtic deity
Saami- the people who live in what is now Northern Norway/Sweden
Sandwic- Sandwich (Kent)
Sarnia- Guernsey (Channel Islands)
St. Cybi- Holyhead
Sampiere -samphire (sea asparagus)
Scree- loose rocks in a glacial valley
Seax – short sword
Sheerstrake- the uppermost strake in the hull
Sheet- a rope fastened to the lower corner of a sail
Shroud- a rope from the masthead to the hull amidships
Skeggox – an axe with a shorter beard on one side of the blade

195

Sondwic-Sandwich
South Folk- Suffolk
Stad- Norse settlement
Stays- ropes running from the mast-head to the bow
Stirap- stirrup
Strake- the wood on the side of a drekar
Suthriganaworc - Southwark (London)
Syllingar- Scilly Isles
Tarn- small lake (Norse)
Temese- River Thames (also called the Tamese)
The Norns- The three sisters who weave webs of intrigue for men
Thing-Norse for a parliament or a debate (Tynwald)
Thor's day- Thursday
Threttanessa- a drekar with 13 oars on each side.
Thrall- slave
Tinea- Tyne
Trenail- a round wooden peg used to secure strakes
Tude- Tui in Northern Spain
Tynwald- the Parliament on the Isle of Man
Úlfarrberg- Helvellyn
Úlfarrland- Cumbria
Úlfarr- Wolf Warrior
Úlfarrston- Ulverston
Ullr-Norse God of Hunting
Ulfheonar-an elite Norse warrior who wore a wolf skin over his armour
Valauna- Valognes (Normandy)
Vectis- The Isle of Wight
Volva- a witch or healing woman in Norse culture
Waeclinga Straet- Watling Street (A5)
Windlesore-Windsor
Waite- a Viking word for farm
Werham -Wareham (Dorset)
Wintan-ceastre -Winchester
Withy- the mechanism connecting the steering board to the ship
Woden's day- Wednesday
Wyddfa-Snowdon
Wyrd- Fate
Yard- a timber from which the sail is suspended on a drekar
Ynys Môn-Anglesey

Maps and Illustrations

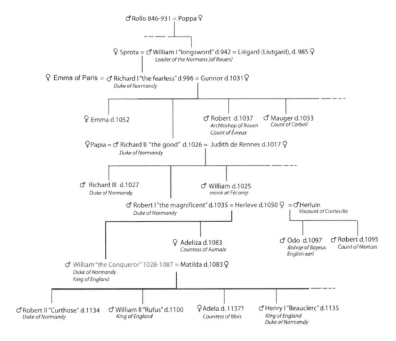

Courtesy of Wikipedia.

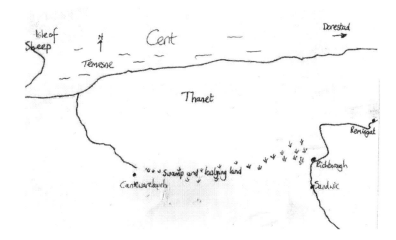

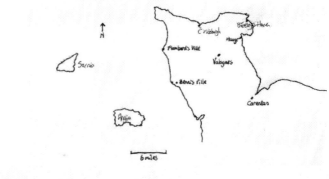

Land of the horse.

The Haugr

Griff 2017

Ragnvald Hrolfsson
Historical note

My research encompasses not only books and the Internet but also TV. Time Team was a great source of information. I wish they would bring it back! I saw the wooden compass which my sailors use on the Dan Snow programme about the Vikings. Apparently, it was used in modern times to sail from Denmark to Edinburgh and was only a couple of points out. Similarly, the construction of the temporary hall was copied from the settlement of Leif Eriksson in Newfoundland.

Stirrups began to be introduced in Europe during the 7th and 8th Centuries. By Charlemagne's time, they were widely used but only by nobles. It is said this was the true beginning of feudalism. It was the Vikings who introduced them to England. It was only in the time of Canute the Great that they became widespread. The use of stirrups enabled a rider to strike someone on the ground from the back of a horse and facilitated the use of spears and later, lances.

The Franks used horses more than most other armies of the time. Their spears were used as long swords, hence the guards. They used saddles and stirrups. They still retained their round shields and wore, largely, an open helmet. Sometimes they wore a plume. They carried a spare spear and a sword.

One reason for the Normans success was that when they arrived in northern France they integrated quickly with the local populace. They married them and began to use some of their words. They adapted to the horse as a weapon of war. Before then the Vikings had been quite happy to ride to war but they dismounted to fight. The Normans took the best that the Franks had and made it better. This book sees the earliest beginnings of the rise of the Norman knight.

I have used the names by which places were known in the medieval period wherever possible. Sometimes I have had to use the modern name. The Cotentin is an example. The isle of sheep is now called the Isle of Sheppey and lies on the Medway close to the Thames. The land of Kent was known as Cent in the early medieval period. Thanet or, Tanet as it was known in the Viking period was an island at this time. The sea was on two sides and the other two sides had swamps, bogs, mudflats and tidal streams. It protected Canterbury. The coast was different too. Richborough had been a major Roman port. It is now some way inland. Sandwich was a port. Other ports now lie under the sea. Vikings were not afraid to sail up very narrow rivers and to risk being stranded on mud. They were tough men and were capable of carrying or porting their ships as their Rus brothers did when travelling to Miklagård.

The Norns or the Weird Sisters.
"The Norns (Old Norse: norn, plural: nornir) in Norse mythology are female beings who rule the destiny of gods and men. They roughly correspond to other controllers of humans' destiny, the Fates, elsewhere in European mythology.

199

Ragnvald Hrolfsson

In Snorri Sturluson's interpretation of the Völuspá, Urðr (Wyrd), Verðandi and Skuld, the three most important of the Norns, come out from a hall standing at the Well of Urðr or Well of Fate. They draw water from the well and take sand that lies around it, which they pour over Yggdrasill so that its branches will not rot. These three Norns are described as powerful maiden giantesses (Jotuns) whose arrival from Jötunheimr ended the golden age of the gods. They may be the same as the maidens of Mögþrasir who are described in Vafþrúðnismál"

Source: Norns - https://en.wikipedia.org

The death of Louis the Pious

In 837, Louis crowned Charles king over all of Alemannia and Burgundy and gave him a portion of his brother Louis' land. Louis the German promptly rose in revolt, and the emperor divided his realm again at Quierzy-sur-Oise, giving all of the young King of Bavaria's lands, save Bavaria itself, to Charles. Emperor Louis did not stop there, however. His devotion to Charles knew no bounds. When Pepin died in 838, Louis declared Charles the new king of Aquitaine. The nobles, however, elected Pepin's son Pepin II. When Louis threatened invasion, the third great civil war of his reign broke out. In the spring of 839, Louis the German invaded Swabia, Pepin II and his Gascon subjects fought all the way to the Loire, and the Danes returned to ravage the Frisian coast (sacking Dorestad for a second time).

Louis fell ill soon after his final victorious campaigns and went to his summer hunting lodge on an island in the Rhine, by his palace at Ingelheim. On 20 June 840, he died, at the old age of 62, in the presence of many bishops and clerics and in the arms of his half-brother Drogo, though Charles and Judith were absent in Poitiers. Soon dispute plunged the surviving brothers into a civil war that was only settled in 843 by the Treaty of Verdun, which split the Frankish realm into three parts, to become the kernels of France and Germany, with Burgundy and the Low Countries between them. The dispute over the kingship of Aquitaine was not fully settled until 860.

I have used the word town as this is the direct translation of the Danish ton-meaning settlement. A town could vary in size from a couple of houses to a walled city like Jorvik. If I had used ton it would have been confusing. There are already readers out there who think I have made mistakes because I use words like stiraps, wyrd and drekar!

The assimilation of the Norse and the Franks took place over a long period. Hrolf Ragnvaldsson aka Rollo aka Robert of Normandy is not yet born but by the time he is 64 he will have attacked Paris and become Duke of Normandy. The journey has just begun.

Viking Raid on the Seine

At some time in the 850s, a huge Viking fleet sailed up the Seine to raid deep into the heart of Frankia. Some writers of the period speak of over a hundred

200

ships. The priests who wrote of the plague that they believe the Vikings to be
ended to exaggerate. I have erred on the side of caution.

Greenways

have used the term greenways in many of my books. We still have them in
England. They are the paths trodden before the Romans came. Many of them
became bridleways.

Books used in the research

British Museum - Vikings- Life and Legends
Arthur and the Saxon Wars- David Nicolle (Osprey)
Saxon, Norman and Viking Terence Wise (Osprey)
The Vikings- Ian Heath (Osprey)
Byzantine Armies 668-1118 - Ian Heath (Osprey)
Romano-Byzantine Armies 4th-9th Century - David Nicholle (Osprey)
The Walls of Constantinople AD 324-1453 - Stephen Turnbull (Osprey)
Viking Longship - Keith Durham (Osprey)
Anglo-Danish Project- The Vikings in England
The Varangian Guard- 988-1453 Raffael D'Amato
Saxon Viking and Norman- Terence Wise
The Walls of Constantinople AD 324-1453-Stephen Turnbull
Byzantine Armies- 886-1118- Ian Heath
The Age of Charlemagne-David Nicolle
The Normans- David Nicolle
Norman Knight AD 950-1204- Christopher Gravett
The Norman Conquest of the North- William A Kappelle
The Knight in History- Francis Gies
The Norman Achievement- Richard F Cassady
Knights- Constance Brittain Bouchard

Griff Hosker
June 2017

Ragnvald Hrolfsson

Other books by Griff Hosker

If you enjoyed reading this book, then why not read another one by the author?

Ancient History

The Sword of Cartimandua Series
(Germania and Britannia 50 A.D. – 128 A.D.)
Ulpius Felix- Roman Warrior (prequel)
The Sword of Cartimandua
The Horse Warriors
Invasion Caledonia
Roman Retreat
Revolt of the Red Witch
Druid's Gold
Trajan's Hunters
The Last Frontier
Hero of Rome
Roman Hawk
Roman Treachery
Roman Wall
Roman Courage

The Wolf Warrior series
(Britain in the late 6th Century)
Saxon Dawn
Saxon Revenge
Saxon England
Saxon Blood
Saxon Slayer
Saxon Slaughter
Saxon Bane
Saxon Fall: Rise of the Warlord
Saxon Throne
Saxon Sword

Ragnvald Hrolfsson
Medieval History

The Dragon Heart Series
Viking Slave
Viking Warrior
Viking Jarl
Viking Kingdom
Viking Wolf
Viking War
Viking Sword
Viking Wrath
Viking Raid
Viking Legend
Viking Vengeance
Viking Dragon
Viking Treasure
Viking Enemy
Viking Witch
Viking Blood
Viking Weregeld
Viking Storm
Viking Warband
Viking Shadow
Viking Legacy
Viking Clan
Viking Bravery

The Norman Genesis Series
Hrolf the Viking
Horseman
The Battle for a Home
Revenge of the Franks
The Land of the Northmen
Ragnvald Hrolfsson
Brothers in Blood
Lord of Rouen
Drekar in the Seine
Duke of Normandy
The Duke and the King

New World Series
Blood on the Blade

Ragnvald Hrolfsson
Across the Seas
The Savage Wilderness
The Bear and the Wolf

The Vengeance Trail

The Reconquista Chronicles
Castilian Knight
El Campeador
The Lord of Valencia

The Aelfraed Series
(Britain and Byzantium 1050 A.D. - 1085 A.D.)
Housecarl
Outlaw
Varangian

**The Anarchy Series England
1120-1180**
English Knight
Knight of the Empress
Northern Knight
Baron of the North
Earl
King Henry's Champion
The King is Dead
Warlord of the North
Enemy at the Gate
The Fallen Crown
Warlord's War
Kingmaker
Henry II
Crusader
The Welsh Marches
Irish War
Poisonous Plots
The Princes' Revolt
Earl Marshal

**Border Knight
1182-1300**
Sword for Hire

Ragnvald Hrolfsson
Return of the Knight
Baron's War
Magna Carta
Welsh Wars
Henry III
The Bloody Border
Baron's Crusade
Sentinel of the North
War in the West

Sir John Hawkwood Series
France and Italy 1339- 1387
Crécy: The Age of the Archer

Lord Edward's Archer
Lord Edward's Archer
King in Waiting
An Archer's Crusade (November 2020)

Struggle for a Crown
1360- 1485
Blood on the Crown
To Murder A King
The Throne
King Henry IV
The Road to Agincourt
St Crispin's Day

Tales from the Sword

Modern History

The Napoleonic Horseman Series
Chasseur à Cheval
Napoleon's Guard
British Light Dragoon
Soldier Spy
1808: The Road to Coruña
Talavera
The Lines of Torres Vedras
Bloody Badajoz
The Road to France

Ragnvald Hrolfsson

The Lucky Jack American Civil War series
Rebel Raiders
Confederate Rangers
The Road to Gettysburg

The British Ace Series
1914
1915 Fokker Scourge
1916 Angels over the Somme
1917 Eagles Fall
1918 We will remember them
From Arctic Snow to Desert Sand
Wings over Persia

Combined Operations series
1940-1945
Commando
Raider
Behind Enemy Lines
Dieppe
Toehold in Europe
Sword Beach
Breakout
The Battle for Antwerp
King Tiger
Beyond the Rhine
Korea
Korean Winter

Other Books
Great Granny's Ghost (Aimed at 9-14-year-old young people)

For more information on all of the books then please visit the author's website at www.griffhosker.com where there is a link to contact him or visit his Facebook page: GriffHosker at Sword Books

.

Printed in Great Britain
by Amazon

62778334R00125